D1825468

Chameleon Uncovered
Book 2 of the Chameleon Assassin Series

By BR Kingsolver
brkingsolver.com

Cover art by Heather Hamilton-Senter
www.bookcoverartistry.com

Copyright 2017 BR Kingsolver

License Notes

Coming late spring 2017
Book 3 of the Chameleon Assassin Series

Other books by BR Kingsolver

The Chameleon Assassin Series
Chameleon Assassin

The Telepathic Clans Saga
The Succubus Gift
Succubus Unleashed
Broken Dolls
Succubus Rising
Succubus Ascendant

Table of Contents

iv

CHAPTER 1

Vengeance and justice are intertwined concepts. Religions and governments have struggled with the proper balance since mankind crawled out of their caves and began building their first social organizations.

Abstract concepts aside, people seemed to have difficulty separating the two things, and a lot of people had always been unhappy with how society defined justice.

Millennia after the first unhappy woman poisoned her mate's breakfast, someone gave Evelyn Olson a phone number. Just a phone number, hand written on a scrap of paper. She didn't do anything with it until one day after a court appearance in her divorce battle. Looking for something in her purse, she found the scrap of paper. She was frustrated and angry, so she called the number.

A woman's voice answered. "Leave your name, phone number, and address. If we can help you, we will contact you."

Evelyn left her information. A week passed, and she forgot about it. Then her phone rang.

"Be at Bistro68 on Tuesday at eleven fifty-five in the morning. Reservations for Evelyn and Elizabeth." It was the same woman's voice as on the recording at the mysterious number.

⊕⊕⊕

In my business, anonymity was important. I never wore my real face to meet a client, as I preferred to avoid unexpected knocks on the door late at night. Some people had no sense of humor when their heirlooms disappeared, and trusting to the discretion of someone who hired a thief or an assassin would just be stupid.

Bistro68 catered to the money-is-no-object crowd and was full on a weekday at noon. I strolled in and sat down across from Evelyn Olson, who looked exactly as she did in all the media pictures. I, on the other hand, looked nothing like myself. Projecting an image eight inches shorter and ten years older than my natural form, I was dressed much the same as the other corporate trophy wives meeting for lunch.

"Good afternoon, Evelyn. I'm Elizabeth. I understand that you have a problem. How can I help?"

I'd done a lot of research on her, her husband, and their divorce before I met her for lunch. Corporate marriages sometimes resembled royal marriages in ages past—a means of cementing alliances and creating acceptable babies. Negotiating teams for prenuptial agreements occasionally employed dozens of lawyers. Evelyn was from a prominent corporate family, and her prenup evidently was airtight, preventing Fredrick from just dumping her on the street.

Fredrick Olson's new playmate was a scandal. Although undeniably beautiful, she was too young, too uneducated, and too middle-class to fit into corporate society properly. No one would have blinked if he wanted to keep her stashed away as his mistress, maybe not even Evelyn. But he wanted a divorce so he could marry the sixteen-year-old kid. Upper-class society was completely aghast.

Evelyn's main complaint was her husband taking

all her jewelry when he left. That pissed her off more than the mistress or the divorce. The divorce judge, a golfing buddy of Frederick's, had denied her motion to have the jewelry returned.

"So, what would you like me to do for you?" I asked.

"I want my jewelry. A friend told me you might have—how did she put it?—a creative solution."

"We might be able to do that," I told her, "but our services are expensive. You might spend more than the jewelry is worth."

She laughed. "I seriously doubt that."

I quoted her a hundred thousand credits, and she didn't bat an eye. When she showed me the insurance photos, I understood why.

Dad always told me to be careful about getting involved with domestic disputes, and I understood the potential problems. Evelyn showed me two pictures, one of her grandmother wearing a necklace, and then a picture of Fredrick's sixteen-year-old sugar baby wearing the necklace. I was about as cynical as they came, but fair was fair.

An aircar rose from the roof, and soon after, most of the lights in the penthouse above the twenty-second floor went out. Time for me to go to work.

I'd spent the previous week scouting the job, following the mark and mapping his habits and movements. It all came down to sitting outside the exclusive apartment building, topped by Fredrick Olson's penthouse overlooking the lake, and waiting for him and his arm candy to head out for a see-and-be-seen charity event. The kind of event where the richer-than-God crowd got together and donated fifteen minutes' income, along with fifteen minutes' lip service, to the "unfortunate among us."

On a scouting foray into the building, I had learned that some of Olson's security guards remained on duty when he went out. That eliminated the easy way in. Climbing a twenty-two-story building was a difficult proposition at the best of times, but I was recovering from a bullet wound and surgery to my left hand. Climbing anything taller than a molehill was still beyond my ability.

For a lot of reasons, I would rather break into a walled estate than a high-rise apartment building. During the day, when Fredrick Olson was at work, his mistress and the housekeeper were at home. In the evening, most of the other residents throughout the building were home, and the place was crawling with 'personal security personnel', also known as bodyguards.

I crossed the road, my chameleon talents allowing me to blend into the darkness. The deepest shadows lay on the southwest side of the building that was closest to the lake. If I kept completely still, even the security cameras couldn't pick me up. I had to move, though, to reach my destination.

An arm's length from the wall, I turned on the personal jetpack I wore—an unanticipated bonus from a previous job—and rose until I reached the roof. I pulled myself onto the roof and lay between the parapet and the greenhouse glass, barely breathing, waiting for some kind of alarm. Nothing happened.

The penthouse covered half of the roof, and the apartment included the entire floor below me. A domed greenhouse with a garden covered the other half of the roof. From the ground, the dome wasn't visible, but the palm trees looked too healthy to be exposed to unfiltered city air.

Shrugging out of the jetpack harness, I crawled along until I reached the gardener's shed. As far as I could tell, it was the only way to go from inside the dome to the outside. The door had an electronic combination lock and a simple alarm contact, but that was it. I bypassed the alarm and disabled the lock. When I pulled on the door, I discovered it hadn't been used very often. Creaking, rusty hinges screamed, and I winced. A panicked glance at the house showed no movement or change. I hoped no one was inside the apartment. If so, I was already screwed.

Another door opened from the shed into the garden. The glass ceiling thirty feet overhead gave the impression of being truly outside. I seriously doubted security cameras or pressure sensors covered the space. Why bother? Breaking through the acrylic glass would've taken a bomb. Such rooftop conservatories were designed to withstand tree limbs blown into them at sixty miles an hour.

Keeping low and blending into the shadows, I made my way past a fountain to an area with several tables surrounded by chairs. No one sat outside enjoying sunny days anymore, at least not in the city, but if you were rich, you could pretend.

The sliding-glass door from the garden to the house didn't have an alarm contact on it and wasn't even locked. I walked right into an entertainment area with a bar, dance floor, and more tables and chairs. Beyond were a formal dining room and a small kitchen. The rest of the rooftop level included a game room and a gymnasium with a lap pool. I took the servants' stairs from the small kitchen down to the main level.

Evelyn told me the jewelry would be in a safe in the master bedroom, and had given me the combination. Frederick hadn't changed it. I took the jewelry that matched the insurance pictures she showed me and put the rest back. Evelyn wanted to send a message. I felt a little guilty, though. The gig was almost too easy.

If I had been working for myself, a lot of the artwork and the rest of the jewelry would have been in jeopardy. Evelyn hoped Fredrick wouldn't realize the jewelry was missing, so I made every effort to leave everything exactly as I found it.

But what were the chances that Fredrick would miss a half-dozen bottles of wine and whiskey? On my way out, I looked into the wine cellar and under the bar. I wasn't a real expert in fancy alcohol, so I used my phone to check his stock against the infonet. I pulled a few of the most expensive wines for Mom and the most expensive whiskeys for Dad. It never hurt to butter up the parents in case I needed a favor.

⊕⊕⊕

Evelyn and I met for lunch the following day at the same charming little bistro as before. I liked the place since the menu proudly boasted that the fish contained no heavy metals or toxins, and she was paying.

We did the so-good-to-see-you air-kiss thing, and I passed her a shopping bag. "Happy birthday!"

"Oh, you shouldn't have," she said, slipping me a payment card.

"I recovered all the pieces except one," I told her after the waiter took our orders. "The diamond and turquoise choker."

"The little slut probably wore it," Evelyn said with a shrug. "Such is life. At least you got my grandmother's necklace and the antique diamond set." She grinned. "I'm going to love seeing Fredrick's face at the museum fundraiser when I wear them."

I chuckled. "Who are you going with?" A man I was dating had invited me, and it suddenly looked as though it might be more interesting than I'd thought.

"Dolores Channing and her brother," Evelyn said. "You know I don't dare go near a man until the divorce is final. It's fine for him to screw around, but he would love to invoke the infidelity clause in the prenup."

"Seems like a silly clause since you didn't have any children," I said.

"Definitely. It turns out that he's sterile." She gave an aggrieved sigh. "You know, Elizabeth, before the world went to hell in a hand basket, there was a movement in North America and Europe that came close to giving women true equality with men. But as soon as the corporations took over, the boys at the top put a stop to that."

I'd read about that in my history classes at the university. It wasn't that women were denied equality, but at the top of the social ladder, women such as Evelyn and her mother, and my maternal grandmother, traded equality for the comfort and luxury their beauty could buy. Very few women cracked the top levels of corporate hierarchies.

Nothing stopped Evelyn from going out and starting her own company, but instead of going to university when she was eighteen, she married a corporate executive eighteen years her senior. I didn't have a lot of sympathy for her, since she was Olson's second wife. He seemed to trade them in when they hit thirty-two.

We ate our lunches, gossiping like a normal pair of corporate trophy wives. After we parted, I went to the ladies' room and changed my appearance, morphing from the woman Evelyn knew into plain old me. With a full purse and a bounce in my step, I ventured forth to hunt down a wicked pair of shoes I'd seen in a shop window.

CHAPTER 2

The Pinnacle was a fancy bar for young corporate types. My best friend managed it, and my other best friend sang there four nights a week. That's where I met James McKenzie, Vice President of Technology Support for Ontario Power and Light. I'd been out to dinner with my father, but didn't want to call it an early night, so I was sitting in the mezzanine overlooking the dance floor, nursing a drink and listening to Nellie sing.

"You're dressed very nicely to be spending the evening alone," a lovely baritone voice said. I looked up and discovered the voice came from a pleasant-looking man with dark hair and blue eyes, who was wearing a very expensive dark suit.

"So are you," I said. "Did you take your mother to dinner?"

He barked out a laugh and said, "No, I didn't. Why do you ask?"

"It was either that, or you got stood up, or you were terribly rude and your date ran away. No one dresses like that and goes out alone."

"Or my date got sick."

"I think I said that, didn't I? Getting sick is the original excuse for bailing out of a bad date. I'm going to have to dock her score for lack of creativity."

"Is that the only clean dress you had, or did you go to dinner with your father?"

I could tell he was trying to return my snark, but he was an amateur. "It was a very nice dinner, but Dad isn't much for night clubs. Or dancing. So why didn't you take her home? Didn't have the bus fare?"

He seemed to think about it. "Maybe you're right.

9

I guess I am a cad. May I join you? I haven't had anyone claw me all night."

"Meow." I gestured to the empty chair. "I tend to erect my defenses when approached by strange men. Are you strange or merely unusual?"

With a bemused smile, he said, "I have been accused of both. I prefer to think of myself as unique. Enjoying the people watching?"

"I'm not sure. I keep hoping someone will ask me to dance, but none of the available men seem to have learned how."

The waiter brought me another drink and took my new friend's order.

He looked down at the dance floor, then looked me over again, obviously taking in my dress and jewelry. Dad had taken me to a really swanky place, so I was dolled out to the max.

"Would you care to dance?"

"Maybe." I turned away from watching the dancers. "Have you known your date long?"

He handled the shift in topic without a problem. "Second date. We were at dinner, and it seemed as though something disagreed with her. Although, the paramedics said it was appendicitis. They weren't too keen on allowing me in the ambulance."

"Really? Aren't you concerned? Don't you want to be there to hold her hand and make her feel she's important to you? Do you care if she lives or dies? Are you going to make her call a taxi to get home?"

"I'll go around to see her in the morning. She's in surgery this evening."

Obviously, he wasn't terribly concerned or broken up about it. "I assume you're still hoping to hook up, then?" I asked, looking around. "What type of woman are you interested in? I suggest you choose someone with a stronger stomach."

His cheerful demeanor took a hit. "I was hoping you might be interested."

"Oh, I am. I think it's fascinating to learn about various men's taste in women. How about the redhead in the green dress?"

He looked. "Not bad, but a little too much." The redhead probably carried an extra ten pounds, maybe a little more, which she'd probably gained since she bought the dress. The effect on her décolletage was rather eye-catching, though.

"Ah, a fitness snob. In that case, how about the brunette with hair down to her butt?" The woman was definitely drool-worthy.

"Nice, but I'm afraid she's married."

"How can you tell that from up here?" I rose a bit out of my chair and tried to see if there was a ring on her left hand.

"The man she's dancing with is her husband. I went to university with him." He gave me a grin that could go a long way toward melting a girl's resolve. "My type runs to tall, slender blondes."

I had to smile. "I'll bet you spent hours in front of the mirror practicing that line." I passed him my business card. "I never go home with men I just met, especially when I meet them in bars. It's not personal. I'd feel the same if I knew your name. I have an aversion to torture and death, so I like to check people out before I agree to games in their personal dungeons. Are any of your former girlfriends on missing persons reports?"

He studied my card, then looked up. "James McKenzie, at your service, Miss Nelson.

Unfortunately, my mother disapproved, so I had to sell my dungeon. We would have to find alternative activities." He handed me his card. Vice President of Technology Support for the local electric company. I thought about the passwords into those control systems, and my interest escalated from mild to hot-and-bothered. Computer hackers have different emotional triggers than other women.

"Impressive, Mr. McKenzie. Is there a Mrs. McKenzie?"

He shook his head. "No, I'm single."

I continued to look at him expectantly. Finally, he said, "I'm divorced. No kids."

I licked the rim of my glass while holding his eyes with mine. "Give me a call sometime. Just don't take me to the restaurant where you went tonight."

James stood on my front porch with a corsage in his hand. The idea of me dating a real, honest-to-God corporate vice president was so absurd that I still hadn't come to grips with it. That was our third date, and I hadn't managed to scare him away.

I turned to my temporary roommate. "Lock it up and don't let anyone in."

Glenda rolled her eyes. "Yes, ma'am. And who would I let in? The only people who ever come here is *Jaaames* and your father, and he has a key."

The way she said James's name kind of bugged me. The kid was starting to act like a smart-ass teenager sometimes. Glenda, a fifteen-year-old street kid I had sort of adopted, was staying with me while I rehabilitated my injured hand. Normally she lived at my mother's brothel and worked in the kitchen as an apprentice. Ignoring her, I smiled at James as I stepped out onto the porch.

"You are so lovely tonight," he said.

"Thank you. You look very nice yourself." He was always nice to look at, with dark hair and blue eyes, a strong jaw and prominent cheekbones. When I wore flats, James and I looked each other in the eyes. His tailored suit displayed his broad shoulders and trim waist. James was more than a pretty face, though. Intelligence went along with the good looks, and his position was unusual for someone still under forty.

He added to my admiration by pinning the corsage on my dress without drawing blood.

His chauffeur drove us to the museum and let us out in front of the building before joining the rest of the drivers. I wondered what the drivers did while their lords and ladies pretentiously pranced around. Most nights I might have been tempted to find out, but the prospect of the Evelyn and Fredrick Olson show had me eager to circulate among the elites.

My parents provided me the training so I could fit in with the upper one percent, while cynically ensuring I understood why they themselves had chosen not to do so. My father had been vice president of security for one of the Fifty—the fifty largest corporations—and my mother's father had been executive vice president of a company in the top two hundred. Such positions paid millions, along with benefits most people couldn't imagine.

Both of my parents were elite in other ways—they were among the top criminals in the world. You didn't find citations for that in the society pages. Mom was possibly the best computer hacker who ever lived. Dad was a cat burglar before taking a fall that left him a paraplegic. They had one child, and they trained me from the time I could first walk and talk. Officially, I owned a security consulting company, riding on my parents' public reputations.

The fundraiser at the Royal Ontario Museum was one of the largest social occasions of the year. Knowing its importance, I'd even bought a new dress and was wearing my best jewelry. I'd put a stack of business cards in my clutch, hoping I'd have an excuse to hand them out. Legal money was the easiest, even if it was rather dull.

We were barely inside and I'd only taken one sip from my first glass of champagne when we encountered Simon and Maya Wellington. She greeted me the way one greets a close friend.

"Elizabeth. It's so good to see you. How have you been?" Maya took me by the arm and bussed me on the cheek.

"Mrs. Wellington." Turning to James, I said, "Mrs. Maya Wellington and her husband Simon. This is my friend James McKenzie. James is with Ontario Power. James, Mr. Wellington is chairman of Hudson Bay."

Maya leaned closer to me and asked, "How is business?"

The question surprised me. "I'm doing okay."

She seemed to scrutinize me. "Did you bring any business cards?"

I smiled. "As a matter of fact, I did tuck a few in my clutch."

"Good." The next thing I knew, Maya was pulling me around and introducing me to her friends.

"Melania, this is Elizabeth Nelson, the best security consultant in the business. You've heard about all the break-ins, haven't you? I mean, the

Carpenters were cleaned out, and no one heard a thing. We had Elizabeth go over our installation, and I feel so much better now."

I handed Melania Makinin my card and smiled. I recognized her husband as president of the largest chain of clothing stores in Ontario. She had a liking for large, heavy jewelry, including some thumb-sized sapphires. I filed the information away.

A dozen introductions later, handing out my cards like candy at Halloween, I glanced at James and found him watching Maya and me with his mouth hanging open.

"I wasn't aware you were so socially connected," James said as he brought me a fresh glass of champagne.

I smiled like the cat who stole the cream.

There was a stir when Fredrick Olson and his teen squeeze showed up.

"Have you heard about the Olson affair?" Maya asked me, obviously disapproving. Maya had a daughter a year older than Olson's mistress.

"I understand it's the celebrity divorce of the year," I replied. I grinned at James. "Was your divorce front-page gossip?"

He shuddered. "No, thank God."

"I don't think you ever told me why you got divorced," I said, baiting him. I was curious. He seemed to be too good a catch to let go.

"It's a long story. Too long for tonight."

About fifteen minutes later, I watched Evelyn Olson walk up to her husband. She was wearing her grandmother's liberated necklace.

"Hello, Fredrick," she said, loud enough to draw attention. "Is this one of your illegitimate daughters?

Aren't you going to introduce me?"

He and the girl turned bright red. Both stared at the necklace, bracelet and earrings Evelyn wore.

"Tell me, darling, do you plan on coming home anytime soon? I'm thinking of redecorating. Do you think the billiards room will look good in pink?"

Several of the onlookers spit their drinks and started coughing.

"I don't believe this," James muttered. A lot of the men looked uncomfortable. Most of the women seemed amused, like sharks amused at a trapped sea lion.

James took my hand and turned to go someplace else. I balked.

"I'm enjoying this," I told him. "Don't you want to see what happens next?"

"James is rather a coward when it comes to confrontations," a woman's voice behind me said.

I turned to see a very pretty woman who came up to my shoulder. She had beautiful shiny brown hair, and I studied it, committing it to memory. The man with her looked embarrassed, but not as embarrassed as James.

"Good evening," she said to James. "Who's the flavor of the month?"

"Hello. I don't believe we've met," I said, extending my hand. "I'm Elizabeth Nelson."

The grin on her face slid, and she looked at my hand as though she didn't know what to do with it.

"Are you one of James's old flames?" I asked, leaning closer and winking at her. "I know there must be dozens of them, but he never wants to talk about his past."

"I'm his ex-wife," she said with a snooty grin.

"Oh." I looked at James, then back at her. "The one who's an alcoholic, or the nymphomaniac?" His expression was shocked, hers was horrified.

"He's only been married once," she sputtered.

"I see." I turned back to James and patted his arm. "I didn't realize that all those stories were about the same woman. You poor dear."

Her face turned scarlet, and she gaped at me with her mouth hanging open.

"It was so interesting to meet you," I said with a smile. "Stop by again sometime when you can't stay so long." I took James's arm and said, "Let's go see the Cezanne they recently acquired."

I motioned toward the glass the ex-wife held and smiled. "Go easy on that stuff tonight. You don't want to embarrass yourself again."

Smiling at her escort, I said, "I do admire a man who is willing to accept a woman no matter how many others she's had. It's so egalitarian."

As we walked away, James said under his breath, "I don't believe you sometimes."

"The bitch shouldn't have tried to embarrass me in public. If she's always that nasty, I can see why you ditched her."

"She can be nasty." A slight smile crossed his face. "That was rather funny."

"My mother taught me that when women get catty, the best strategy is to show them the size of your claws right at the beginning."

"You don't seem to care what you say or who you say it to."

I gave him the smile I usually used as a warning. "You're starting to catch on, darling."

As we admired the Cezanne, James asked, "Do

you consult to museums about their security?"

"Sometimes."

"What do you think about the security systems here? Any chance someone might steal this painting?"

I appraised him out of the corner of my eye. He seemed to be mildly curious, but nothing more.

"All the major museums have good security," I said. "Contrary to what you see in vids, most major art thefts from museums aren't meticulously-planned burglaries. Usually a gang pulls out some guns, takes the pieces they want, and makes their getaway while hundreds of people watch. With that many eyewitnesses, any consensus about the perpetrators' descriptions is accidental."

"I'm disappointed," he said. "The vids always make it look so exotic. Elaborate plans to defeat the laser detectors, rappelling through the skylights, exact replicas of the statue they plan to steal. You know what I mean."

I laughed. "Indeed, I do. I loved watching that sort of thing when I was growing up." I waved my arm about me. "Do you see anywhere to hide laser detectors?" The walls were solid stone.

Then I turned back to the Cezanne. "Don't you think it would be a little awkward climbing a rope up to the ceiling carrying that? I'll bet the frame alone weighs twenty pounds. Much easier to haul it out the side door to a van."

"I see what you mean. Couldn't you cut it out of the frame?"

"Only an amateur would do that. Of course, if a collector wanted it badly enough, I'm sure he could find someone to steal it for him. Most major art thefts are done on commission, you know. That way the thief doesn't have to worry about selling it."

CHAPTER 3

I thought about that conversation concerning art thefts a week later when my friend Wil called from Chicago. Wilbur Wilberforce was the Deputy Director of Security for the North American Chamber of Commerce. The big corporations all had their own security forces, but they paid into a pool to fund the local police, whose major functions were to deal with traffic, and keep the lower classes from causing disturbances that disrupted the upper classes and their businesses.

The Chamber acted to mediate disputes between businesses and deal with security issues that extended beyond a single corporation's affairs. I hadn't seen Wil since we worked together in Toronto on a case involving a particularly lethal new street drug.

"Are you busy?" Wil asked when I answered the phone.

"Not at all. Are you in town?" I kept telling myself that I didn't want to get involved with him, but any woman who didn't get excited thinking about him hadn't met him.

"I meant busy as in business busy."

"Oh." I tried to keep the disappointment out of my voice. "Nothing going on at the moment. Why?"

"The Art Institute wants to hire a consultant to evaluate their security. Interested?"

I didn't have to think twice. The Art Institute of Chicago was the foremost museum in North America, maybe in the world.

"You're kidding, right? Of course, I'm interested."

"Can you fly down here by Wednesday?"

"Absolutely. Do you have a recommendation as to

a hotel?"

"The Institute will take care of it. Just let me know when you'll be flying in."

After we hung up and I finished dancing a jig all over the house, I called my dad and told him.

"You're going to work with me on this, aren't you?" I pleaded. "This is way larger and more high profile than anything I've ever done." Dad had trained me in security systems, and he'd probably forgotten more than I would ever know. A gig at a museum like that could either make your reputation or ruin it.

"Of course. I'm a little surprised. The big security companies usually get that kind of job."

"I think it's Wil," I answered. "The museum didn't contact me directly."

"I hope he keeps it on a professional level," Dad said. "He doesn't expect anything in exchange, does he?"

I couldn't imagine what. It wouldn't have taken a million-credit contract to convince me to let him in my pants.

"I don't think so, Dad. Anything he might want from me he could probably get with dinner and a couple of drinks."

"Too much information," Dad said.

"Then don't bring up that kind of topic."

"Touché. Call me if you need to, and don't sign any contracts before I review them."

⊕⊕⊕

Glenda couldn't stay at my place alone. She was fifteen and really needed a structured environment.

21

Truth be told, more structure than she probably got living with me. I told her to pack up, and Mom sent a car to take her home. Glenda had been a huge help, but it was nice to have my space back. I'd been living alone for seven years and didn't realize how set in my ways I'd become.

Dad and I spent a day going over publically available information about the museum. Two hundred years before, it was considered one of the top two or three museums in North America, but as Manhattan and Washington were threatened by the rising oceans, curators began seeking dryer and safer places for their most important works. New museums were built in alternative locations, and major museums in places such as Chicago and Toronto were expanded.

The inundation of Montreal caused most of the museums there to move their collections to Toronto. The Art Institute of Chicago grew over time to more than a million square feet to accommodate the art from museums in New York, Boston, Washington, and Philadelphia.

The sad part was the many masterpieces that weren't moved to safer places in time. At first, cities built seawalls and moved their collections to new facilities on higher ground. Then, on a single day, all those great seaport cities in the old United States disappeared in nuclear fire, along with the great cities and museums of London, Paris, St. Petersburg, and Rome.

The facility in Chicago was massive, and at any given time, at least two-thirds of the art was in climate-controlled storage. Those areas were the most susceptible to the type of burglary James envisioned. The major trick for a thief there would be gaining access to the warehouse and inventory records. If you couldn't find a treasure, you couldn't steal it.

Dad drove me to the airport. I hadn't flown enough for it to become routine or boring for me, so I still felt a bit of excitement getting ready to board a plane for the seventeenth time in my life. Airplanes were one of the few machines still fueled by petroleum, which made flying wildly expensive. If I'd been paying my own way to Chicago, I probably would have booked an electric train, which would have taken fifteen hours but been a lot cheaper and safer. At least a dozen jets a year crashed because they got caught in storms too strong for them to navigate.

Wil met me at the airport in Chicago. He wasn't difficult to spot, his shaved bronze head sticking up above the crowd. I could have found him by simply following the line of sight of every woman between fourteen and eighty-four. I didn't understand why he wasn't a vid star. Men who looked like that didn't need any acting talent.

To my surprise, embarrassment, and immense pleasure, he caught me up with his hands around my waist, swung me around, and enveloped me in a hug. "Libby! It's so good to see you. How was the flight?"

"It was okay." I looked around. Based on people's expressions, I guessed that half of the women in the place hated me. I took solace in knowing I was probably the only person in the place, other than Wil and the security guards, who was armed, so I could fend off any jealous attacks. I couldn't figure out why a man who could have any woman he wanted, sometimes acted as if he wanted me. Or maybe he made all women feel that way.

Wil drove an expensive hybrid hydrogen-cell-and-electric European sports car when I met him in Toronto. In Chicago, he escorted me to a sedan that cost even more. I let him put my check-in bags in the trunk, but I didn't want him to feel the weight of my carry-on bag.

"If I get the contract," I told him, "we'll come down on the train. Some of the equipment would be too heavy and expensive to bring on a plane."

He nodded. "We?"

"I don't know what you told the people at the museum about me, and really, Wil, I am very grateful for the recommendation, but this job is a lot bigger than anything I've ever done. My dad is going to be working on it with me."

He chuckled. "I'm surprised to hear you admit that anything is beyond your abilities."

"Aw, come on. I'm confident, but I'm not arrogant. Overconfidence will get you killed."

"True." He grinned at me. "I have reservations at the best steakhouse in Chicago tonight. I hope you brought an appropriate dress."

"Of course I did, but not with the intention of wearing it for you. I brought it to look nice for Museum Director Zhukoff. I do know how to act around the kind of people who populate museum boards of directors."

Wil laughed. "Miss Libby, will you do me the honor of letting me escort you to dinner this evening?"

"Well, I do have to eat, but I'm going to speak to that Deborah Zhukoff about how I'm being treated," I said with a smile. I leaned over and gave him a peck on the cheek. "Thanks for picking me up."

He took a route through town to avoid the backup from a wreck on the freeway. What should have been an hour's trip turned into three times that.

"Have you seen the AIC before?" Wil asked.

24

"I was at the Art Institute once in high school, once in college, and the last time a couple of years ago," I told him. "That time in college, I spent a whole week viewing the exhibits. You know that my minor was Art History, right?"

"Yes, it's in your official bio."

"And my university records, which I know you've read."

"Those are private."

I couldn't believe the prim way he said that, and I couldn't contain a burst of laughter. "Oh, come on. Don't give me that bullshit. I know your shoe size and when you went to the dentist last. I'm in the business, remember? The only things you don't know about me are things that aren't in any computer, or that you're not good enough to hack into."

He blushed and then laughed. "You got me there."

⊕⊕⊕

I'm tall for a woman, six feet two inches, but I had to wear stiletto heels to look Wil straight in the eyes. It might have been my imagination, but it seemed that people turned to watch us as we walked to our table in a secluded corner of the restaurant.

The other patrons were dressed to be seen, as were we. He wasn't lying when he said it was one of the ritziest restaurants in town. If all the women pooled their jewelry, we could have bought an island complete with cabana boys. I doubted I could have calculated the bill without a computer's assistance. Of course, that was only a guess, since my menu didn't include prices. Typical corporate treatment of women as fashionable ornaments.

25

My filet was tender enough to cut with my fork, the wine Wil ordered exploded like sunshine and fresh fruit in my mouth, and the atmosphere was as elegant as any restaurant I'd ever seen.

The best thing was the company. I had always appreciated Wil's effortless grace and elegance. Combined with his vid-star good looks, dinner with him was the kind of experience girls dreamed about. The wine filtered into my brain, and I began to feel very romantic. I backed off on the wine.

I had no desire to be a corporate trophy wife, not that I fit the profile. I was pretty, but not beautiful, and the marriage market for corporate executives didn't have a mutant aisle. I had even less desire to be a kept woman. The only other option for a relationship with a man in Wil's position was to be an occasional bedmate. With his looks, I was sure he already had plenty of applicants. As much as I liked sex, I usually wanted it to mean a little more than a good time. I had the same problem with James, who gave me the feeling he did want a wife.

When we finished our dinner and the waiter cleared our dishes, I started feeling itchy and uncomfortable in a vague sort of way. I never knew how to describe it, but I'd felt it before.

"Wil, let's go somewhere else for dessert," I said.

He cocked his head and asked, "Is something wrong?"

"I don't know. It's been wonderful. I mean, I'm really enjoying this, but, well, I don't know. I'm uncomfortable. Can we go somewhere else? Please?"

His brow furrowed and he studied me. I could see that his mind was working.

"If you like," he finally said and held his hand up. The waiter instantly appeared. "Check, please."

26

The waiter handed him the bill, and Wil swiped his card. I stood, and Wil hurried around to pull out my chair.

"I'm sorry," he said as we walked to the exit. "I should have known you'd be tired after your flight."

"It's not that," I answered. "I don't know how to describe it. Sometimes I get sort of itchy, as though something isn't right and I need to move."

The air in Chicago was much worse than in Toronto. We stopped to put on our masks, then stepped outside. Wil handed his claim check to the valet, and the world exploded.

Actually, the restaurant did. Glass and flame and the pressure of an explosion burst forth from inside the restaurant, slamming into me. I felt searing heat on my back and I flew through the air, hit the street, skidded, and rolled. When I finally stopped moving, I felt as though I had just received a good beating. I lay there, my mind blank and unable to focus on any thoughts.

People were screaming. Pushing myself to my feet, I looked around at a nightmare. Bodies littered the street, but I was only looking for one. I spotted Wil lying in a twisted heap against a limo, entangled with the valet attendant and a woman in an evening gown. The fire raging inside the restaurant lit the whole scene.

I started to rush over to him and almost tripped over my high heels. I reached down to take them off, then noticed the sparkling shards of glass and debris all over the pavement. Deciding I was lucky I still had my shoes, I tottered over to where Wil lay.

Something niggled at the back of my mind that there could be another explosion. Throwing caution to the wind, I peeled Wil away from the other people and dragged him around the limo to the side away from the restaurant.

I checked his pulse and his breathing, and heaved a sigh of relief. The skin over a large bump on his head was split and leaking blood, but otherwise he looked okay. Rolling him over, I saw that his back was completely clean except for a couple of shards of glass embedded in his right shoulder. That's when I realized that my back still felt as though it was on fire. I had been standing between him and the restaurant.

Reaching behind me and brushing my hand down my back, I felt pain in my fingertips and in my back. When I looked at my hand, I saw it was covered in blood. My first thought was that my dress was ruined. My second thought was how dumb and inappropriate my first thought was.

I fished in Wil's pocket and pulled out his phone. I pushed the speed dial button and then punched one.

"Explosion at Torbert's on Rush Street," I said when someone answered.

"Who the hell are you?"

"The woman Wilbur Wilberforce took to dinner. He's unconscious and the restaurant is on fire."

Silence, then, "We have people on the way."

⊕⊕⊕

It was late morning before they would let me see Wil. I walked into his hospital room and said, "You certainly have a unique way of showing a girl a good time."

He looked over at me and did a double take.

"What the hell happened to you? You look like a mutie."

28

I ran my hand over my bald head. "It's my new look. Don't you like it? It's all the rage this season." In addition to dealing with bruises and scrapes over most of my body, the doctors had spent more than two hours picking glass and splinters of wood and metal out of my backside, including my scalp. My shoulder-blade-length blonde hair was gone.

"My head hurts," he groaned.

I tried to be upbeat. "Lucky you landed on your head. The doctors were afraid you had a fractured skull, but I told them it was solid bone, so no problem."

Wil gave me a sickly grin. "Are you all right?"

We were wearing matching hospital gowns. I turned around and held the back open so he could see the bandages that covered me from head to ankles.

"Nothing terribly serious or deep," I said, turning back to face him, "but since I was covered in blood, they kinda freaked out. I won't be sitting down or lying on my back for a while. They actually gave me a transfusion. I asked if they had any blood from a mutie who could fly, but no such luck."

Lying on my stomach across the foot of his bed, I asked, "Who is Democracy Now?"

He blinked at me. "What are you talking about?"

"The bomb at the restaurant. The news feeds say that a group called Democracy Now is claiming responsibility."

With a groan, he said, "A bunch of stupid terrorists."

"Well, they certainly know how to pick their targets. Boatloads of corporations are scrambling to figure out their new organization charts this morning."

29

The news was subdued, a lot less than I would have expected for such a catastrophic event, but some information escaped before the corporations clamped down. Several independent news feeds reported that at least two chairmen of the board and three chief executive officers of different corporations died in the explosion, along with at least a dozen more corporate officers of various ranks. No one mentioned the restaurant staff or the women patrons, but the reports put the body count between eighty and a hundred. I assumed that Wil and I were lumped in with the "forty people injured."

I handed Wil his phone. "If you feel up to it, you should probably call Deborah Zhukoff and tell her we need to reschedule our appointment." It was ten o'clock and we had a meeting scheduled for eleven. I had no idea if people at the museum would know about the bombing.

He made the call, setting a new appointment for Monday. When he hung up, he asked, "What happened?"

I knew that a person with a concussion often had gaps in their memory. "What is the last thing you remember?"

He got a pained look on his face and thought for a while, then said, "When I picked you up at the hotel."

"We had a wonderful dinner, I gave you a blow job under the table, then you asked me to marry you and promised to sign a prenup giving me all your worldly possessions."

Wil stared at me, then said, "No, really."

I sighed. "I knew I should have gotten your signature before you could weasel out of it." He just glared at me.

"We finished our dinner and went outside to get

your car," I continued. "We were standing at the valet stand, and I was behind you when the restaurant blew up. Major explosion with some kind of flammable explosive. I don't see how anyone in the main dining room could have survived."

"That bad?"

"Truly nasty. I've played with explosives a little bit, but I've never seen anything like that." I shifted onto my side, trying to find a comfortable position where I could see his face. "Do you think you could ask where my stuff is? After the doctors cut off my clothes, I think my purse and stuff were confiscated by your people or the police."

"Yeah, I'll ask." He made a call on his phone.

A nurse came in and shooed me out, but I hung out down the hall and snuck back in after she left. Wil was sleeping, but I lay on his bed and used his phone to surf the infonet. About an hour later, a man showed up with a box.

"Elizabeth Nelson?" he asked. "Or are you Jasmine Keller?"

Jasmine Keller was a disguise I had used for an undercover gig the Chamber of Commerce hired me for in Toronto. The identification was totally authentic, issued by the Chamber.

Wil stirred and opened his eyes. "Hi, Devon."

Devon held out the box. "Here are your companion's belongings."

Wil motioned to me, but Devon put the box on the bedside table.

"An interesting collection." He held up my garrote. "They found this in her hair." Next, he put my stiletto and hat pins on the table. "These were in her bra. And this," he pulled out a compact thirty-two

31

caliber polymer pistol, "was strapped to her thigh. Then we have the purse, which in addition to identification for two different individuals, had a phone, a can of mace, a can of skin-seal, another pistol with a silencer and extra ammunition, an ejector knife with a spring strong enough to break your wrist, and a jet injector filled with a fast-acting barbiturate. Quite the fashionable range of accessories for a young lady going out to dinner."

He and Wil looked at me expectantly.

"After last night, you can't tell me that Chicago isn't a dangerous place," I said. Wil opened his mouth but I hurried on. "And don't tell me that you'll protect me. Hell, I ended up shielding you with my body. I should get a medal. I'm a hero."

Devon rolled his eyes, and Wil just shook his head.

I jumped up, gathered all my stuff, and put it back in the box. "Thank you," I said to Devon, then hurried out and down the hall to my room.

CHAPTER 4

Most of my bandages came off after three days. I had lots of half-healed scars and I was sore, but nothing to keep me in the hospital. Online shopping and delivery provided clothes so I could leave the hospital with some dignity. I wasn't about to ask Devon to get clothing from my hotel room. He was likely to check my other suitcases, and one held equipment even harder to explain than the contents of my purse. I would feel naked if I traveled without a sniper rifle, but I'd probably have a hard time explaining that to people.

The doctors kept Wil until Sunday, and the Chamber sent a limo for him. The doctors strictly prohibited him driving until his headaches stopped.

I rode with him to his home, dying of curiosity all the way. I had long fantasized about what kind of mansion he had. His position was the equivalent of a corporate associate vice president, which meant a salary and bonuses large enough to pay even my fees if he wanted to.

We drove to what they called the West Loop and a fancy apartment complex. Wil's place was nice, new, modern and shiny, but a major step down from most of the places I'd robbed. As far as I could see, the main attractions of the apartment complex were the bar and a health club on the roof, which Devon told me provided a lot of opportunities to meet the opposite sex.

"I'm disappointed," I told Wil. "I figured you had a thirty-room mansion nestled in acres of unspoiled wilderness."

"I apologize," he said. "I'll have my realtor find something suitable immediately."

33

"Sounds good. I'll design your security system. Ten percent off because you're a friend."

"You'd charge me?"

"You had your chance to get it free, but you weaseled out of the prenup."

He just rolled his eyes.

We had delivery pizza, and then his limo took me back to my hotel.

Bright and early Monday morning—or bright and early for me—we showed up at the Art Institute to meet with Deborah Zhukoff and Malcolm Donnelly, chairman of the museum's board. Donnelly was also Chairman and CEO of Tarden Corp., a manufacturer of steel building materials.

Wil seemed to think ten o'clock was fine for a meeting and couldn't figure out why I hadn't eaten breakfast yet. I'd barely had time to get in a quick workout in the hotel fitness room, the first time since I was injured. I hoped my stomach would stop growling before our meeting.

"You have hair," he said in a slightly shocked voice when I walked out of the hotel and got in his limo.

"I'm part lycan, didn't I tell you?"

He scrunched his lips and said, "You bought a wig."

I shrugged. "I don't want to walk into an interview looking like I got jumped by every gangbanger in Chicago." I hadn't bought a wig, of course. My chameleon abilities covered up all the bruises, scrapes, and other damage.

Usually, official online pictures are heavily doctored, reflecting how the person looked when they were ten years younger, and/or were staged in the most flattering of ways. Deborah Zhukoff looked good

34

in her picture. In person, she looked better—strikingly beautiful, especially for a woman in her forties. A voluptuous hourglass figure encased in a form-fitting designer dress didn't hurt her first impression.

Donnelly was a bit shorter than I was, slender, with salt-and-pepper hair and brown eyes. According to his bio, he was fifty-two years old, but he looked older, his face creased and weather-beaten.

We sat in a conference room and exchanged pleasantries, talked about how awful the bombing was, and the weather in Toronto. When my stomach growled loud enough that people looked around for lions, we finally got down to business.

I told them my rates, and said I would need to spend a week, possibly two, at my base rate to define the scope of the assessment. After that, I'd give them a quote, and my associate and I would delve into the details.

"And how long do you think the entire assessment will take?" Zhukoff asked.

"My guess is six to eight weeks once we get started, if you include all of your storage facilities. I'll provide a draft report of my findings two weeks after that."

Zhukoff and Donnelly exchanged glances. "We were hoping we could get it done sooner," she said.

"Securitas installed your systems, is that correct?" I asked.

"Yes, they did."

"They're one of the best in the business," I said. "Of course, on a project this size, there's always the possibility they screwed something up, or missed something. My guess is that at worst, you're only ninety-nine percent secure. If you're willing to live with that, then you don't need my services at all."

They squirmed in their seats and looked uncomfortable.

"What I'm saying," I continued, "is that any holes in your security aren't going to be glaring. A firm like Securitas doesn't make obvious mistakes. If you want complete assurance, then my company will have to check a hundred percent of your installation and compare it to their specifications and a complete risk profile. That's going to take time. Some other firms might have more people so they can do it faster, but the level of expertise we provide is uncommon. It's up to you."

Zhukoff looked at Wil.

"I don't have any arguments with anything she's saying," Wil told her. "Her associate retired as Director of Security at MegaTech, and one of MegaTech's subsidiaries is a competitor to Securitas. You're not going to find anyone more knowledgeable."

In the end, I got the go-ahead and signatures on a contract I had prepared in advance for the initial assessment. The sun seemed to shine brighter when we walked back outside. Even my bruises felt better.

⊕⊕⊕

When I showed up at AIC the following morning, a secretary type led me to a small office in the basement, and I balked.

"This won't do. I need large tables to spread out blueprints and schematics. Don't you have an unused conference room?"

She called Zhukoff, who came down to talk to me.

"I'm going to be asking for blueprints of every

building you own, lease, or borrow, and I need space to spread them out. I need room for the schematics for all of your security installation, and to keep them neat and separated. If this is my workspace, I'll need to block off the hall so I can use the floor."

She regarded me with a twinkle in her eye and a twitch at the corners of her mouth.

"We do have a space such as you describe, but it's in our oldest building and hasn't been used in years."

"May I see it?"

"Certainly." She led me out of the new modern part of the museum, across an elevated walkway, through another building, down a long flight of stairs, up another flight of stairs, through a dark back hallway, across a glassed-in terrace that served as a surrogate for an outdoor café, down more stairs, and finally to a locked door at the end of a hall. She keyed in a security code and pushed the door open.

Inside the large room were empty bookshelves, several large wooden tables, and half-a-dozen old wooden chairs. And dust. Lots of dust. One dirty window provided some light, but when Zhukoff flipped a switch, half of the fluorescents on the ceiling came to life.

"This would be perfect," I said. "Do you supp—"

Her laughter interrupted me. She had a wonderful laugh. "That we could get it cleaned up a little? Yes, I think we can manage that." She turned to the secretary type. "Jess, get hold of housekeeping and tell them to spruce this up and replace the lights."

Jess pulled out a radio and gave the orders.

"Do you have a map showing how to get here?" I asked.

Zhukoff laughed again. "Yes, but there are shorter

ways. This is part of the original museum, and your car can drop you off right down there." She walked over to the window and pointed down at a parking lot.

She put her hand on my back in a friendly way and said, "I apologize that we're not ready for you this morning. Why don't you come over to my office and we can discuss what else you need while we get this space cleaned up?"

I tried to hide my wince. My back was still very tender.

We trooped back through the labyrinth along a different path to Zhukoff's office. I had always loved the museum and was secretly relishing the chance to thoroughly explore it. At one point, I stopped, and Deborah didn't notice until she had walked on quite a way.

I stared at the incredible necklace in the case—a gold, enamel, opal, and amethyst creation of René-Jules Lalique crafted in the late nineteenth century. The main motif, repeated in nine pendants, was an attenuated female nude, whose highly-stylized curling hair swirled around her head, and whose arms sensuously curved down to become a border enclosing enamel-and-gold swans and an oval cabochon amethyst. Shorter pendants, set with fire opals mounted in swirling gold tendrils, separated the nudes.

"Incredible, isn't it?" Deborah asked.

"I love his work. I wish I could own something of his."

We continued on to her office, where she made me tea and we sat on a comfy couch next to each other. I explained all the documentation I would need, as well as an escort to take me around and show me things.

"I probably don't need the tour guide until next week," I said. "Somebody from your maintenance staff who has access to everywhere would be ideal."

"Not someone from security?" she asked.

"No, I want the guy who crawls around in the ceilings or under the floor when the lights or the plumbing aren't working. I want the guy who knows how the trash gets out of the building."

She cocked her head and in a flat voice said, "The trash."

"Two paintings were stolen from the National Museum in Brasilia last year. They recovered the paintings and discovered they were smuggled out of the building in the trash. If you aren't doing a security screen on your garbage, you've got a major hole that needs to be plugged."

I could see the 'Oh, crap!' thought by the expression on her face. "I'll check on that immediately."

She put her hand on my knee, smiled, and said, "I can already see this is going to be worth the money. Thank you, Elizabeth."

We had lunch in a staff dining room off the main restaurant, and then went back to inspect my workspace. The dust was gone, and the window was clean, but otherwise the place was bare. Just the way I wanted it.

⊕⊕⊕

I spent the week reviewing the blueprints and schematics, scanning them, and sending them to my Dad. First major security problem. Why did their system allow me to do that? I carried a roll of

39

blueprints out of the building and took it back to my hotel one night. Even though I brought it back in the morning, no one should have been able to carry anything out of the building unchecked. I could have easily rolled a Rembrandt into the middle of those blueprints.

I was healing nicely, and by Wednesday, I could even sit on one of the hard, wooden chairs in my workroom. I took a break at lunch and called Wil. The doctors hadn't let him go back to work. I had talked to him a couple of times, and he still had episodes of double vision and headaches.

That afternoon, Deborah stopped by.

"How's it going?"

"Making progress," I told her. "I'm finding a few things you should pay attention to."

"Problems with the system?" She moved from relaxed to alarmed in two seconds flat.

"Oh, no. Just some procedural things, training of your staff, things like that. The system stuff looks fine," I hastened to reassure her.

Her shoulders slumped. "Well, that's good to hear. We spent a huge amount on the upgrade."

"But you wanted my assessment anyway?"

She shook her head slightly. "That was Malcolm. He said that unless everything was verified and validated by an independent expert, we were just guessing as to how well the job was done."

I nodded. "That is standard procedure for large computer systems projects."

"He's very smart, and a good businessman. We're lucky to have him on our board." Her voice changed on that last part, almost as though she were reciting a slogan rather than something she believed.

"What are you doing tonight?" Deborah asked, changing the subject.

"Just back to the hotel, dinner, hot bath. Maybe read up on some of Securitas' specifications until I fall asleep. If you ever have insomnia, system specs are a good cure."

She laughed. "I thought I might take you out to dinner. We could get to know each other. We're going to be working together for quite a while if your schedule is correct."

I straightened from the blueprint I was leaning over and turned to her. "Can we go someplace that doesn't have a lot of corporate bigwigs? I don't think I could handle being bombed two weeks in a row."

"Oh, you poor dear," she said, reaching out and stroking my shoulder and upper arm. "Of course. I have just the place. Great food, casual atmosphere, and not a CEO in sight."

"Sounds good. How should I dress?"

"Oh, casually. Nothing fancy. I'll stop by your hotel for you about six-thirty."

$\oplus\oplus\oplus$

I knew my definition of casual and that of a woman such as Deborah Zhukoff were vastly different. Her choice in clothes was decidedly feminine and fashionable. A lot of pink and other pastels, with skirts and dresses rather than business suits. In short, Deborah was a girly-girl, with elegance and sex appeal oozing out of her pores.

I also wasn't naïve. I had watched her with other people, and not once did I see her touch another woman. Hands-on wasn't her standard personnel management style. I also noticed the looks I was getting from her secretary. If looks could kill, I would've needed body armor around Jess.

After my shower, I put on a red blouse with a broad, open collar, black stovepipe pants that fit my butt like I was poured into them, and a belt-length black jacket. With a pair of four-inch heels, I would be a head taller than Deborah and rather masculine-looking standing beside her and her curves. To emphasize that, I set my illusory hair into a tight bun at the back of my head.

My instincts proved correct. Deborah showed up in a sports car wearing a dark green pleated skirt with a hemline well above the knee, and a bright yellow blouse that showed plenty of cleavage.

"My, don't you look nice," she said with a bright smile. "Very sexy."

I laughed. "Very practical." I pulled up the leg of my trousers to show my bruises and scars. "I won't be wearing anything that shows much skin for a while. And my back and ass make this look good."

"It's a miracle you're up and around," she said.

I agreed. Wil might not remember why we were outside the restaurant, but I did. It haunted me. I couldn't remember the feeling I had, just that I was uncomfortable.

Deborah took me to a Mediterranean restaurant with many small rooms with small alcoves and candlelit tables set far apart. I quickly noticed that almost all the parties were couples, and at least half of those were same sex couples. I understood her promise that we'd avoid the titans of industry.

"I'm curious," I said as we waited for our meals. "Your official bio indicates you've never been married." For a woman of her class that was highly

42

unusual, as was her position as head of a major institution.

She took a sip of her wine. "By the time you get a PhD, you're a little too old to make a traditional marriage. Truth to be told, I'm not against marriage, but I've never met a man I loved more than art."

A sly smile crossed her face, and she looked at me over the rim of her glass when she said, "You're rapidly passing marriageable age. No panic? No regrets?"

I laughed. "I come from very unconventional parents. A very unconventional mother. Mom never presented becoming a corporate wife as a goal. Quite the contrary."

To my surprise, Deborah blushed. Evidently, she had researched me and found my mother's history. I wouldn't have thought a single woman would be scandalized. Director Zhukoff was a bit more conventional than she was trying to project.

"How long have you known Wilbur?" I asked. "I'm a little surprised that a non-profit institution would seek a vendor through the Chamber of Commerce."

Tossing her shoulder-length brown hair, she said, "You shouldn't be. Museums, the Symphony, and other artistic endeavors, have a special relationship with the Chamber. We can't support ourselves, but the elite classes need something other than money to set themselves apart. High culture has always depended upon the moneyed classes for patronage. The Chamber helps us organize and coordinate that and ensure our survival."

"Well, that makes sense. So, that's how you met Wil?"

She blushed again. "He is very fond of art. I met him at a gallery show for a young local artist."

$$\oplus \oplus \oplus$$

After dinner, Deborah asked, "Back to your hotel, or are you interested in seeing some more of Chicago?"

I acted as though I was thinking it over. "Is your taste in music confined to opera and the symphony, or do you ever go slumming to listen to common tunes?"

Laughing, she said, "Chicago has a rich blues tradition. Do you like blues?"

"Twist my arm," I said, returning her laugh.

We drove to a club and turned her car over to the valet.

"Don't wander too far," Deborah cautioned me, her eyes scanning the neighborhood around us. "We're on the edge of a mutie district. Friends of mine tell me it's safe, but I just never feel that way."

We went inside and found a table. It was a very upscale club, but the band was playing some great down-and-dirty blues. The patrons were casually well dressed, even though the crowd contained a fair sprinkling of mutants. Among the obvious mutations, I spotted more than a dozen bald women and several chimeras—people with multi-colored skin and hair. Those weren't necessarily mutations, since both could be due to developmental abnormalities, but anyone who wasn't normal was usually classified as a mutant. The vamps and lycans were definitely mutants.

"The mutant community is either more affluent here than in Toronto, or less inclined to hide their abnormalities," I observed.

44

Deborah looked around. "A bit of both, perhaps. Scientists noticed mutated animals and fish in Lake Michigan three hundred years ago. The percentage of mutations here is higher than any other North American city, except Denver. Unless, of course, you want to consider what's left of Mexico City a city."

I watched a man in a business suit walk up to the bar on four hands, like an ape. He stood upright to order a drink, then returned to his table walking upright, looking quite normal.

We ordered drinks from the automenu. After taking a sip of her colored thing with a bunch of fruit on a toothpick, Deborah continued. "There's a mutie district in the southwest part of the city and another one near Gary. I've never been near either one, and they are basically lawless. Here, on the North Shore, a lot of mutations crop up even in the better families. Those that are viable have the same opportunities available to them as everyone else."

I was so used to the prejudice that I didn't have to bite my tongue. What she meant by viable went beyond the ability to function. A child would also have to be physically whole and presentable. Even healthy mutants from rich families might get turned out if their mutations were unsightly. At the best, they had no chance at moving up the corporate ladder, so the mutant janitor could be the brother of the CEO.

I wondered why Deborah took me there instead of a more mainstream club. I was glad she did, as I was more than comfortable and planned to come back on my own. Then she asked me to dance, and I realized that she didn't expect to meet anyone she knew. Me? I didn't care what anyone thought about me.

We stayed for a couple of hours, dancing a few times and enjoying the music. Then a couple of fools got in a fight over a girl. It didn't appear to me that she had an interest in either one of them, but the alcohol-testosterone mixture bathing their brains wasn't helping them to pay any attention to reason. Unfortunately, they started their little game near our table.

I grabbed my beer and stood up, facing the pugilists and shielding Deborah.

"I think we should move," I told her. "I don't want to get caught in this thing."

I felt her stand behind me. "I'm ready," she said.

About that time, a couple of one fighter's friends joined in the fray, which caught the attention of the other guy's buddies. I turned, grabbed Deborah by the arm and headed toward the exit. We almost got there.

Then a chair flew across our path, followed by a man staggering into me and knocking me off balance. I grabbed his arm and steadied us both, then pushed him away from me. Instead of thanking me, he cocked to throw a punch. Some people don't recognize courtesy. I kicked him in the knee, and he screamed as he went down.

I tried to turn back toward Deborah and the door, but two more idiots decided they wanted to show a girl how tough they were. I could have told them that wasn't the way to impress a lady.

I took one out with a roundhouse kick to the head and hit the other one in the throat with the edge of my hand. My recently healed left hand. It hurt. I kicked him in the stomach out of spite. A man as tall as I was looked down at the three on the floor and then up at me.

"I'm out of patience," I told him, putting my hand in my purse. "Anyone else comes at me, I'm going to start killing people."

"Right," he said and turned away.

I backed up until I ran into someone. Looking down, I saw it was Deborah, standing next to a bouncer.

"Let's get out of here," I said, draining my beer and handing the glass to the bouncer.

We collected her car, and she drove me home.

"That was quite a performance," she said once we were on the road.

"I don't provide bodyguard services, but my dad made sure I knew how to protect myself," I told her. "These shoes make it hard to demonstrate my best move, though."

"Oh, what's that?"

"I have long legs and I can run like hell."

CHAPTER 5

I spent the rest of the week going through the documents AIC gave me and sending them on to Dad. Other than lunch with Deborah one day, and Friday dinner with Wil at his apartment—he cooked, something no man except my dad had ever done for me—I spent my time working.

The museum was busy on Saturday, and I wandered around in the crowds, observing the docents, staff, and security guards. That night I made my first efforts to hack into the computer systems. The public-facing computers were easy. I worked from Saturday evening until almost midnight Sunday to get into the administrative systems. I was impressed, but I did get in, using only tools and techniques available to anyone on the infonet.

I didn't even try to access the security system. They were secure against most attacks. Mom and I had built specialized tools to hack into Securitas' systems, but no one needed to know that.

My second week in Chicago, I organized and wrote my initial report and prepared my bid for the main assessment. After running it by Dad, I presented it to Deborah and Malcolm Donnelly on Thursday, and flew back to Toronto Friday morning.

Dad picked me up at the airport and did a double take at my new hairdo.

"What the hell happened to you?"

I turned around so he could see the almost-healed scars on the back of my head. "I got a little too close to the action. Chicago's an exciting town."

On the way into town, I told him about the bombing. By the time I finished, I could see his agitation.

"Why didn't you call me?" he asked.

"And what?" I returned. "There wasn't anything you could have done except worry."

"Does your mother know?"

"Oh, hell no. She would have been on a plane before she hung up the phone." My mother talked a good game. But in spite of projecting a devil-may-care attitude, and telling me I was a big girl who didn't need mama to take care of me, she was over-protective to the max.

"Dad, do you think you can tap into your contacts and find out how dangerous those terrorists are? If we're going to be working in Chicago, I'd like to be a little better informed. What's available publically is pretty slim."

"Will do. We don't have anything like that here in Toronto, but Chicago is five times as large."

After Dad dropped me off and I got unpacked, I called James.

"Hi," I said when he answered. "I'm back in town. Did you miss me?" Even though we'd had a third date, I figured a subtle nudge to remind him I existed wouldn't hurt.

"Of course, I missed you. What was your name again?" I could hear the smile in his voice.

"Alice. Or maybe Karen. Or Susan. I get so confused sometimes," I replied.

"I get confused, too," he said. "Ever since a woman named Libby broke my heart, I spend my nights searching for tall blondes, but it's never the same." He gave a dramatic sigh.

I had to laugh. "Would it interrupt your schedule if I asked you to dinner tonight?" He didn't answer immediately, and then the silence extended. "Oops.

49

Did I hurt your masculine ego by asking you out? Am I being too forward? Should I play harder to get?"

He laughed. "No. I was just checking my schedule. I have a meeting that runs late, but no blondes waiting for me afterward."

"Oh, good. No place fancy. I don't feel like dressing up. An Poteen Stil? Do you know it?"

"Sure. I can be there by eight o'clock."

⊕⊕⊕

When James arrived at the bar, the band playing that night was starting to warm up. We went through the "what happened to your hair" routine. I wanted him to see me au naturel for a reason.

We punched our orders into the automenu, and he looked around. "I don't think I've been in here since my university days."

"Too low brow for a corporate big wig?"

"Too much fun for us corporate types," he said with a smile. "You know that we have to pretend we like charity receptions and the opera. Anything as raucous as an Irish pub must be left to the lower classes."

With a big sigh, I said, "Yeah. Probably no chance at all of getting blown up in here. Where's the excitement?"

He shook his head. "I can't believe you almost got killed."

"I can't either. I didn't even know that such terrorist groups existed in North America. It seems like something that would happen a long way from here."

50

"What makes you think it was a terrorist act? It sounds like a gas explosion." His expression was a little too flat, his voice a little too neutral.

"It was a bomb attached to a gas line. A group called Democracy Now took credit, or blame, for planting the bomb. My friend Wil said they're a terrorist group agitating for an elected government."

Wil had shown me the forensic reports. The bomb itself wreaked havoc, but the secondary natural gas explosion killed most of the victims. I figured that if any corporation would be paranoid about terrorists, it would be the electric company. In James's position, he would have to be aware of security risks.

"Do you know of any groups like that in Toronto?" I asked.

He shook his head. "No, not that violent. There's a small chapter of Democracy Now at the university, but they're all talk. Most radicals sober up when they graduate and discover living without mommy and daddy's money is too uncomfortable for them. They cut their hair and put on a suit and go find a job."

I noticed he didn't mention any ghetto groups as being a threat. "So, you're not worried at all about sabotage."

That got a reaction. "Of course, we are. We spend a huge amount of time and money on physical and cyber security. We're the ultimate target for a terrorist group."

"And you get regular briefings on those groups and other security threats?" I asked.

He nodded, though he seemed a bit reluctant.

"So, spill. That bombing in Chicago killed a hundred people, and the corporations suppressed the news. What's the real scoop?"

With a sigh, he said, "Chicago and Toronto are different. The large southern cities have larger excluded populations, and of course, that breeds instability."

Our food slid out of the chute in the automenu box. I was starving, so I took a big bite of my burger.

"What do you mean 'excluded populations'?" I asked as soon as I swallowed.

"Those who aren't included in a corporate or other institutional ecosystem. Here in Toronto, that's about fifteen percent. In Chicago, it's over a third of the population."

"People like me."

"Oh, no. Corporations depend on the expertise of independent consultants. I'm talking about people completely outside normal society. The mutants, criminals, those without jobs or education. You know, those people in the slums and ghettos."

In other words, people like me. I didn't tell him that.

"How about the couple down the street from me who run a small convenience store? Or how about a family-owned funeral home?"

"Well, yeah, I guess they would fit the definition of exclusion, but people like that are the cream of excluded society. I mean, they aren't out agitating for change and blowing up restaurants. They do contribute to society as a whole."

I almost asked him if he considered the owner of a high-class brothel part of the cream of excluded society, but bit my tongue. No need to drag my mother into it.

"So, who is blowing up restaurants and threatening power plants?"

"Ideologues, such as Democracy Now or the Communists. Jihadis. You know there's still a lot of hate out there over what happened in the Middle East. Radical Christian groups, such as the Army of God, ecoterrorists, like The Sierra Club. The Chamber puts out a monthly bulletin covering about a hundred fifty groups on their watch list."

I filed it away to check the Chamber's computer system when I got home.

After we finished eating, we danced a few times, had a few more beers, and then he walked me out to the taxi stand.

"I can give you a ride home."

I turned to him and put my arms around his neck. "And then I'd have to make a decision about inviting you in. But I'm still not sure if I want to do that, and I'm definitely not healed enough to do that."

"Not sure if you like me enough?"

"Oh, I like you. And you're very sexy. But I'm not a one-night-stand kind of girl. I have to decide how much I like you, and how much you like me. Besides, I'm headed back to Chicago next week, and I'll be gone for two months. If you still remember me when I get back, and you don't have another girlfriend, then we'll see."

I leaned forward and kissed him. Very thoroughly. He did a damned good job of returning the favor and making sure I would remember him. Breathless, I pushed away from him and said, "See you when I get back." Then I jumped into the waiting taxi before I did something I would regret.

As I bounced my butt against the hard taxi seat, it affirmed that I was not healed enough to do too much bouncing. The last thing I needed was to fall for someone who didn't accept my differences. I

53

wondered how interested James would be if he knew just how "excluded" I actually was. I could stop being a criminal, but my mutations weren't a coat I could take off.

CHAPTER 6

I felt like I was going on safari in some old movie as I watched a robot load four large crates on the train.

"Are you sure we need all of that?"

Dad chuckled. "Since you don't have twenty so-called experts to impress your clients, you need to do it with technology. Being competent isn't enough, Libby. You have to have some showmanship." Some of the equipment was mine, some his, but half of it was borrowed. He had good connections.

"Fine for you to say," I grumbled. "You'll just sit around and issue orders while I have to go out and set all of that up."

"And someday you'll be able to abuse your kids the same way. It's a millennia-honored tradition."

I shot him a sour look.

"Don't worry," Mom said. "If you've forgotten anything, let me know and I'll ship it down to you. Did you remember to pack the kitchen sink?"

The twinkle in her eye that she always got when she pulled my chain made me want to growl at her.

Through a misunderstanding, the trucking company delivered the crates to our hotel instead of the Institute when we got to Chicago the next day. I had to call Deborah, who sent over a truck with some of her crew to haul the stuff to the right place.

For convenience, I had reserved rooms for Dad and me at a place closer to the Institute. Either I forgot to tell Deborah we were at a different hotel, or she forgot, but she sent the truck to the hotel I'd stayed in before. By the time everything got straightened out, it was late afternoon. I had the crates open in my conference room at the Institute, and with Dad looking over my shoulder the whole time, assured myself none of the equipment was damaged.

"Is everything all right?" Deborah's voice came from the doorway.

"Finally." I turned and gave her a smile. "Doctor Deborah Zhukoff, this is my assistant, Doctor Jason Bouchard."

She walked over to Dad with a smile and her hand out. As they shook hands, she said, "Your assistant? You don't introduce him as your father?"

"He says I need to be more professional," I said, and everyone laughed.

She did the standard survey of my father and his power chair, which most people did. Then she asked, "Did you get checked in?"

"Yes, but we haven't had a chance to unpack or change clothes yet."

"Well, why don't you do that, and I'll send a car around about seven to take you to dinner." She looked down at Dad. "We can get to know each other. I have a meeting set up at ten in the morning to kick off the project."

⊕⊕⊕

The place she took us was really fancy, and I must have looked nervous as we sat down.

"Don't worry, Libby," Deborah said, reaching out and taking my hand in hers. "I called ahead, and they swept the place for explosives this afternoon."

I wanted to lash out, but managed to simply say through clenched teeth, "I'm sorry, but I don't think that's very funny."

She straightened, and blinked at me, then said, "Oh, my, I wasn't trying to be funny. It's true. Most of the best places are doing that now. Getting into one of the country clubs is worse than going to the airport."

My turn to blink stupidly. "Really?"

"No one was going out to eat," Dad said.

"Or anywhere else," Deborah chimed in.

"I talked with a couple of people I know in Chicago," Dad continued, "and security firms have had a bonanza on the North Shore." He winked at Deborah. "Lucky you got us when you did. I had two offers for Libby to put in new systems here in Chicago. Had to tell them all we were too busy."

I wasn't sure whether to believe him or not. That was the first I'd heard about it. Even with such precautions, the restaurant was only half-full.

During dinner, Deborah asked, "Why did you change hotels? Didn't you like the Shoreside?"

"It was fine, but I wanted a place that was closer. The Shoreside had a nice gym and a swimming pool, but nowhere to run. At the Winston, I can go running in the park." The Art Institute was surrounded by parklands on the shore of Lake Michigan.

"When do you run?" Deborah asked. "I run in the evenings after work."

"That works for me. I'm not fanatical about it, though. I only run twice a week." I had noticed that she used the same expensive filter masks I did, the kind that were marketed to athletes and people who worked outside.

Later, standing outside waiting for the car, Deborah put her hand on my back and said, "Do you want to go running tomorrow evening before dinner?"

"Yeah, sure. That would be nice," I said.

⊕⊕⊕

Dad and I met with members of the Institute's board of directors the next morning, and then with the staff that afternoon. Dad gave an excellent presentation to the board. He had a lot of experience with people at that level, and I felt the board went away feeling good about the money they were spending.

After the morning meeting, we planned to have lunch in the staff dining room. Dad and I started over there, then I remembered that I wanted to tell Deborah to get a facility map for the afternoon meeting.

"Dad, just go on down this hall, and past the double doors, take the hallway to your right. You'll see the dining room on the left. Okay? I'll catch up to you. I need to tell Doctor Zhukoff to get me a map for this afternoon."

I headed back toward Deborah's office. Jess wasn't at her desk, so I walked past it. Just before I got to the doorway, I caught a reflection in the glass of the open door.

Deborah was leaning against her desk with her arms around Malcolm Donnelly's neck. He had his hands on her ass, and they were kissing.

I backed away quickly. I had met Mrs. Donnelly on my previous trip to Chicago. She was about Deborah's age, but not nearly as beautiful. I wasn't surprised at Malcolm's morals, but I'd thought Deborah had more self-respect.

Going back to the hallway, I leaned into the

reception area and called, "Doctor Zhukoff? Is anyone here?"

"Just a minute," her voice came from the back. I waited until Deborah came out. "Yes, Libby. What can I do for you?"

I told her what I needed, then headed back to the dining room to meet Dad. I had admired Deborah for reaching such a powerful and prestigious position. It made me a little sad as I wondered if sleeping with Donnelly was part of the deal.

About thirty people attended the afternoon meeting. I introduced Dad and myself and explained what we were doing and what unusual things might happen while we were conducting our assessment.

"As part of our testing, we'll be setting off alarms all over the place, doors will lock unexpectedly, lights will flash or strobe," I told them. "Just wait a couple of minutes and things will return to normal."

When I was finished, we had a smaller meeting, with Deborah, Jess, David Wilson, the Chief of Security for AIC, and Aubrey Henderson, the Head of Maintenance.

"I think this is a waste of time," Wilson said. "Securitas certified the system, and we signed off on it. It seems we're just spending money for nothing."

"It's standard practice to have an outside firm verify new systems," Dad said. "But our review will cover more than the electronics. We'll be looking at procedures, staffing, training, and all the practices in place here at the museum."

"Nothing wrong with my staff or their training," Wilson said. "There hasn't been a theft here in over fifty years, and that guy was caught before he left the parking lot."

Wilson had come up through the ranks during a thirty-year career, and from what I'd already seen, most of the museum's weaknesses were due to his staff and their practices. He was already validating my fear that he would get defensive.

⊕⊕⊕

The main museum complex included some storage facilities. The rest of the warehouses were thirty miles away. I planned to treat them as a separate assessment. With over a million works of art, there wasn't any way to display them all at the same time, so most of the museum's collection was in storage.

Dad roamed around in his chair telling me what to do and inspecting my work, while I did all the equipment installation. Luckily, Aubrey loaned us a couple of large men to do all the carrying for me.

After my first full day of equipment installation, Deborah stopped by.

"Are you up for a run this afternoon?"

Even though I prided myself on being in shape, I was sore from bending, lifting, stretching, and a lot of other motions I wasn't used to. A soak in a hot bath sounded better than running.

"Go on," Dad helpfully chimed in. "We can catch dinner after your run."

Thanks, Dad. I needed to have a talk with him about that sort of thing.

"I'll need to go back to the hotel to change," I said. "I didn't bring my running clothes with me."

"You'll have to do that from now on, won't you?" Dad cheerfully said. "Go on, go get them. I'll finish up here and see you later."

"I'll walk over with you," Deborah said. "I can change at your place, can't I?"

Yes, Dad and I really needed to have a talk.

The weather was warmer in Chicago than in Toronto, but not as humid, so it sort of balanced out. Dark clouds were building in the northwest, and the wind started to rise. Halfway to the hotel, it started to rain. By the time we reached shelter, drops the size of my thumb were pummeling us, driven by gusts of wind that made it hard to keep our feet.

Drenched to the skin, we took the elevator up to my room, laughing like schoolgirls.

"The storms get worse every year," Deborah said. "I guess that's the tradeoff for not having snow anymore."

"Did the clothes in your bag stay dry?" I asked her.

She unzipped her gym bag and pulled out her running gear. "It's a little damp, but not bad."

I went to the closet as I shed my clothes. "I'm not sure what I have that will fit you. Maybe a skirt."

"Not a chance," Deborah said with a laugh. "I haven't been as thin as you are since high school."

I came out of the closet with the largest skirt I had and found Deborah stripped to her bra and underwear, the same garments I still wore. I held the skirt against her, and it became very apparent that it wouldn't fit.

"I told you," she said.

When I looked up from the skirt to her face, I saw she was looking at my breasts. I took a step back and turned toward the closet.

"You'll have to do with what you have in your bag.

61

I think I can send your wet things down and get them dried."

"I'll send for a car. My running clothes will do to get me home," she said from very close behind me.

Slowly, I turned around to find her standing less than arm's reach from me.

"You have the most incredible body," she said. "I always wanted to be an athlete, but I got this."

'This' was an hourglass figure with world-class curves. She was built even better than my mom, and that was saying something. The comparison was apt, since they were about the same age.

"And you have the kind of body men drool over," I said. "When I was a teenager, I'd have killed to have curves." I noticed her skin was covered in goose bumps. "You're cold. Get out of those wet things and either dry off or take a hot shower."

I put my hands on her shoulders and turned her away from me, guiding her toward the washroom. I pulled towels off the shelf and handed her a couple, then took one myself and went back into the bedroom.

The room phone rang and I answered it.

"Libby?" It was Dad. "Did you make it back before this storm hit?"

"No, we got soaked. Deborah doesn't have any dry clothes."

"Well, as soon as things settle down, I'll have a car take me over there, and she can go home."

"Okay. Call me when you leave."

I heard the shower start. By the time Deborah dried herself and came back into the room, I had dried off and dressed. She looked disappointed.

Room service brought hot tea and pastries, and took our wet clothes. We watched a news feed about

62

the storm while we had our tea and chatted.

Dad arrived at about the same time as the hotel staff delivered Deborah's and my dry clothes. The intensity of the storm had died down to a steady, pounding rain, and Dad said he would rather have dinner at the hotel than go out. Deborah declined and said we'd go out another night.

I walked Deborah down to her car. As we said our good nights, she suddenly drew me into a hug, then turned and walked away. I went back upstairs to have that talk with Dad.

CHAPTER 7

"Other than a few minor issues, which we've fixed, the electronic security system installed by Securitas is solid. You got your money's worth," I told Director Zhukoff and Board Chairman Donnelly as I pushed a thin report across the table.

I took a deep breath. "We do find significant vulnerabilities due to staffing, training, and procedures in use by your security office."

Dad and I had worked six days a week for a month testing and documenting our test results. We found a loose camera here, a nicked cable there, an unconnected door contact, and half a dozen other minor problems, none of which could be exploited by themselves.

The museum's leaders paged through the report that identified those issues. None of them had taken me more than fifteen minutes to rectify.

"And the report on staffing issues?" Donnelly asked.

"It's not completed yet. We would like your permission to perform two black-hat incursions, one here and one at your warehouse complex."

Donnelly's eyebrows rose. "And what value do you think that would provide? Can't you simply detail the issues and provide a plan to remedy them?"

"To be honest," Dad said, "in more than forty years, I have yet to see a corporate management team take such a report seriously enough. Our interactions with Chief Wilson and his commanders leave us with a lack of confidence that he will consider our recommendations at all. Black hat operations destroy the denial, the excuses and justifications."

"Do you remember my warnings about your trash?" I asked. "Has anything been done about that?"

Deborah squirmed in her seat. "I gave orders to have all the trash screened."

"And?"

She glanced at Donnelly. "I'm not sure how much has been done."

"Are you aware," I spoke slowly to capture their attention, "that in almost two months of me working in this facility, no one has ever checked to see what I was carrying out at night?"

I let them chew on that for a while. "Your blueprints and security schematics are stored on your computer network."

"Such documents are protected by appropriate security," Donnelly said.

"Yes, but anyone with access can send the documents outside of your network. I have done so, sending them to my own off-site account."

"How did you get into our network?" He glowered at Deborah. "Did you give them access?"

I handed them a much thicker report. "The computers controlling your security system are practically impregnable. Your administrative computer systems are not. I've detailed the tools and methods I used to break into the system. You can duplicate everything I did. That includes access to your warehouse inventory database. I know where all your treasures are located."

The stunned looks on their faces told me we had finally broken through their complacency.

Donnelly paged through the report for a few minutes while we waited. When he looked up, he asked, "How do you want to run these black-hat things?"

⊕⊕⊕

The voice over the public-address system announced, "The museum will close in fifteen minutes." The docents and security guards began ushering people toward the exits.

I went to the women's restroom. Inside, along with all the normal fixtures, was what appeared to be a locked door. An hour earlier, my lock picks had made short work of opening it to reveal mops, brooms, cleaning supplies, and enough toilet paper to open a store.

Pulling the door closed behind me, I made myself comfortable sitting on a barrel, plugged in my earbuds, and called up a book on my tablet. A package of jerky and some dried fruit served as dinner.

Between ten-thirty and eleven, fresh guards would come on and the current guards would go home. When that happened, they would turn off the door alarms.

At ten o'clock, I exited the closet and slipped through the shadows to my target, *Starry Night* by Vincent van Gogh.

I quickly cut the screws holding the frame to the wall and gently lowered it to the floor. Using a screwdriver, I pried off the plaque on the wall identifying the painting, and put it in my pocket.

I put on my gas mask while walking down the stairs to the back entrance.

At ten-thirty, three security guards came through the employee's entrance. I rolled a canister emitting smoke down the hall toward them, and just to make sure, shot each of them. Trotting toward the guard station near the main entrance, I shot a guard who came around a corner toward me. I tossed another canister of smoke into the guard station, and shot both guards as they flushed out into the hallway.

The sergeant in charge looked down at the splash of red paint on his chest and back up at me. "Damn!"

My answer was a grin as I shoved the paintball gun into the holster at my waist.

I hit the employee entrance door at a dead run. A white van pulled up to the door and I jumped in. Giving Dad a thumbs-up, I turned to Deborah and Malcolm in the back seat and handed them the plaque.

Deborah's eyes bulged. "Where's the painting?" she asked in a panic.

"Sitting on the floor where I found it. I took the frame down from the wall, but even touching it made me nervous as hell."

"Any problems?" Dad asked.

"No. The guards were angry that I got them, but everyone was well behaved."

"And if it had been a real robbery?" Donnelly asked.

"If I used drug darts, they'd all be asleep. If I used bullets, you'd have six dead guards."

⊕⊕⊕

The insides of the warehouses were divided into pods, each with its own climate control system. The

67

settings varied depending on what was stored in each pod.

I targeted a pod containing small stone sculptures and jewelry, art objects least susceptible to temperature and humidity fluctuations. Art that was also difficult to damage. The idea was just to show their vulnerabilities, and I didn't want to take any chances with harming any of the art.

Three nights after my 'theft' of *Starry Night*, I stood fifty yards from the ten-foot-high chain-link fence surrounding the Institute's warehouses. Razor wire coiled along the top, and there were sensors every three yards. The guard station at the entrance was manned around the clock.

That was just the first obstacle. Getting inside the warehouse would be more difficult.

I had considered several different ideas, but in the end, chose the most direct approach. At four o'clock in the morning, I walked up to a stretch of fence out of sight of the guard shack. Pulling a laser welder out of my backpack, I used it to cut a hole in the fence. The sensors didn't detect anything touching the fence because nothing ever did.

The next obstacle involved the guards at the locked entrance. I stripped out of the black coveralls I was wearing to reveal the security guard uniform underneath, then walked up to the front door and pushed the buzzer. Inside, the guards would be watching me on their cameras, and there really wasn't any reason for me to be there. I was counting on human nature. I had made it through the front gate, so I must be legitimate.

"What's your business?" the speaker at the door barked out.

"Special delivery." I held up a bag often used by

the museum to transport small objects. "This was supposed to be brought over this afternoon, but someone screwed up and forgot it. Wanted it brought over before all the stuff was inventoried this morning."

I waited a couple of minutes, then the door clicked. Pushing against the door, I pulled out my paintball gun and shot both guards as soon as I stepped inside. They stared at me incredulously.

"You've been had, boys," I said.

Entrance to the various pods required a keyed entry code, but the security guards had little electronic wands that could override the locks. I took one of them and headed into the facility. Curiosity drew the two 'dead' guards along in my wake.

It took me a few minutes to find the pod I wanted. The wand opened the door, and I walked in. Stacks of shelves, reaching three stories high, surrounded me in all directions. The air was cool, but dry. Nothing in that pod needed water or humidity.

Access to the upper shelves required use of three-story rolling metal staircases. I searched until I found the aisle, location and shelf of the statue I wanted. Pushing the staircase into place, I found the wooden box with the correct bar code. It fit in my hand and only weighed a couple of pounds.

From my research, I knew the granite carving was swathed in bubble wrap and steel straps reinforced the box. The statue would survive unharmed even if I dropped it three stories.

After I put on my dark coveralls again, I walked out of the building and through the hole I'd cut in the fence. A half-mile walk around the outside of the fence brought me to the entrance gate as the sunrise began to lighten the sky.

"Hey, how's it going?" I called to the guards as I approached them. I held out the box. "I think the museum lost this. You should probably call the director and tell her you found it."

The next thing that happened was they pointed guns at me, and I ended up spread-eagled on the ground while they searched me.

"Careful, boys. This is only a drill," I said as one of the guards started to get a little too personal. "Watch where you put your hands."

Deborah showed up half an hour later, and Dad made his appearance immediately after. He'd been watching from the trees nearby. The guards handed her the box.

"What is it?" she asked me.

"A ten-thousand-year-old fertility goddess." No one could put a price on such an object. It was the definition of priceless.

⊕⊕⊕

"Parlor tricks," David Wilson yelled. "You gave them all the information about our systems and procedures, and turned them loose. Of course they were able to exploit what they call vulnerabilities. My men would have responded differently if those were real robberies. They knew it was only a test. What were they supposed to do, shoot her?"

He glared at me and Dad. I got the impression he wasn't happy about our intrusion testing.

"We understand the difference between a test and an actual situation," Deborah said. "The fact remains that she did manage to penetrate our facilities."

"You gave her everything except the damned key," Wilson grumbled. "Not a fair test at all."

⊕⊕⊕

Dad wrote up his recommendations for a reorganization of the security staff, along with new processes and procedures, and a training program. I prepared a quote for securing their administrative network. We submitted our invoice, and the museum paid it. I felt as though I was walking on air.

Deborah and Malcolm indicated that they would quickly approve my quote for the computer work, so I decided to stay in Chicago rather than do a back-and-forth to Toronto.

I had seen Wil a few times, but I'd mostly been busy, and with Dad on site with me, I felt kind of uncomfortable when I took any time off. But after I put him on the train with all of our equipment, I decided I deserved a little rest and relaxation.

"Hey, are you busy tomorrow evening?" I asked when Wil answered his phone.

"I have a couple of dates, but nothing I can't break for you," he replied.

I snorted a laugh. "I'd hate to be the cause of any supermodel suicides."

He laughed. "What's going on?"

"We finished the gig with AIC, and I wanted to take you out to dinner and thank you for the recommendation. Choose your favorite place."

He said he would make reservations. "The place is nice, but more dressy-casual than upscale fine dining. I'll pick you up about seven."

I did an infonet search on 'dressy-casual in Chicago'. How was I to know what that meant? After looking at some pictures, I went out and bought a new dress.

Whether I got it right or not, Wil greeted me with a wolf whistle when I walked out of the elevator in the hotel lobby. I felt my face burn as everyone turned to look.

Cajun food was a new experience for me, and even though it was really spicy, I liked it. We lingered over strong bitter coffee and cognac while I listened to a story he told about traveling in Europe and fantasized about taking him to bed.

It remained a fantasy. His phone rang.

He gave it a quick look, then said, "Damn. I'm sorry, Libby. I have to take this."

I watched him stand and walk out to the lobby with the phone to his ear. He was only gone a short time, but he grabbed the waitress on his way back to our table.

"I'm sorry, but I have an emergency. I'll ask the host to call you a cab."

"What's the problem?"

"Not sure. Maybe a terrorist attack."

Later, I blamed it on the brandy. "Screw the taxi. I'll go with you and watch your back."

His eyes widened in surprise, but before he could say anything, the waitress brought the check. He paid while I grabbed my coat and purse.

"You need to keep your schedule more private," I said as I got in his car.

"What are you talking about?"

"I think the terrorists are planning their attacks on nights we go out."

With a chuckle, he pointed the car into the air and headed north.

"Dear, God," I breathed, checking my seatbelt. "I

73

didn't know this is an aircar."

"Prevents traffic issues," he said, leaning forward and flipping a switch on the dashboard. People began talking, and I realized we were listening to some sort of emergency security channel.

"What happened?" I asked.

"A bomb in a bar near the University of Chicago. It doesn't sound too bad, not like the one at Torbert's," Wil said.

I tried to make sense of the voices on the radio, but except for one very clear voice giving orders, everything seemed garbled. Wil was listening closely to it, so I kept quiet.

In spite of the terrible circumstances, flying over Chicago was a treat. I couldn't help but be impressed by all the pretty lights stretching away to the horizon in all directions except for the dark of the lake.

An explosion of static came over the speaker. It took me a moment, but then the screaming and cursing from different voices told me that it really was an explosion.

"What the hell's going on?" Wil shouted into his microphone.

Everything coming over to us was unintelligible confusion. Then a voice broke through. "There's been another explosion."

"Where?" Wil barked.

"In the street. Busy. I'll get back to you," the voice on the radio said.

"First responder targeting," I said.

Wil shot me a look. "What?"

"It's an old terrorist trick. Set off a bomb, then when the emergency personnel show up, set off another one. Wil, there could be more."

He clicked his mic. "Warning. Everyone be aware, there may be more bombs. Extreme caution."

"We have massive casualties," a voice answered. "At least thirty or forty down."

Wil looked over at me again.

I shook my head. "Any new responders should come from the same direction as the original ones," I said. If there are more explosives, the chances are they're waiting for people to come from the other direction. Wil, I know it sounds callous, but you should hold people out of the area until you can secure it."

He turned back to his driving, or flying. I didn't know what to call it. I'd never driven or flown an aircar. His face looked like it was set in stone, and I could almost hear his teeth grinding together.

"How far away are we?" I asked.

"Another twenty minutes," he answered.

⊕⊕⊕

Wil brought the car down near a cluster of emergency vehicles two blocks away from the scene of the bombings.

"Stay here," he said, then got out and went around to the back of the car. He came back, opened my door, and handed me a combat vest like the one he was wearing. It didn't match my dress, but I put it on anyway. One of his men handed him two helmets, and he handed one to me. Luckily, I had worn boots with low heels.

"This really isn't fashionable," I told him. "Do you think you can find the budget to redesign your assault wardrobe? You're never going to attract many female recruits if you dress them like this."

He just rolled his eyes.

I followed him and some SWAT team personnel forward. We reached about a dozen men hiding behind a couple of armored vehicles. Some of the men wore Chamber SWAT uniforms, others were from the Chicago police.

I peered past them and saw several vehicles, including a fire truck and three ambulances, sitting in the street. I counted five bodies lying about, and I could see the blackened storefront that must have been the bombed tavern.

"Status," Wil ordered.

"About fifteen minutes after the first medical and security personnel arrived, a second bomb went off," one of the Chamber men said. "We checked like you told us, and we've identified at least one more device planted on the block beyond. We can't get any closer, though, because of the snipers."

"Where?" Wil asked.

"The copter took out a couple of the bastards on a rooftop over there," the man pointed. "But the guys on that rooftop," he pointed again, to a closer building, "are under a metal awning on the roof. They can't get out without exposing themselves, but we can't get to them. No place to land, either."

As if to add a punctuation mark to his report, I heard several shots in quick succession and bullets bouncing off the armored cars and pavement around us.

"Wil, this isn't fun," I said.

"You're the one who insisted on coming along."

"That's not a very chivalrous answer. So, what's the plan? We're going to sit here all night hoping they're stupid enough to jump out of their cover and be gunned down by the helicopter?"

Everybody gave each other blank looks, which told me that I'd hit the nail on the head. I grabbed Wil's jacket sleeve and pulled him toward me.

"What you're going to do is cover me. Lay down suppressing fire so that I can get to the base of that building in one piece. Understand?"

"How the hell do you know so much about this? First responder targeting. Suppressing fire. You sound like some kind of commando."

With a sigh, a big sigh to express my frustration with someone asking stupid questions, I pulled out my phone and did a search. Then I shoved the display in front of his face.

"*Counterinsurgency Tactics* by Jason Bouchard. He's written fifteen books, including five on the history of different terrorist movements. Other little girls read books about ponies and princesses, but I had fucking quizzes on this shit when I was growing up." I shook my head. "I never doubted my father loved me, but he had zero idea about how to raise a girl."

At first, he just stared at the screen, then the laughter sort of bubbled up from inside him. "Oh, hell, Libby. I'm so sorry," he gasped between bursts of laughter. "I'll never doubt you again."

"I'll remember you saying that. Wil, if I don't know what the hell I'm doing, or if I don't know something, I'll tell you. All my pride is bundled into what I can do. Okay? I'm more than happy to back off and let experts take care of things."

"Okay." He flipped up the visor on his helmet, then flipped up the visor on mine, leaned forward and gave me a quick kiss on the lips. "Suppressing fire.

What are you going to do?"

I winked at him. "Surprise the hell out of everyone, I hope."

Crouching low, I moved toward the end of the armored car on our right and readied myself to run. I looked back at Wil.

"You ready?" he asked.

"Yes, I'm ready. Don't I look like I'm ready?"

All of the men popped up and started shooting at the snipers. At the same time, the helicopter swooped in and added its machineguns to the effort. I jumped up and sprinted down the street. When I reached the sniper's building, I dodged into the side street next to it.

The building was fairly new, and the mortar between the bricks was fairly smooth. But the window sills and headers above the windows provided hand holds. I pulled my pistol out of my purse and strung a length of nylon through a ring on the butt, tied it off, and hung it around my neck. Then I took off my boots and sat them down next to my purse.

Luckily, I don't wear tight skirts, so my dress didn't bind my legs as I began my climb. It wasn't the easiest climb I'd ever done, nor was it the hardest. About twenty minutes after I started, I pulled myself over the parapet onto the roof of the three-story building.

From where I lay, I couldn't see the snipers, though I could see part of the metal awning they hid beneath. I looked around and saw the helicopter about two hundred yards away and preparing to turn back toward me.

I invoked my chameleon ability and blurred my form, becoming invisible against the background of the roof.

Taking my pistol in hand, I checked to make sure the silencer was securely in place. I crept toward the snipers' hiding place as carefully as I could, trying to keep the vestibule where the stairs exited to the roof between us.

When I peeked around the vestibule, I saw two men with assault rifles on tripods to hold the barrels of the guns steady. They were sitting on a spread-out blanket, and they had a picnic cooler. Half a dozen empty beer bottles lay about.

The lack of professionalism offended me. Holding my pistol in a two-handed grip, I sighted on the head of the man closest to me and pulled the trigger. He slumped forward and lay still. The other man turned to look at him, a startled expression on his face, and I shot him in the chest.

Holding my breath, I waited for any reaction. Since I couldn't see the door leading to the stairs, I didn't know if any of their friends waited inside. The helicopter made another pass, but didn't come too close. The snipers had fired at it several times.

I was concerned that the copter might decide to shoot at me. From the time I started climbing the building, I had been out of its sight. Dropping my camouflage and becoming visible might not be the best idea.

My phone was in my purse. Too late to fix that oversight. Crawling back down the wall wasn't an option. I pondered for a few minutes what I should do, then decided that my best option was to try the stairs.

Slipping around the side of the vestibule, I stooped to pick up one of the discarded beer bottles. I couldn't hear anything inside, so I took the chance and tossed the bottle through the doorway. It made a hell of a racket as it bounced down the steps, and I winced as I heard it break in the distance. I listened hard, but only heard silence.

I peeked around the corner into a darkness much deeper than that on the rooftop. A stolen glance toward the snipers showed that neither of them had moved. If they weren't dead, they were either incapacitated or the best actors I'd ever seen.

Although I had left my purse and boots, I still had a few tricks and I pulled the stiletto out of my bra. Crouching as low as I could, with a knife in one hand and a pistol in the other, I began making my way down the stairs.

At the bottom, I found a narrow landing with broken glass and a door that opened outward. Shuffling my feet to try and prevent stepping on any glass, I moved behind the door, turned the knob, and pulled it toward me. Faint light from beyond lit the landing and allowed me to see the glass on the floor. Even better, I couldn't hear anything past the doorway.

But I did hear something above me. The man I had shot in the chest stumbled down the stairs, and for the first time I got a good look at him. Blood from his mouth covered his chin and stained the front of his shirt. He shouldn't have been walking, but pseudo-vampires are tough.

I raised my gun and fired, but only grazed his cheek. Then he crashed into me and grabbed my arm, pushing my pistol away from him. I stabbed him in the abdomen as my back hit the wall behind me. His free hand reached for my throat and succeeded in slamming my head against the wall.

Everything went black. My legs turned to jelly,

and I tried to slide down the wall, but he held me up. That was a bad decision. He should have let me pass out. I managed to pull my knife out of his belly and stabbed him in the side of the head. His eyes bulged and he started shaking. His hands loosened, and I was able to push him away from me. Placing the muzzle of my pistol against his forehead, I pulled the trigger.

The vamp wasn't the only one with the shakes. I was none too steady, and my vision was a little blurry, but I looked up the stairs, afraid his buddy might be waiting his turn to try and kill me. Mercifully, the stairs were empty.

I had to move the body out of the way to pull the door open again. When I did, I saw a young woman standing there with a pistol and a frightened expression. She wasn't any older than I was, and the top of her head barely reached my shoulder. I didn't bother to ask her politics before diving at her legs and knocking her off her feet.

After I pinned her down and shoved my pistol in her mouth, I growled, "Drop the gun or I'll blow your head off." She let go of her pistol.

"When I get off you, I want you stay right where you are. Do you understand?"

She nodded.

I backed off and stood. "Now, roll over on your stomach."

Like a good girl, she complied.

"Okay. I want you to get on your hands and knees, and then stand up with your hands in the air." She did as I asked. "Are there any more of you in this building?"

"No." Her voice shook. "Are Dan and Wally..."

"They're dead, which is what you're going to be if

you make one wrong move."

She stiffened, and I heard what sounded like a ragged sob.

"You're going to walk ahead of me and take me on a safe route out of this building. Do you understand? If anyone attacks me, I'll shoot you first. Now move."

She took me to the end of the hall, past what looked to be offices closed for the night, then down two flights of stairs. By my reckoning, we were at the back of the building, away from the street where the bodies lay in the aftermath of the bombings. We stopped in front of a door.

"Where does that lead?" I asked.

"To the alley."

"Open it. Slowly." I pressed the muzzle against the back of her head. "I don't plan to die tonight. As far as I'm concerned, you and your friends deserve your own dungeon in hell, so don't think I won't pull the trigger."

She pushed the door open and stepped out. I waited a moment, then looked around the corner. No one was there, so I grabbed her shoulder and pushed her out past the open door. I guided her around the corner of the building and retrieved my boots and purse, and my phone.

"Wil?" I said when he answered. "The snipers are down. I have a captive on the side of the building. Can you send someone to take charge of her?"

It only took a couple of minutes until SWAT troops surrounded me and took the girl away. Wil walked up and looked me up and down.

"Are you all right? Is any of that yours?"

I looked down at myself. The vamp had bled all over me. "You know, every time we go out, I have to buy a new dress." Turning around, I put my hand up to the bump on the back of my head. "Does that look too bad?" It hurt like hell when I touched it.

"No," he said. "It'll probably look worse in the morning."

With a sigh, I said, "Lovely."

"We need to talk," he said, "but not tonight."

"About?"

"Climbing walls like a spider, turning invisible, overwhelming armed insurgents, that sort of thing. Libby, the things you do aren't normal."

"Yeah. Well, there are a lot of normal girls in the world. You don't have to hang around with me if you don't want to."

"That's not what I meant."

"I'm kinda tired. I think I'm going to go sit in your car until you get through here."

I had no idea what in the hell I was doing playing hero. I looked around at all the emergency personnel who were getting paid to be there and then down at my ruined dress. And Wil wanted to talk about things I didn't want to talk about. I wondered what it felt like to be normal. I wondered if I knew anyone who was normal that I could ask.

CHAPTER 9

I was gimping around my hotel room the next afternoon feeling sorry for myself when Deborah called. "Libby? Are you still in town?"

"I told you I was going to stick around. What's up?"

"The board approved your proposal, and I have the contract drawn up. As soon as you can come by to sign it, you can start work on the computer system."

"They approved all the hardware?"

"The entire thing."

"I can stop by this afternoon."

"That would be wonderful. I'll be here."

"Whoooo hoooo!" I yelled after hanging up the phone. I stood to earn another half-million by hardening their administrative systems and databases. It was turning out to be a very good year.

That stopped me for a moment. I was in line to earn as much as Deborah, and I didn't even have a PhD or a fancy title. Not only that, but most of the money was legal. That had never happened before.

After a scalding-hot shower, and feeling much better about myself and the world, I dressed, had some breakfast, and headed over to Deborah's office.

"Here's the contract," Deborah said, indicating I should sit on the couch. She handed me a stack of papers, then went over to her sideboard and came back with two flutes of champagne. "And this is to our ongoing relationship." She handed me one of the flutes and clinked hers against mine.

"I was just thinking today how much I've benefitted from the museum," I said as I took a sip. Holding up the contract, I continued. "I'm glad you

84

have such faith in my work."

"Oh, darling, you and your father were wonderful to work with. The entire board was impressed." She sat down beside me, smiled, and leaned close. "Malcolm was impressed. You may end up getting some business from Tarden Corporation."

I read through the contract while sipping champagne, and Deborah kept refilling my glass. After we both signed the agreement and took our copies, she said, "Now, let's go celebrate."

She drove us to a restaurant where we had a nice dinner and more wine. From there, we hit a place with desserts to die for, accompanied by espresso and liqueurs. The next stop was a dimly lit bar with a quartet playing soft jazz. Deborah ordered dark chocolate and a carafe of a fiery liqueur that complimented the chocolate to perfection.

Deborah poured the booze into tiny glasses, handed me a piece of chocolate the size of my thumbnail, and said, "To a beautiful partnership." She popped the chocolate in her mouth and followed it with the liqueur. I tried it, too. The taste and feel of the combination was indescribable.

When she leaned over and kissed me, I didn't think anything of it and I kissed her back. The next thing I knew, her hands were all over me, including some very sensitive places. I was drunk, and she made me feel good. I went with the flow.

Her home turned out to be the thirty-room mansion I had imagined for Wil. A butler answered the door, and I got a quick glance at some of the house before Deborah dragged me upstairs to her bedroom.

⊕⊕⊕

I couldn't remember the last time I'd been that drunk, but the hangover reminded me of one reason I didn't like to drink that much. Another reason was that when you're drunk, you aren't in control, and I'm a bit of a control freak.

We got up disgustingly early, and Deborah was disgustingly cheerful for such an early hour. She dropped me off at my hotel on her way to work, and I went back to bed.

That afternoon, I submitted the orders for the hardware I needed for the museum's computer systems, then went back to bed again. I made a note to myself not to try and keep up with Deborah. The woman could probably drink a troll under the table.

Wil called and woke me up about sunset. I told him I was busy, but he insisted he needed to see me. I finally agreed to meet him the following evening. Remembering his comment the previous night, I wasn't in a hurry to answer his questions.

By the following morning, my head cleared and my appetite returned. While I was eating breakfast, Jess called and told me the first of my equipment had arrived. Since a lot of what I ordered was manufactured in the Chicago area, I had expected quick delivery.

I ambled over to the museum after breakfast, unpacked and tested the equipment, then set it aside. After logging into their network, I installed half a dozen software programs and began configuring them. By the time I stopped working that afternoon, the computer systems were already more secure than they had been that morning.

As I picked up my coat and headed toward the door, Deborah came into the room.

"Knocking off for the night?"

"Yeah. I'm supposed to meet Wil."

"Tell him I said hello." She pressed her body against mine, put one hand between my legs, and with her other hand pulled my head down to kiss me. "I wanted to thank you for the other night."

She let me go and stepped aside. "Have fun."

When I walked out into the hall, I found Jess standing there. She didn't look happy. I turned back to see a smiling Deborah following me. She stepped between us, put her arm around Jess's shoulders, and they walked away.

I didn't plan to ruin any more of my clothes. When Wil came to pick me up, I wore black jeans, a black shirt, and black waterproof jacket made from ballistic cloth. It wouldn't stop a bullet, but it would turn a knife blade, and blood washed right off. The same clothes I would have worn for a break in.

He looked me up and down while I gave him my best defiant look, daring him to comment on my non-sexy garb.

"Damn, Libby, did you pour yourself into that, or paint it on?" he finally asked. "I should have brought a fire extinguisher."

I felt my face flush. He'd seen me in those clothes before. That's what I'd worn regularly when we worked together the previous summer.

With a curtsey, I said, "I'm glad you like the outfit. I figured I'd save my nice clothes for someone who doesn't consistently take me to a disaster."

It was gratifying to see him blush, though with his

dark skin it wasn't as apparent as it was with mine.

We went to hole-in-the-wall kind of place that had a young and hip clientele, great hamburgers, and a girl singing with her guitar. I liked it a lot. It didn't look like the kind of place that would get bombed by unhappy radicals, either.

While we waited for our food, Wil said, "About the other night—"

"Yeah, about the other night," I said, cutting him off. "I've been thinking about that. I realized I was the only one out there who wasn't getting paid to risk my neck. You're right, I won't do that again. My dad always said that altruism was an insidious vice, and I have to agree. No one even said thank you."

He opened his mouth and closed it a couple of times, then tried to recover. "You climbed up that building like some kind of spider."

"What did you do the last time you went on holiday?"

"Huh?"

"Holiday. Vacation. What do you do? What did you do the last time you had time and money?"

"Went to Europe. I like history and museums."

"On my last holiday, I went to the Bruce Peninsula on Lake Huron and climbed cliffs," I said. "Have you ever done any technical climbing?"

"Uh, no."

"That's why my nails are so short." I held out my hand with the closely-trimmed nails painted a pretty red. Taking a drink of my beer, I asked, "Do you have any more silly questions?"

He gave me a sheepish look.

"I don't know what the hell you're thinking," I said, leaning close to him, "but the way you're coming

88

at me isn't appreciated."

Wil leaned back in his chair, biting his lip. "I'm sorry."

"You should be. I don't ask how the hell you got to your position, now do I? I could make insinuations about your age. Wonder if you're a psychic. Ask if your boss is a woman and if you're trading your favors. Such questions would be insulting, and you'd be right to take offense."

He had the grace to look embarrassed. "I'm sorry, Libby. Truly, I am."

"Good." I reached out and took my meal as it slid out of the slot. "Order me another beer, if you please."

After I finished my burger, I said, "To answer the question you wanted to ask, my abilities to climb walls, shoot people I don't like, and get into more trouble than any rational person should, have nothing to do with any mutations."

His head snapped up, and he blushed deeply.

I smiled and winked at him. "I'm just a fun sort of girl."

⊕⊕⊕

Deborah came to my conference room on Friday afternoon. We talked for a while about how my work was progressing.

As I pointed out something on one of the schematics, she came up behind me, wrapped her arms around me and put her hands on my breasts, pulling me tight against her.

"I don't understand anything about those drawings," she whispered.

She brushed lightly over my nipples through my blouse. They tightened in response, so sensitive that shivers ran through my body. One of her hands slid down, over my stomach and under my belt. Her clever fingers caused me to gasp.

Her breath hot on my neck, she continued to whisper. "I can't stop thinking about how you felt when you were beneath me. How you taste."

Even though I was cold sober, what she was doing to me, the images her voice recalled, sent hot lust coursing through me, enveloping my mind with longing. All the time I'd spent fantasizing about Wil probably contributed to my susceptibility as well.

"We can go to my place and have dinner in bed. Tomorrow's Saturday. We don't have anywhere we have to be."

I whirled about and crushed her to me, covering her mouth with mine. Soon after, we spilled out of the building and into her car. She gave it the order to take us home, and then we were all over each other.

At her house, she gave brief orders to the butler to bring us food and drink, and then pulled me by the hand after her up the stairs. We started shedding clothing before we even closed the door to her bedroom and fell together on the bed.

We stayed there most of the weekend.

CHAPTER 10

I woke up Wednesday morning to someone hammering on the door. Before I was half out of bed, the door opened, and half a dozen Chamber Security men, a couple of Chicago police, and Wil burst into the room with drawn guns.

"Hands in the air," one of them barked.

I complied, even though the sheet slid down to my waist. "Whoa. Hold on. What's going on?"

No one answered me as they spread out and started looking through drawers and the closet. Two of them tried to fit into the washroom. In general, there wasn't enough room for all of them.

I looked to Wil, who returned an angry glare, and asked him, "Can you tell me what's going on?"

"The museum was robbed last night," one of the other men said.

"And so, the first person you suspect is the security expert they hired to plug their holes? That makes sense. How stupid would I have to be?"

"Or how smart," Wil said. "The last person anyone would suspect."

"Obviously that strategy didn't work," I said, slowly lowering my hands and pulling the sheet up over my body.

Wil searched my clothes before he gave them to me, and didn't include a bra. They watched me get dressed, handcuffed me, then hustled me out and down to a waiting car.

We ended up at the city jail, but they took me to a part away from the other prisoners. Once they put me in a cell, one of the policemen threw a switch on the wall near the door and warned me that the bars were electrified. That's when I realized I was in a special section for mutants.

I tried not to smile. Please don't throw me in that briar patch.

After they all left, I took in my surroundings. The space contained six cells, and only one other cell was occupied. The girl, or young woman, I'd captured at the bombing watched from the cell across from me.

With good light, I realized she was a chimera. Her hair was two colors in patches, dark blonde and light brown. Her skin had a swirling mosaic pattern with one color almost as light as mine, and the other a couple of shades darker. One eye was blue and the other was brown. Although she had long hair and looked female, there was no telling what she looked like with her clothes off. Chimeras' gender might be anything on a continuum from pure male to pure female, and how she looked on the outside would tell me nothing about her internal organs. All that said, she was a very pretty girl, to some eyes exotic enough to call beautiful.

"Welcome to hell," she said.

"Thank you. Is there a schedule of events and entertainments?"

She snorted a laugh. "No schedule that I've figured out, but they come and ask me questions and yell at me a couple of times a day."

"Wonderful. I love being yelled at."

Standing up from her bunk, she approached within a foot of the bars. "You're the woman who put me here. The one who killed Dan and Wally."

"They weren't playing nice with others. You have to expect consequences when you take an assault rifle and start shooting innocent people on the street." I searched her face, trying to read her reactions. "They couldn't have expected to get out of there alive."

Various emotions played across her face, from anger to sadness to resignation.

"What do you really expect to gain by bombing and shooting people?" I asked.

Her eyes slid up and to the side. I followed her gaze and saw the cameras lining the passage between the cells.

"Do they turn the lights off at night?" I asked.

"Yeah. They feed me twice while the lights are on. That's how I know how long I've been here." Her diction was educated. She hadn't grown up in one of the mutie ghettos, or at least not one of the blight areas.

"Food any good?"

"Bland, but plenty of it. What did you do? I thought you were one of them."

"I think they just don't like girls."

She told me her name was Carly, and she watched me as I checked out my cell. Her dress was dirty and a bit ragged, and I could smell her even though ten feet separated us. Water for washing was a rare commodity in many of the mutant slums, and after a week, the cops still hadn't allowed her a shower. I didn't consider that a good sign.

Shortly after I arrived, two armed jailers and another man brought us unsweetened oatmeal, a peeled hard-boiled egg, and water.

"Yum," I said after they left.

"Same thing every morning," Carly said.

Dinner wasn't much better. A slab of fried soy cake with fried squash and applesauce. She was right about the size of the servings. The soy cake was enough for two people.

In between the meals, nothing happened. No one came to ask me questions or yell at me. I kept expecting Wil to at least come and glower in disapproval, but he didn't.

Without warning, the lights went out.

"Must be night time," Carly said. "Good night."

I waited a few minutes, then grabbed hold of the bars of my cell, shorting them out, and hitched myself up so I could reach out and touch the camera trained on me. I shorted out the camera, but wasn't sure if that had any effect on the other cells and cameras. I couldn't know if the guards monitored the electricity, but figured I'd find out soon enough.

My mischief done, I sat on my bunk waiting for visitors. Eventually I fell asleep.

I awakened to the lights coming on, and shortly afterward, the guards came with our breakfast. As they opened the door, I heard one say, "...sometime during the night. They were working yesterday."

"Any idea when they'll get them fixed?" another voice asked.

"Dunno. We'll probably have to wait until someone can come look at them."

I assumed they were talking about the cameras. One of the guards threw the switch that would turn off the current to the bars of our cells. After we received our food, he switched the electricity on again. I reached out and made sure the bars of my cell were still cold.

"Carly? How strong is the current running through the bars of your cell?"

"Knocked me on my ass the only time I touched them."

"Can you do me a favor and check them out again?"

She gave me a sour look. "Why don't you do it if you think it sounds like fun?"

I reached out and grasped a bar. "Mine are cold. No current."

Her brow furrowed. Walking up to the bars, she waved her hand close to them, then tentatively reached a finger out to touch one. Next, she took hold of it like I had. "You're right, it's cold."

"Cameras aren't working either," I said, taking a bite of my egg.

After thinking about it, she cocked her head and asked, "What did you do?"

I thought that was an interesting question. I look normal, and since I went to corporate schools and university, I never lived in the mutant ghettos. I do hang out in mutie bars sometimes and rarely have a problem. Maybe my height makes me enough of an oddball that I'm accepted.

But Carly found it easy to believe that I could disable cameras and electric security enclosures. Normal humans would never make that leap.

"Do you know people who can do that sort of thing?" I asked. "Mess with electrical devices?"

She regarded me suspiciously. "You're one of them. They just put you in here hoping I'd tell you something."

With a sigh, I began spooning oatmeal into my mouth. As bad as it was, I couldn't imagine it would get any better when it hardened into a cold lump.

"Why don't you tell me why your friends wanted to kill people," I said.

After she thought about it, I guess she decided

answering my question was harmless. "The corps are killing us. Some of us fast, some of us slow. They don't give a damn about us, so why not let them feel a little pain?"

"Who's us? Are you part of Democracy Now, or some other group?"

"Us. People like me and Dan and Wally. Mutants."

"Which one was Dan?" I asked.

"The vamp."

"And what kind of mutie was Wally?"

"A trog."

She meant a troglodyte, sort of a catch-all for photosensitive people, those who didn't do well in the daytime or outside. A vamp and a trog would make a great nighttime sniper team.

"Which one were you in love with?"

The question caught her off guard. I saw her eyes glaze over, she shuddered and drew a ragged breath. In a voice so low I could barely hear her, she said, "Wally."

"Sorry," I said. "He shouldn't have shot at me."

"Why are you here?" she asked again.

"They seem to think I stole art worth millions of creds from a museum."

"Did you?"

"No. It's just a mix up." I changed the subject. "You're educated. You could get a corporate job, or a job with an indie. You don't have to play martyr."

"I'm different. I'd always be different. How would you like it if people always stared at you?"

I stood up and her head bent back so her eyes could follow my face.

"They do. Get over yourself," I said. "The boys

used to call me a giant and a troll and throw rocks at me. When I was fourteen, I was the tallest person in the school, including the adults."

I resumed my seat and continued eating my breakfast.

"Well, I might have a chance in the normal world," Carly said, "but a lot of muties don't."

"Not arguing that," I said. "So, you just like hurting people. Maybe you should become a dominatrix. Make good money beating up norms but stay out of jail."

"I don't like hurting people." Her sullen, muted demeanor suddenly changed to animated agitation. "Sometimes you have to do radical things to make people pay attention. We're nothing, not even background noise. We need to make people aware of the problems we face."

With a sigh, I said, "Carly, I have one piece of advice for you before they get those cameras working again. The only witness they have that you were with Dan and Wally is me. They actually haven't asked me anything about you. Deny everything. Tell them you were just in the wrong place at the wrong time and I jumped to conclusions. The pistol wasn't yours, you just picked it up after my fight with the vamp."

She opened her mouth to say something, then stopped. "Seriously?"

"Do you like living?"

⊕⊕⊕

Four guards came for me after breakfast. They led me up two flights of stairs and into a room where Wil sat behind a table. He motioned to the chair opposite

97

from him.

"I've been sitting a lot," I said, pacing across the room and back. "I want a lawyer."

"What good do you think a lawyer will do you?" he asked.

"He's going to sue your ass off. Neither the Chamber of Commerce nor the Chicago Police have any right to detain me without filing formal charges."

"Calm down, Libby."

"It's Miss Nelson to you, and I'll be damned if I calm down. Who in the hell do you think you are? Whose idea was it to barge into my room like a bunch of storm troopers? Somebody steals something from the museum, and instead of investigating it properly, you assume that I did it?" I realized I was screaming when I heard the echo of my own voice.

"The robbers used weaknesses you identified in your report," Wil said.

"Wow. Those weaknesses were so unique. Do a little research on the past two hundred museum robberies and notice the similarities. So, I assume everyone who read that report is also in jail? The entire damn board of directors? No? Gee, you're falling down on the job. Why is it taking you so long to round them all up?"

The room was too small. I could only take three paces in one direction before I had to turn around. "I can't believe this. There were ten copies of that report plus the original on a chip, and God alone knows who might have read it. I guess I should feel lucky that you didn't literally shoot the damned messenger."

I stopped, leaning toward him with my fists resting on the table, and calmly said, "If I was going to rob that damned museum, nobody would even know anything was gone."

He held my eyes for a few moments then looked down.

"Do you have a copy of the report?" I asked.

"Yes." He reached into a briefcase by his feet and pulled it out.

"Look at page fifteen," I suggested. That was where I documented that no one had ever checked me when I left the museum. "After that, take a look at page thirty-two." On that page, during a discussion of some of the sloppy inventory work, I revealed that I had found an undocumented Gauguin behind a door in a workshop in the basement of the original museum building. The damned painting was worth millions, and as far as anyone could tell, had sat there for more than a hundred years. I had immediately called Deborah, who then called security and the head curator.

Wil read those passages in the report, then looked up at me.

"Nothing stopped me from walking out with a painting they didn't know they had. Nothing but my own damned integrity. Now, I want a lawyer."

He reached for me with his right hand.

"Touch me, and they'll be charging me with murder," I said through gritted teeth. He pulled his hand back.

With that, I pulled out the chair, sat down, crossed my arms, and refused to say anything else. An hour later, they took me out to the street and let me go.

CHAPTER 11

One of the Chamber Security goons drove me to my hotel. The people at the front desk didn't act happy to see me, but they did give me a key card.

The room was a mess. My clothes were tossed around, and every piece of equipment I owned, including my phone, tablet, and computer, were missing. So was my purse, with all my identification and credit cards.

I used the room phone to call my dad and tell him what had happened. He said he would find me a Chicago lawyer.

After taking a shower, I took the stairs to the floor above me and picked the lock on the housekeeping room using a piece of wire I took from the electric cord of the ice machine. Climbing up shelves stacked with fresh towels and sheets, I moved a ceiling panel and pulled down the suitcase I'd stashed there.

I felt somewhat better with a pistol, knives, a tablet, a burner phone, a spare set of identification, and a valid credit card. The rest of the weapons and the fake IDs stayed in the suitcase. After stuffing it back in the ceiling, I returned to my room and began a search on the tablet.

It didn't surprise me that the museum robbery hadn't made the news.

The phone rang about two hours after I talked to Dad.

"Miss Nelson? I'm Orlando Ortega. MegaTech asked me to call you. I understand that you might need a lawyer."

"Yes. Are you employed by MegaTech?"

"No, I'm not," he said. "I'm a criminal lawyer they

keep on retainer. My understanding is that you are also independent."

"That's correct. I'm independent of MegaTech." That was important. Although Dad was retired from the corporation and they'd take care of him to his grave, I wasn't part of their 'family' past graduating from university. "My business is incorporated, though, and I'm a paid-up member of the Chamber."

"Then you understand that my rates are five hundred credits an hour."

"Mister Ortega, I may need a criminal lawyer. I definitely need someone who isn't afraid to sue the Chamber of Commerce and possibly the Art Institute of Chicago. I have the money to pay."

"I would be most happy to be of service." I could hear the shark's smile in his voice.

"Then please come to the Winston Hotel, and bring a camera."

He showed up forty minutes later with a young woman in tow. Ortega was a weaseley sort of man with dark red hair and a mustache. The top of his head came to my chin. To my surprise, he was a vampire. I tried to control my smile as I thought, *Here's someone who won't mind going after blood.*

His assistant introduced herself as Molly McGuire. She was about my age, mid-twenties, as flame-haired and voluptuous as my mother, and I detected a bit of an Irish accent. She took one look around and said, "Oooh, I like what you've done with the place. Hotel rooms are so cold and impersonal unless you redecorate." Then she started taking pictures of everything.

I couldn't help but laugh. My clothes were scattered across the room, the bed was torn apart, and the closet looked like a bomb had gone off inside it.

Ortega listened to my story then asked, "What is your most pressing concern?"

"They've stolen everything of value. My phone, tablet, computer, all of my equipment, and my weapons. The computer alone has hundreds of thousands of credits worth of proprietary software tools and data. I not only want it back, I want them enjoined from accessing or copying any of it. My client files are confidential."

"And after that?"

"I have a half-million credit contract with the museum. I don't want them backing out on it. And if they do, I'm concerned about my reputation. I'd want to sue them for defamation. Sorry I can't provide you with the contract, because the Chamber's thugs took my copy."

"And the Chamber?" he asked with a sparkle in his eyes.

"Assault, theft, false arrest, kidnapping, humiliation, and whatever else you can sue them for. I may be an indie, but I pay my dues to the Chamber, so there should be some kind of breach of contract."

"I can start as soon as I receive a ten thousand credit retainer," Ortega said.

I fished in my pocket and handed him my credit card.

Ortega and Miss Molly finished up and left. I tidied up the room, put on a jacket, and hiked over to the museum.

Jess had her back to me looking in an open filing

cabinet when I walked into her office. "Is Deborah in?" I asked.

She whirled around, her eyes wide and a frightened expression on her face.

"What are you doing here?"

I gave her the kind of grin that scared men in bars. "I work here. I have a contract. Now, is Deborah in?"

Jess stammered and cast enough glances at Deborah's closed door to let me assume her boss was in. I didn't ask if she was busy or if she wanted to see me.

I beat Jess to the door and walked into Deborah's office. She looked up from whatever she was working on, and the blood drained from her face. Taking a seat in front of her desk, I said, "If I wanted to rob museums, I'd make a lot more money than I do designing security for them. But I don't. I think great art is one of the things that keeps us halfway civilized. I've always loved this museum. I'm grateful I can come here and see the beauty it contains. I can't do that in rich people's private collections."

I leaned forward and spoke slowly. "I didn't steal anything from this museum. Not even a paperclip. But I'm damned sure going to help you find who did."

She relaxed slightly. "I'm sorry, Libby, but surely you can understand our suspicion, considering how the works were stolen and what was stolen."

"No, I can't. I don't know what was stolen, how it was stolen, or when it was stolen. No one has told me a damned thing, just accused me of being a thief." I do righteous indignation well. I'm especially good at it on those rare occasions when I'm innocent.

Deborah blinked at me, then sighed. "The

custodian's closet trick. The thief took six pieces, including that Lalique necklace you drool over every time you pass it."

"Oh, no." I felt sick. "Not that." I thought furiously, then said, "That was a stupid thing to steal. You couldn't wear it anywhere because it's instantly recognizable." I tried to imagine what someone would do with that necklace. "Deborah, truly unique jewelry doesn't have a resell market. Usually major pieces are broken up, the gold melted, and the stones sold separately. But the stones in the Lalique piece aren't inherently worth very much. The necklace is simply a work of art. What else was taken?"

"A Modigliani, two Renoirs, a Degas, and a Monet."

"Were they all in the same section of the museum?"

"In the same wing, but not on the same floor. The necklace was on the fourth floor, the Modigliani on the third, and the French artists on the second."

I mulled that over. "So, it wasn't just a quick snatch. The works were targeted. I'll bet my virginity that the theft was commissioned."

She finally smiled. "Do you remember where you left your virginity?"

I grinned back at her. "In a dorm room at the University of Toronto. I'm sure someone has swept it up and tossed it in a rubbish bin by now. Can I see the list?"

She picked up a piece of paper from her desk and handed it to me.

Jeanne Hébuterne
Amedeo Modigliani
1919
Oil on canvas
36 x 28 3/4 in. (91.4 x 73 cm)

Necklace
René-Jules Lalique
ca. 1897–99
Gold, enamel, opals, amethysts
Overall diam. 9 1/2 in. (24.1 cm) 9 large pendants: 2 3/4 x 2 1/4 in. (7 x 5.7 cm) 9 small pendants: 1 3/8 x 1 1/4 in. (3.5 x 3.2 cm)

The Dance Class
Edgar Degas
1874
Oil on canvas
32 7/8 x 30 3/8 in. (83.5 x 77.2 cm)

Two Sisters (On the Terrace)
Pierre-Auguste Renoir
1881
Oil on canvas
39.6 in × 31.9 in (100.5 cm × 81 cm)

The Grands Boulevards
Pierre-Auguste Renoir
1875
Oil on canvas
20 1/2 x 25 inches (52.1 x 63.5 cm)

On the Bank of the Seine, Bennecourt
Claude Monet
1868
Oil on canvas
32 1/16 x 39 5/8 in. (81.5 x 100.7 cm)

I recognized the pieces. But... "This list doesn't make sense," I said.

"Not as a whole, no," Deborah said. "The Monet and the Degas might bring three or four hundred million at auction, as would Renoir's *Two Sisters*. The other Renoir might be worth a few million at most. The Modigliani, well, I can see that a collector might want it. It is one of his most famous works. Maybe two hundred million."

"Over a billion credits," I breathed. "I didn't realize it was so much."

She shrugged. "It's been ages since works like this have hit the open market. As you said about the necklace, you can't display them in public, so your guess about having a collector commission the theft makes sense. I can't think of a collector of impressionist art who has that kind of money, though."

"Or a collector so eclectic," I said. Indeed, it looked like a list my father might put together from different orders by different collectors. I'd hit a private collection once with a list. I bypassed some of the most valuable pieces in favor of someone's personal favorites.

"Who's investigating?" I asked. "Other than the Chamber and the police, of course."

An expression of disgust passed over Deborah's

face. "The insurance company. The police didn't even recognize the names of any of the paintings."

"How did they steal them? You said someone hid in a custodian's closet?"

"Hid someplace. After the housekeeping staff went home, he, or they, shot the guards with tranquilizer darts. Then they took the paintings, waited for the replacement guards to come on shift, and shot them. Exactly the way you did it."

I glanced toward my report sitting on the corner of the desk.

"Did Wilson implement any of the changes we recommended?"

Deborah shook her head. "We were still arguing about them. He maintained that your demonstration was just a circus trick and no one could ever pull it off."

"Have you fired him?"

She shook her head.

"Why ever not?"

She bit her lip and said, "I don't know."

I shrugged. "Easier to shoot the messenger? Blame me?"

The stricken expression on her face told me that was exactly the plan.

"Well, I still have a contract to harden your computer systems. If you would please tell the Chamber to give me back all my equipment, not to mention my phone and my bank card, then I'll go back to work."

"Things are still under investigation."

"Then my lawyer will be filing suit for breach of contract. I will also be going to the press about this robbery, the fact you were warned about the security weaknesses, and that you did nothing about them." I leaned forward and put my elbows on her desk. "Let's get something straight here. I'm not playing scapegoat for anyone."

Her eyes took on a hard glint. "Are you threatening me?"

"No, those were promises. I've already engaged a lawyer who should soon be talking to the Chamber. I thought you might be reasonable and save both of us money, but I see that you'd rather spend the museum's money than take any blame for your negligence."

I stood and said, "Your call, Deborah. The press will love the angle that you're accusing me because you're a jilted lover."

As I walked out her door, I turned and saw her picking up the phone. I would have given a lawyer's retainer to know whom she was calling.

⊕⊕⊕

My route back to the hotel took me through the park surrounding the museum campus, across Michigan Avenue, then three blocks past the Symphony, stores, restaurants, old government buildings, and new office buildings. The day was humid, windy, and generally nasty.

The assassins were amateurs. I spotted the guy following me as soon as I crossed Michigan Avenue. He talked on his phone as he walked, so I wasn't surprised when a second man with a gun stepped out from between two buildings on the next block.

He didn't indicate what he wanted me to do, so I

had to guess. Probably go with him somewhere so he could kill me without witnesses. Instead of playing his game, I shot him in his right shoulder and he dropped the gun.

I blurred my image and dropped to the sidewalk as I whirled about to face my follower. He stared with his mouth open at his buddy while struggling to pull his pistol out of his pants pocket.

I shot him in that pocket. He screamed, lurched, and fell down. I left him writhing around on the sidewalk and turned my attention back to the first man.

My image still blurred and hugging the wall of the building next to me, I sprinted up to him, grabbed him by the hair, and dragged him into the space where he'd been waiting.

"Who hired you?" I asked as I pushed the barrel of my pistol between his eyes.

"I don't know," he practically screamed. It must have been scary to have a woman he could barely see pointing a gun at his head.

I lowered the pistol and shot him in the knee. Disregarding his scream, I moved the gun back up to point at his face. He and his friend were both louder than my silenced pistol.

"Let's try this again. You tell me everything you know, and I don't blow your balls off. Fair enough?"

"I don't know who the money man is," he sobbed. "Joe Wilson hired us, but he ain't got no money."

"How much were you paid?" I asked.

"Five grand in advance, five grand after the job's done."

I was insulted. "How do I find Wilson?" I pulled out my phone, punched record, and put it next to his mouth.

My informant stuttered out a phone number, a rough address, and the name and location of a bar. I also collected his name and that of his buddy. I searched him and found a picture of me, taken by one of the museum's security cameras. After taking his wallet and his phone, I peeked around the corner and found several people clustered around the wounded man.

Time for me to go. Inching out onto the street, I moved slowly next to the wall until I reached the next street over. I heard sirens as I unblurred and hurried to the hotel.

Without my computer, I only had my spare tablet to access the infonet. Everything took longer, and I didn't have the tools to get me into secured databases. It still didn't take long to find a Joseph Breshard Wilson living on the street my assailant gave me.

I decided I was getting cynical, because it didn't surprise me that Joe's brother was David Wilson, the chief of security at AIC.

CHAPTER 12

I didn't have the same confidence going out into Chicago to roust someone as I would have had in Toronto. I didn't know the neighborhoods, and most maps don't tell you if your destination is in the middle of Vampireville or an area where druggies regularly kill each other over a pair of shoes.

On the other hand, taking a taxi would leave tracks, and I wasn't on a mission I could easily explain to any sort of authority.

The bar my unlucky assassin told me about was a different story. I looked it up on the infonet and disregarded the reviews about the quality of the food. Nothing in the other reviews suggested that a death wish was required to enter the neighborhood. A number of nearby establishments were equally silent about their murder and mugging rates. I couldn't find any news stories or police reports highlighting the area.

With that sketchy background information, I morphed into a thirty-five-year-old man, who looked exactly like one of my mother's ex-boyfriends. I walked a couple of blocks to catch a train and then a bus to Lou's Lounge. The surrounding neighborhood looked marginally respectable. At least none of the buildings were burned out or falling down, the people on the streets wore shoes and filter masks, and some of the men shaved occasionally.

The difference between a neighborhood pub and a dive bar has always been difficult to define. Lou's was a dive bar. A few lights needed fixing, the floor could have used a good cleaning, and the washrooms' lack of basic hygiene was apparent before you opened their doors. The liquor behind the bar was basic, and I had no interest in finding out what they were pouring from under the bar. The clientele was a little rough, a little loud, and a little crude. To be generous.

I asked a couple of people if Joe had come in yet, and a waitress directed me to a back corner near the washrooms. Why anyone would want to sit that close to them was a mystery.

The family resemblance between Joe and his brother Dave was apparent, though I estimated Joe was ten years younger. He looked pretty happy, partying with two girls half his age. My cynicism raised its head again. Joe looked like a guy who had just come into some unexpected money.

"Hey, Joe," I called out as I approached his table. "I heard you're a man who can get things done."

He preened. "Some people think so. It depends on what you need done."

I slid into the booth on the other side of him and the girls. "Maybe your friends should go take a powder."

I received an up-and-down look, then he turned to one of the girls. "Why don't you go order another bottle of champagne for us."

Both girls got up, each of them gave him a kiss on the cheek, and headed toward the bar.

"So, what are you looking for?" he asked with a smug grin.

"Sonny and Huang told me you're the guy to see for a hit."

His grin lost some of its smugness as his eyes nervously danced around the place.

"I have a pistol under the table aimed at your balls," I said and watched the grin slide off his face. "We're going to go outside and have a conversation.

Do you understand?"

"Look, mister, I don't know what you're talking about."

"Joe, Joe. Sonny has two bullets in him and Huang has one. They were still able to answer all my questions, so I figure you'll talk just fine with a bullet in the balls." I tossed Sonny's identification on the table and watched Joe blanch. "Shall we go?"

We went out the back door into the alley, walked down to the end, and turned the corner. Joe glanced back once, saw the gun, and kept walking.

I morphed back to my normal self. "That's far enough. Turn around." His eyes about bulged out of his head.

"Who paid you to kill me?"

"Nobody. I don't know what you're talking about."

I aimed at the bottom of the zipper in his pants and pulled the trigger. He stumbled backward and fell on his butt. I let him stare at his bloody lap for a moment, then stepped up to him and held the muzzle of the pistol against his head.

"You paid two men to kill me," I said. "I take such things very seriously. Now, who paid you?"

"M-m-my brother," he said.

"How much did he pay you?"

"Twenty-five thousand."

"When?"

"This m-morning."

"How did Sonny and Huang know where to find me?"

"Dave called me. Told me you were at the museum." He was crying, his words coming out between broken sobs. "Oh, God, please don't kill me."

113

I couldn't imagine a single reason why I should let him live. I definitely didn't want him tipping off his brother.

I pulled one of my hatpins out of its sheath in my bra, put it in his ear, and pushed. Six inches of stiff stainless steel coated with a neurotoxin penetrated the temporal lobe of his brain. He seemed to freeze, staring straight ahead, and stopped crying. I withdrew the pin and wiped it clean on his shirt. I took his wallet, keys, another picture of me, and his phone, then walked out of the alley and went looking for his car.

David Wilson certainly had reasons for wanting me out of the way, but he didn't strike me as a guy with twenty-five thousand credits in spare cash. That put Deborah and Malcolm squarely in the picture. The timing, according to Sonny and Joe, meant the hit had been contracted as soon as I got out of jail.

Back at my hotel, I retrieved the suitcase from the linen closet again, then walked over to the museum. The buildings across Michigan Avenue were all at least twenty stories high. I blurred my form and entered the building closest to the staff parking lot. Fifteen minutes later, I was on the roof.

During my time at the museum, I'd become familiar with the staff, their schedules, and their habits. I knew when people came to work, when they left, and what method of transportation they used.

David Wilson called his brother's phone twice that afternoon. I didn't answer it.

The sun slid toward the horizon, and the shadow of the building I sat on fell across the parking lot. The museum closed, and the last of its patrons left the building. Shortly thereafter, the staff left through the employee exits, most headed to the train station a couple of blocks behind me.

Wilson finally emerged from the building, and I tracked him through the telescope on my rifle. When he reached his car, he stopped to unlock it. I centered my crosshairs on the back of his head and waited for the computer controls to adjust for the height, angle, and distance. The crosshairs turned red and the scope beeped. I took a breath, let half of it out, and slowly squeezed the trigger.

His head slammed forward, hit the car, and his body bounced backward and fell to the ground.

I broke down the rifle and packed it back in the suitcase, then in my blurred form, I descended the stairs to the ground floor and went out the loading dock. I set off the alarm, but I didn't care. I would rather have anyone who investigated look at that escape route than think a ghost went through the security desk and the front door.

⊕⊕⊕

The knock on the door came while I was eating breakfast. I answered it and was gratified to see the surprise on Wil's face. I knew he didn't expect to find me awake, let alone dressed, at six-thirty in the morning.

"May I come in?" he asked.

"No," I said, turning away and going back to my food. He followed me into the room and shut the door behind him.

"I used to think you were a gentleman," I said as I took my seat, "but it was all an act, wasn't it? You're actually one of the rudest sons of bitches I've ever met."

115

His face flushed, and he stood in the middle of the room, acting as though he didn't know what to do.

"You thought I'd still be asleep, didn't you? And you came at this time on purpose. Deputy Director Wilberforce, you'd better hope your guts are never on fire."

His face hardened, and he flushed as dark as I'd ever seen. His jaw muscles worked, and I was sure if I listened closely enough, I'd hear his teeth grinding together.

"David Wilson is dead," he finally said.

"Oh? This is a tough town. I told Deborah she should fire him, but I didn't mean literally."

"He was shot by a sniper."

"Well, you wouldn't expect a cultured lady like Director Zhukoff to do the job herself."

"Are you saying you didn't kill him?"

I set my fork down on my plate and looked up at him. "Is this the new normal? Paintings are stolen, let's roust Libby. Someone dies, accuse Libby. I'm surprised you aren't trying to pin the bombings on me. How about any old shoplifting cases?"

My stomach churned, and I pushed my plate away.

"You didn't happen to bring my stuff that you stole, did you? You took everything I own, so I don't know how I managed to buy a rifle and assassinate someone. You've had people following me since you let me out of jail. Did they see me rob a bank?"

"They lost you in the first five minutes. Said you just disappeared. How did you know Wilson was shot with a rifle?"

"Lots of incompetents in this city. Your men. Wilson. You. I assumed it because I never heard of a

116

sniper using a derringer, you dumbass." I was getting so sick of this whole mess.

"What do you hope to accomplish by sending that damned lawyer around to harass me?" he said with a lot more passion than I'd seen before.

"He's not harassing you. He's protecting my rights, and getting ready to sue your ass off." I got up and walked over to the window. It was looking like a wet and gloomy day ahead. "You don't seem to get it. I'm not some bimbo you can treat any way you want. My corporation is a member of the Chamber, and as such, we have a contractual relationship. I also have a contract with AIC. I have contacts, including a member of the Toronto Chamber's board of directors."

I turned back to face him. "The large corporations control the Chamber, but all of the small corporations give you legitimacy. You treat your smaller members like shit, and you'll get a rebellion that makes a few muties throwing bombs look tame."

His brow was furrowed, and he seemed to be having a problem understanding me. "What do you mean, your corporation?"

"Do you ever do any research, or do you just hope that your good looks will cover for your blundering around? I'm the CEO and Chairman of Fly by Night, Incorporated. We pay our ten percent tithe to the Chamber just like Hudson Bay or MegaTech. You truly think I'm some kind of idiot, don't you? Some little girl playing around."

Two strides took me within inches of his face. "You better get your act together. I want my personal effects and my equipment. I want my weapons, for which I have Chamber permits due to my position as my corporation's chief of security. I want AIC to pay me the money they owe me. And if you can't do those simple things, then I'm not only going to have that lawyer bite your ass, I'm going to the media and tell them about the art theft."

"We don't want the public to know about the theft," he said.

I gave him a smile and batted my eyes. "Then I'll be sure to give the media your name as a point of contact. I'll also tell them that the museum buried my company's assessment of their security rather than implement the recommendations. I'm sure their insurance company will be interested in that."

His eyes widened, then narrowed. I realized I was right. He thought I was some kind of dumb blonde bimbo. Then it hit me. He didn't think I pulled the robbery. They, he and the museum board, had latched onto me as a convenient scapegoat. I could understand why Deborah and Malcolm would want to cover up their incompetence, but the idea that Wil was willing to sacrifice my life to his career caused something to break inside me.

Slipping around him, I went to the door and opened it. "Get the hell out. And don't come back without my equipment."

After I closed the door, I felt like I wanted to throw up. As much as I'd always pushed Wil away, I couldn't deny that I had a schoolgirl crush on him. His voice on the phone or a smile from him made me feel hot and numb, thoughtless and breathless. How in the hell did we get to a place where we were enemies?

CHAPTER 13

David Wilson's murder made the news, though the stories I read attributed it to a mugging. Joseph Wilson's murder showed up on the Chicago Police report, but no one considered it important enough to make the news. I was sure Wil and Chamber Security didn't pay any attention to it. My experience with Chamber Security in Toronto had shown they were oblivious to anything that didn't affect their corporate masters. As a result, I considered it doubtful anyone would link the two deaths.

I used the tablet to send Dad the list of stolen art works. If anyone had a clue as to the buyers, it would be him. I hoped he also might have some suspicions as to who pulled off the heist.

With time on my hands, I felt restless. Out of curiosity, I blurred my image, snuck out of the hotel, and headed over to the museum.

I rarely tried to maintain invisibility for very long in public, especially in the daytime. It required moving slowly, staying close to objects or buildings I could use for a background, and avoiding getting close to anyone. I made it unseen into the museum and past all the security to the wing with the administrative offices.

Few people who knew me would have considered me a patient person, but they had never seen me work. Casing a potential break-in or profiling the movements of a target often required days or even weeks of observation. I settled into the doorway of an empty office down the hall from Deborah's office.

Over the next two hours, I watched Jess leave and come back twice. Three different people from the Finance office and one from Payroll went to the washroom. Shortly before noon, Jess left again, and then Malcolm Donnelly came down the hall and went into the office. I slipped through the door right behind him.

Malcolm didn't bother to knock before opening Deborah's door, and I slid a stapler from Jess's desk into the doorjamb before the door could close.

"What's going on?" Malcolm asked.

"Wilberforce called me this morning. Nelson is threatening to go to the press and the insurance company," Deborah said.

"That's not good."

"No, it's not. How are we going to explain not informing the insurance company?"

"We use the same reason we always planned on," Malcolm said. "We delayed telling anyone because we thought the Nelson woman was responsible and we were trying to convince her to return the paintings."

Deborah's laughter sounded harsh and a little shrill. "That excuse might have flown if we were only talking about two paintings. I was crazy to let you talk me into this in the first place, but what in the hell were you thinking? A billion credits worth of art. Your damned greed is going to do us in."

"It's a little too late for second thoughts. Two paintings or five, it doesn't matter. We still have the necklace."

"You fool. Do you still think you can plant that on her? Wil has her under constant surveillance. He's searched her room repeatedly. Throw the damned thing away. All it can do is incriminate us."

I heard Deborah's heels click across the floor, stop, and come back. "Mal, we've got to call the insurance company. Wil thinks we already have. If we delay any longer, people are going to wonder why."

The door opened behind me. I slowly, ever so slowly, bent over and pulled the stapler out of the door. It slowly closed without a sound, but didn't latch.

"Deborah?" Jess called. "They didn't have chicken salad today so I got you salmon."

I inched backward into a corner and watched as Malcolm and Deborah came out of her office, Malcolm left, and Deborah took her lunch back to her desk. I had to wait another hour and a half until Jess went to the washroom before I could sneak out. That gave me a lot of time to think.

⊕⊕⊕

Since I'd recently done a security audit of the entire facility, I probably knew the museum as well as anyone. I wandered down to a vacant office with a working phone. Feet up on the desk, I called North American Insurance and asked to speak to the claims adjuster in charge of the AIC robbery.

After being transferred a couple of times and then put on hold, a man came on the phone and asked, "To whom am I speaking?"

"Jasmine Keller," I said. "I'm a reporter for the Chicago Daily News. I'm trying to get some information on the investigation into the robbery at the Art Institute of Chicago earlier this week."

"I'm sorry, but we don't comment on ongoing investigations," the man said.

"Can you confirm that a billion credits worth of art was stolen?"

"We will make a press release available through

the Institute at the proper time." Then he hung up.

I smiled. At that point, I couldn't see any benefit to me of doing anything Wil or the museum wanted me to do. The next call I made was to the Chicago Daily News, the largest news media organization in the city. I was quickly passed to someone on their Arts desk.

"What was this event you said we missed on our calendar?" a woman asked.

"Not an event. The robbery. I was wondering why I couldn't find anything about the stolen Monets and Renoirs on the infonet."

We chatted for a few minutes, then I hung up, morphed into a fifty-year-old woman, and made my way out of the museum.

The news that Wil was searching my hotel room every time I left disturbed me. I hadn't worried about it too much, since I didn't have anything left to steal, but it bothered me. It also bothered me that I was being followed, even if it was easy to fool any tail they set on me.

An hour of research led me to a decent hotel in a middle-class mutie district not too far from the blues bar I'd visited with Deborah. I took a bus over there in my disguise as Jasmine Keller and checked it out, then rented a room for the rest of the month. On my way back to the Winston Hotel, I stopped into a cheap recycled clothing store and spent a hundred credits on shirts, pants, dresses, and underwear.

I packed everything I still owned, using the new clothing to replace my stuff in the closet and drawers. I doubted a man would notice the difference. After retrieving the suitcase from the upstairs linen closet, I morphed into a likeness of a five-foot-tall, dark-haired woman in conservative clothing wearing a hijab headscarf. I had seen her at the museum a couple of weeks before. Hanging a 'Do Not Disturb' sign on the door, I took my luggage down to the lobby and called for a taxi.

Only my mom and dad, and Orlando Ortega, had the number of my spare phone. Only Mom and Dad could reach me through secure email. I called all of them and told them I was no longer at the Winston, and why, but didn't tell them where I'd gone. I also sent an email to Mom, asking her to ship me a replacement computer. The tablet worked great for most people, but I had serious systems I needed to crack.

I turned on the screen in my room, tuned in the news feed, and settled in to wait.

⊕⊕⊕

I waited for two days. The hotel café served what they called "Southern Comfort" food. Evidently, that was a euphemism for "fried." The second night I went out and found a place that served pizza. The other options in the neighborhood were primarily Asian and various preparations that tried to disguise soybean curd as some kind of animal, bird, or fish.

Sticking with my Jasmine persona had a number of benefits. She wasn't homely, but she wasn't pretty enough to attract unwanted attention. On the other hand, Jasmine was as tall as me, but forty or fifty pounds heavier, which tended to intimidate people. And since she was only an illusion I projected, Jasmine had my speed and strength.

The morning of the third day, I morphed into a redhead that looked like my mom when she was young. I grabbed a subway down to the train station, where I met Mike Di Blasio, one of the bouncers at my mom's brothel. He handed over my new computer, and I handed over the pint of human blood I'd bought fresh that morning.

"Oh, wow, Lizzie," Mike said, his smile showing his fangs, "you didn't have to do that. That's really nice of you." Most respectable vamps rarely drank human blood. It was expensive, unless they had a lover to donate on a regular basis. Of course, there were those select few at high corporate or criminal levels who could afford a harem of blood whores.

"It's the least I can do, Mike. I really appreciate you making the trip all the way down here."

"It's nothing. I get paid, and I mostly sleep. Kinda breaks up the monotony, ya know?" He leaned close and dropped his voice. "Your mom said that if you need someone to watch your back, I should stay. Gave me a message for you. Said to tell you that, now these is her words not mine, you understand?" I smiled and nodded. "She said to tell you that only a damned fool turns down help when someone's trying to kill you."

"I really appreciate the offer," I said, and I did. The problem was all my changes. Very few people knew about my abilities. Mike knew me as Lizzie, my mom's sweet redheaded daughter, and also as Libby, the tall blonde with the smart mouth. He didn't know we were the same person.

He handed me an envelope and said, "Let's go someplace a little more private."

That I agreed with.

We found an Asian restaurant with private rooms and I ordered lunch. Mike drank the bag of blood while I went to the washroom and read the letter from my mom. In addition to the letter, the envelope included a credit card to a Swiss account with a hundred thousand credits, and a set of identification. I studied the photo and committed it to memory, along with Prisha Kumar's vital statistics.

It gave me a warm feeling to know that I was still Mom's baby girl and she was looking out for me.

The letter was short.

Libby, Mike is completely trustworthy. He worked for your father at MegaTech, is a trained bodyguard, and nothing you do will surprise him. If needed, he excels at wet work. He knows you are a chameleon.

Don't be a damned fool. If you need to run, do it. Cleaning up messes is much easier when you're alive.

Love,
Mom

I went back to our little room to find my pho and eggrolls, and Mike with a satisfied expression on his face.

"So, you used to work for my dad?" I asked before spooning some of the soup into my mouth.

"I worked for MegaTech for twenty-five years, the last twenty for Jason. After his accident, things just weren't the same, so I retired. Your mother was gracious enough to offer me a position as her head of security."

My head snapped up and I stared at him. His diction had changed completely from ghetto vamp to educated corporate.

"You're educated," I blurted out.

With a chuckle and a nod of his head, he continued. "Yes. Both of my parents worked for

MegaTech. My mother was a technician, and my father was a designer. I majored in electrical engineering. I can trace my family tree back to the first mutations in the late twenty-first century."

"So, why the act?"

"Most people are more comfortable with vampires who are intellectually inferior to them. It helps them to deal with our physical superiority. Father thinks people are more afraid of smart blood-sucking monsters than of dumb ones."

The top of Mike's head was even with my mouth when he stood next to me, but he was built like a block of granite. I knew vamps were faster and stronger than normal humans. They also lived longer. Mike looked to be in his thirties, no older than forty at most.

"You worked for MegaTech for twenty-five years after you graduated? Do you mind my asking how old you are?"

He gave me one of his toothy smiles. "I'm fifty-six. My parents are in their nineties. Mama still runs half-marathons, and Father races sail boats."

"In her letter, Mom said you know about my mutations."

"Mutations?" He cocked his head. "I know you're a chameleon. I've known that for years. You have more than one?"

"You seem to accept that rather easily," I said. "Have you known other chameleons?"

"I've known that Lizzie and Libby were the same girl since before I went to work for Miss Lilith. That seems to be very different from what most consider a chameleon. I've known two people who could blend into the landscape, like the lizard, and become almost invisible. I've never heard of someone who was a true shape shifter."

I shook my head. "I'm not. Lycanthropes change their shape more than I do. It just looks as though I'm different." I let go my disguise and morphed into my real self. "This is what I really look like, but I don't physically change."

"That is...astounding. It's instantaneous."

I changed my peach-fuzz blonde hair back to its former long wavy red. Then I changed my clothing into a gold satin evening gown. "I can manipulate or hide what I touch, up to a point," I said. "But nothing really changes." I morphed into Jasmine. "This is the persona I'm using at the moment, the one I used to check into my hotel."

"So, if you walked through a security camera like that, the people monitoring it would see the real you."

Ah, the paradox. "Actually not, and I don't know why. Dad hooked me up to a bunch of sensors, and they showed that nothing about me changed. But cameras see me the way people see me. Have you ever known a psychic who could manipulate electronics?"

He shook his head. "Only your mother."

"Hmmm. I have her gift, but I don't think that it's psychic. It's a measureable physical ability, like an electric eel, only in reverse."

"Maybe your ability is an interaction between two or more mutations," Mike said. "The electrical manipulation and a chameleon mutation."

"I've wondered that. Dad says that he's never heard of anyone like me. On the other hand, no one has ever studied a chameleon. Dad said that all the ones he's met or heard about were thieves. I know that I don't have any desire to walk into a university

127

research department and tell a scientist what I can do."

His chuckle was very dry. "After what happened in the late twenty-first and early twenty-second centuries, no mutant volunteers for that."

Some of the experiments scientists conducted on mutants were sickening to read. The backlash included mutants slaughtering whole staffs at some research institutes. The suspicion on both sides had never disappeared.

CHAPTER 14

Orlando Ortega called that evening.

"Deputy Director Wilberforce has asked for a meeting tomorrow morning," he said.

"Are they planning to arrest me on some new trumped-up charge?" I was lying on my bed watching a vid on the screen. Mike had the room next door, but I didn't know if he was in or out. Vampires usually don't wake up until after dark.

"No, I don't think so. He said that he wants to release all the evidence they gathered and formally drop all charges. He also said he wants to talk to you about the insurance company's investigation into the robbery at the Institute."

"Damned decent of him, considering that they never formally charged me with anything."

He chuckled. "I did ask what charges he was talking about, and he was evasive."

So, Mike and I grabbed a train and braved the morning rush-hour trip downtown to Chamber headquarters. Ortega and Miss Molly awaited us on the sidewalk in front of the building with Federal Reserve Bank of Chicago chiseled into the stone above the entrance. Only the strongest banks survived the dislocations of the twenty-first century, and I guessed that wasn't one of them, in spite of its impressive, enormous Corinthian columns framing the massive front portico.

A sign showed that the Chamber shared the ancient building with the International Monetary Fund and the International Court of Settlements.

Ortega broke out in a big smile when he spotted us. "Michael! Long time no see. How have you been, my friend?"

"Lying back, enjoying retirement," Mike said with a smile as the two men shook hands. "Feeling a little bored, so I thought I'd come down and pester one of my many goddaughters."

I stood there with my mouth hanging open watching Mike and the lawyer catch up. I glanced at Molly, and she looked as bewildered as I felt.

Mike eventually turned to me and said, "Orlando and I were roommates at McGill. Our parents all worked for MegaTech." Turning back to Orlando, he said, "Shall we go in and see what the mighty Chamber has in store for our Libby?"

"They say it's a small world," I muttered to Molly as we climbed the steps to the building.

"Aye, they do say that."

To my surprise, Wil was waiting for us at the front security desk and waved us through, even though Mike and I set off the metal detectors. I made introductions. Orlando and Molly in their business suits looked like lawyers, but Wil looked askance at Mike.

"Mr. Di Blasio came down from Toronto at my parents' request to watch my back," I explained.

Mike stepped forward and shook Wil's hand rather vigorously. I thought I saw Wil wince.

"Good to meet ya, Mistah Wibberferce," Mike said with his best idiot bouncer smile.

Wil led us to a conference room on the second floor where three boxes with my possessions sat on the table.

"Check it all out," Wil said, waving at the boxes. "I don't know if that computer is still functional or not. The electrical charge almost killed one of my techs. No one has tried to touch it since. The general opinion is that the booby trap probably fried the computer as well."

"That equipment is very valuable," Orlando said. "If you've harmed it, I assure you we will be presenting you with a bill."

I opened it and turned it on, assuring myself that the insulation between the case and the internal components had served its purpose in protecting the electronics and data.

"It's working," I announced. "If you'd ever bothered to ask, I would have told you it's secured against thieves." Only Mom and I could get through the security, since we weren't affected by the electrical charge. The voltage could have killed the tech if he had a heart condition. It certainly knocked him on his butt. If he'd handled it with rubber gloves and managed to open the case, the charge when he tried to turn it on would have fried the computer, and possibly killed him even with the gloves.

My phone was still locked, as was my tablet. My credit cards, identification for both me and Jasmine, my jewelry, makeup, toiletries, and everything else appeared to be present and undamaged.

"It's all good," I told Orlando.

"Well, in that case, I think we're clear with each other," Wil said.

Orlando looked to me and I gave him a raised eyebrow and a slight shake of my head.

"Not exactly," Orlando said. "We'll still be suing the Chamber and the Institute for assault, false arrest, illegal imprisonment, kidnapping, and defamation, in addition to damages for loss of income, professional reputation, humiliation, emotional and physical trauma, and stress."

"Don't forget breach of contract," I said.

"Of course," Orlando replied. "Mr. Wilberforce, if I were you, I would engage a good attorney. The Chamber's lawyers are going to feed you to me without a second thought."

"You should have signed that prenup," I told Wil. "You know what they say about a woman scorned."

Molly, who had been staring at Wil with glazed eyes, snickered.

"Mr. Ortega said you wanted to talk to me about the insurance company's investigation," I prompted.

Wil tore his eyes away from Ortega and said, "Yes. Myron Chung is their lead investigator. He would like to meet with you at the Institute this afternoon, if it's convenient."

"Convenient for me? When did people around here start caring about my convenience?" I shrugged. "Sure. About damned time someone decided to investigate the robbery."

"Someone tipped off the news media about it," Wil said.

I nodded, and looked up to meet his eyes. "I don't threaten. I told you I was going to call them. Are you aware that the Institute didn't notify the insurance company?"

"So I found out."

"Think about why. There'll be a quiz."

He didn't say anything, but he looked profoundly unhappy.

⊕⊕⊕

We put all my stuff in Orlando's aircar, and he

gave us a ride to the Institute.

Jessica met us at the entrance and guided us to a set of offices in the administrative wing. We walked to an inner office past a woman and two men working at desks. An Asian man, Chinese maybe, around fifty years old greeted us. His black hair formed a ring around the bald top of his head.

When he stood to welcome us, I realized he couldn't be much taller than five feet. He looked at my entourage and said, "If you please, Miss Nelson, you're not a suspect in my investigation. But I really need to speak with you privately."

"I don't need a lawyer?"

"I hate to disappoint you," he said with a thin smile, "but no, you don't need a lawyer."

Mike took the hint quickly. "That's great. We'll have time to see some of the exhibits. Call me when you finish, okay?"

"Sure thing, Mike." I watched him and the lawyers back out of the office.

"I'm Myron Chung," the small man said and pointed to a chair. "Won't you please have a seat?"

My reports—the ones my dad and I wrote—sat on his desk. Also on his desk were all three of my contracts with the Institute, pictures of the missing art works, and a dossier with my name on it.

"I'm surprised you've ruled me out so early in your investigation," I said. "Everyone else seems to think I'm the obvious suspect."

He shook his head. "Actually, I ruled you out as soon as I read your report. You're far too intelligent to pull a stunt as stupid as this. Besides, Jason Bouchard is too smart to let you do it. You have a fine career ahead of you, and I'm sure you saw this contract as a

133

feather in your cap that you could use to truly make your mark."

I released my breath in a whoosh. "Yeah, that's what I thought. Things haven't exactly worked out how I expected."

We went through several things in my report, trends rather than individual items. Then he turned to my current contract.

"I've informed Director Zhukoff that I believe you should be allowed to complete your work. If you don't do it, someone needs to. Hiring another firm would just delay things. She said she would inform the board, and she should have a decision in the morning."

"Thank you. That would be a relief."

"You're welcome. I hope that we can speak again if I have any questions. Or any theories. It's sometimes helpful to bounce ideas off an outside party."

"Of course." I was so filled with relief that I thought I'd burst. I wanted to jump up in the air and cheer, but that wouldn't have been terribly dignified. Mr. Chung didn't look like the type who'd appreciate a hug. Instead, I went and found Mike and showed him some of my favorite parts of the museum.

CHAPTER 15

It felt good to get back to work. No one had messed with the equipment I left at the museum, so it didn't take me long to get back on schedule.

On the other hand, I didn't feel comfortable in Chicago, especially knowing what I did. Mike stuck around, and we continued to stay at the hotel in the mutie district. With his background, he proved to be a big help in installing new equipment and fixing some of the physical issues that needed correction.

Seeing Deborah every day was uncomfortable, but Jess seemed friendlier now that her boss wasn't so obviously trying to seduce me. Jess and Deborah's relationship struck me as rather unprofessional, but who was I to judge?

Mike came around in Joe Wilson's old car and picked me up after work.

"Change into that Jasmine girl," he said as we headed south. "I want to take you to a restaurant I remember."

"But you don't eat regular food," I said.

"Maybe not, but the food smells great, and they serve fresh pig blood."

Okay. I could live with food that smelled good. I hoped it also tasted good. But as we drove, I began to have my doubts. Some of the neighborhoods along our way were worse than the worst areas I'd seen in Toronto.

"Nice neighborhood. Bet we could get some deals on real estate," I said, looking at block after block of crumbling row houses.

Mike chuckled. "Even the cockroaches and rats have abandoned parts of this city. This area, was a slum even before the wars. Back then, poor people of various ethnic descents were often confined to ghettos, much as the muties are now."

The history of The Fall had always fascinated me. Areas such as the one we drove through were decimated by the plagues and food shortages in the late twenty-first century.

"Are we going to a mutie district?" I asked.

"Yes, a rather affluent one compared to anywhere in Toronto. There's almost another economy going on in parts of the city, and Chicago's southwest side pretty much ignores the corporations. Muties moved in and took over businesses in the old ghettos. Along with the Africans already there, and the Mexicans coming north as a result of the desertification of the Southwest, it's an indie ecosystem."

The neighborhood we stopped in looked a lot better—the buildings were in good repair, and the people out on the street were well dressed and most wore filter masks. Some businesses were still open even after dark, lots of boutiques, bars, restaurants, a corporate pharmacy, and a non-corporate grocery store.

We parked on a side street, and Mike led me to a place called John's Barbeque. It didn't resemble the fancy barbeque place I knew in Toronto at all. Butcher paper covered the tables instead of linen, the patrons were casually dressed, and we ordered through an automenu instead of with a live waiter.

The food was different, too. Lots of meat—pork, chicken and sausage—but with reasonable prices, which alerted my sense of self-preservation. God only knew where cheap meat came from, or what kind of poisons it contained, and I'd grown up hearing about people dying from eating contaminated food.

I looked up from the menu and met Mike's eyes.

"It's safe," he said. "Your father introduced me to this place. It's a total family operation. The meat is all raised on their own farms outside the city and fed corn and soybeans they grow themselves. Jason usually ordered the ribs, but sometimes he got chicken."

The food was incredible, tender and smoky, with a sweet, spicy sauce, potato salad and baked beans. I ate until I thought I'd explode, washing my food down with a good dark beer. Mike's meal came in a glass, like the ones some places used to serve milkshakes, and it even had a silly umbrella.

At least half of the clientele had dark skin, with enough vamps that Mike and I didn't stand out. Mercifully, the lycans and trolls were seated in another room so I didn't have to watch them eat.

After dinner, we lazily strolled back to the car. Although I didn't think we stood out in any way, I noticed a number of people watching us. Stopping in front of a closed shop to look at the goods displayed in the window, I saw that several of our watchers were following us.

"We're being tracked," Mike said.

"So it seems." I still maintained my Jasmine persona, and she should have been virtually unknown in Chicago. "Do you have any enemies here?" I slipped my hand into my purse and curled my fingers around my pistol grip.

"I haven't been in Chicago in ten years," he said. "Let's try to get to the car."

We picked up our pace, but before we reached the street where we left the car, a group of people seemed to coalesce around us. I recognized one person, Carly, the young woman with whom I'd shared the hospitality of the Chicago Police. She'd only seen me in my own form, though. Jasmine should be a complete stranger.

"Hi, Libby," she said.

"The name's Jasmine."

"Whatever name you want to use, I know you."

That was unnerving. No one had ever seen through any of my personas.

"We need you to come with us," Carly said. "We need to talk."

A quick scan showed me there were about twenty people surrounding us, including a couple of vamps and half a dozen lycans, most shifted into their wolfman form. I could take a vamp one-on-one, and likewise a lycan. They might have been stronger than I was, but few people had the training I'd received. That said, fighting my way through a group that large was out of the question.

I wasn't alone, though. I glanced at Mike, and he spoke up.

"I don't think so. Call in the morning, and we'll set up an appointment," he said.

"You don't understand," a man said, stepping forward. "You're coming with us now." He was thin and of average height. Nothing especially intimidating, but he had the swagger and air of a bully about him. The way he held himself. The smirk on his face.

"Eel," several people in the crowd said, and I didn't like the grins on their faces when they said it.

He moved forward, his hand extended to grab me.

I took him off guard by stepping toward him. My left hand shot out and took him by the throat. A bolt of electrical energy surged from him to me. He had a

138

mutation for bioelectrogenesis, similar to that of an electric eel. The shock was enough to knock most people down, but it didn't affect me at all. My hand closed on his throat and I shook him like a dog would shake a rat, then tossed him away from me.

Out of the corner of my eye, I saw a lycan move toward me. Mike spun and delivered a snap kick to the lycan's chin. The mutant fell to the ground, his head at an unnatural angle, and his open eyes staring at the sky.

We both pulled our pistols, and Mike moved behind me, facing the other way.

"As my friend said, you should call and make an appointment."

Carly nodded. "I'm afraid I don't have your number."

"Come here," I said, crooking my finger toward me.

She came toward me, stopping a couple of feet away. I leaned close to her and said, "Come to the Art Institute in the morning. Ten o'clock. Tell the guards to call the director's office and tell them you have an appointment with Libby Nelson. You can bring one other person with you. Understood?"

Carly nodded her head. Then she turned and said, "Let them go. We don't need a fight."

We followed Carly, and the crowd reluctantly parted to let us through. When we were in the clear, she stepped aside to let us walk past her.

"What's this about?" I asked her.

"Mutie business. You need to know what we're fighting for."

"I think I have a pretty good idea," I said, "but you're going about it the wrong way."

Mike and I hurried to the car, got in, and he drove away. We abandoned the car a few blocks from the hotel, left the keys in it, and walked the rest of the way. It was convenient, but now that we were associated with it, it was a liability.

"Is my illusion slipping?" I asked Mike.

He shook his head. "All I see is Jasmine."

"That woman had never seen Jasmine, but she walked up to me and called me Libby."

"She's a mutant," he said.

"Obviously. She's a chimera, but that's not necessarily a mutation. You're saying that she has an ability to see through my illusions?"

"That's the obvious explanation. We'll see tomorrow morning."

⊕⊕⊕

Jess stuck her head into my office the next morning.

"A woman says she has an appointment with you."

"Yes. Thanks, Jess. Where is she?"

"At the front desk."

I walked out to the entrance and found Carly and a very tall man in his fifties. They both looked very nervous. I signed them in with security and led them back to the conference room I'd converted into my office.

When I said the man was very tall, I meant he was a head taller than I was and didn't outweigh me by much. Skeletal would be an apt description. His hair was receding and graying, and his face was lined and weathered.

140

I ushered them into the office and found that Mike had made tea for us using the electric teapot Dad bought when he was working with me.

We all sat down at the table and I said, "Okay. What's so urgent that you tried to kidnap me last night?"

"We weren't trying to kidnap you," Carly said with a pouting set to her mouth.

"Turning an electrogenic loose on me wasn't very friendly."

She looked down at the table and hunched her shoulders. "That wasn't my idea."

"Okay." I waited while the silence grew uncomfortable.

"I saw you," Carly said, "and I didn't know how to find you, so I had to talk to you before you got away and I lost you again."

"Well, here's your chance."

"You're a mutant," she blurted out, "but you're inside the corporations."

Mike chuckled.

"Well, you're half right," I said. "But suppose that's true. So what? There are a lot of muties working for the corps."

"But you don't work for them."

I shook my head. "You're confusing me."

"We need you." The tone in her voice reminded me of Glenda whining that something wasn't fair.

I turned to her companion. Neither he nor Carly had introduced him. "Do you need me?"

"She says we do." He had a German accent, and his voice sounded like he was gargling gravel.

"And she's that important?"

He looked at her, and I saw his face relax into what I read as love and compassion. The way my dad looked at me sometimes in his tender moments. Then he turned back to me.

"Yes."

"Let's start at the beginning," Mike said. "Who are you, and who do you represent?"

The man turned his head, scanning the room.

"There aren't any cameras or listening devices," I said, pointing at piles of schematics on a side table. "Believe me, I would know."

"I'm Carlotta Cardoza," Carly said. "I represent a group called Democracy Now."

"A terrorist organization that came close to killing me twice," I said. "I'll tell you, I'm not a fan of your methods. And you, sir?"

"Gustav Alscher."

I saw Mike give him a sharp glance.

"I read your infonet site," I said. "I didn't see anything about you being a mutie organization." Indeed, the whole thing had been a convoluted manifesto about democracy and socialism, and ranting about the corporations. I could have found the same ideas posted by dozens of people on the infonet.

"Mutants are worse than second-class citizens," Carly said. "We need equality, and to get that, we need the corporations to pay attention to us."

"Oh, they'll pay attention," I said. "You're going to ignite a war and a genocide. Don't you understand? They don't care about you. You can't make them care about you. Your only chance is to build your own society like I saw in that neighborhood last night. The corps will ignore you, and that's fine. Take care of your own, educate your own."

I stood. "I can't help you. If you continue on the road you're on, no one can help you."

Mike escorted them out of the museum, then came back.

"Was I wrong, Mike?"

He shook his head. "No, you were entirely correct. Eighty percent of the world's population depend on the corps for tomorrow's meals. Alscher was a radical in Europe twenty years ago, until things got too hot for him and he dropped out of sight. It doesn't surprise me that he's involved in this. You don't want to be anywhere near those people. Sooner or later, they'll go too far. They don't understand how the corps think. The corps wouldn't blink at scrubbing an entire city down to bedrock if they decided it was necessary."

CHAPTER 16

My relationship with Deborah remained frosty, but Jess was a lot friendlier. I saw Wil once when he came to meet with Myron Chung, and he refused to meet my eyes. I just put in my time at the museum and went back to the hotel. Mike and I avoided the mutie areas of the city.

A couple of days after Mike came to Chicago, I received an email from Dad.

Libby,

About the list you sent. The Modigliani is easy. Frank Gomez, Chairman of Valient Corp. in Kansas City, has a standing order for any Modigliani paintings. One of my sources tells me he's twice tried to buy that piece from AIC.

The most probable buyer for the Renoirs is Florence Alberts in Atlanta. Her father was Chairman of Southern Foods, and she's the widow of a Chairman of Royal Beverages.

As for the Monet and the Degas, who knows? I've attached a list of about twenty private collectors with the funds to buy such paintings. I have no idea why anyone would steal the necklace. It has zero resale value.

My guess is the four major paintings will bring fifty million each, and the minor Renoir about two to five million. On the other hand, Gomez offered AIC one hundred million for the Modigliani, so I could be wrong.

As for who could have organized things, I would bet on Margarita Martinez. She's local in Chicago, a well-known 'patron of the arts' and a contributor to

144

the museum. She's brokered some fairly large acquisitions.

There are two strategies to consider. The paintings are still in Chicago, and the thieves are lying low waiting for things to cool off, or the art lovers took them out of the city before anyone knew the robbery occurred. In either case, the people who actually took the paintings are going to want to get paid. Follow the money.

Dad

I wandered down to Myron Chung's office and gave him the list.

"My source tells me that Gomez tried to buy the Modigliani piece from the museum," I said.

"Really?" Chung's eyebrows shot up. "I wonder why Director Zhukoff didn't mention that."

"Maybe it slipped her mind."

"Maybe." He pursed his mouth as he perused the list. "Alberts for the Renoirs would make sense. For the Monet, I would guess either DeGruen or Rostikov, or Hollande, and the Degas could be Hollande, Partridge, or Itagaki." He glanced up at me. "Your source knows his collectors."

"Any idea who would want the necklace, other than me?" I asked. "My source says it has no resale, which was my own take."

"I agree with you and your source. I think a lot of people would want it if they could acquire it legitimately, but no one can wear it if it's stolen."

"Exactly. I love that necklace. To think I'll never see it again makes me sick."

Chung studied me. "It was on a different floor from any of the other pieces taken."

"Yes, I know. It was targeted, but why? Someone might be able to wear it in China or Africa, but I don't know if someone from those cultures would find it attractive." I acted as though a thought had just struck me. "Unless they wanted it to throw suspicion on me."

He nodded. "My thoughts exactly. Miss Nelson, who knew that you admired that necklace?"

I shrugged. "Anyone who saw me around it. Director Zhukoff, her assistant, Jessica Prior, and my dad all saw me admire it." I shook my head as I tried to think. "I can't think of anyone else, really. A young schoolgirl who was here with her class one day. We stood and drooled over it together."

That evening, I started researching Margarita Martinez. She was thirty-eight years old, daughter of a corporate executive vice president, married once and divorced, no children. Her mansion was in Glencoe, north of the city, near someplace attractively named the Skokie Lagoon, and the Chicago Botanic Garden, sandwiched between two golf courses. The neighborhood definitely had thief appeal.

Known primarily as a socialite and arts patron, Margarita had two years of university education, and had never worked. Her money came from inheritance and a favorable prenup. Lots of gossip about her love affairs, mostly with much younger men. A hint of scandal concerning the fourteen-year-old boy-and-girl twins of another wealthy corporate family, and the thirteen-year-old daughter of a country club ex-employee.

Her carnal tastes didn't seem to harm her social standing. As far as I could tell, her parties and the

146

other soirees she organized were a must-go for Chicago's upper crust. She'd thrown a fundraising event that raised millions at the museum just a few months before the robbery. Deborah and Malcolm would have known her well.

Checks on the whereabouts and schedules of the potential buyers on Dad's list didn't show anything unusual. That didn't tell me anything. People with that kind of money didn't stick their fingers into the messy details. Either the thieves would take the paintings to the customers, or their underlings would come to Chicago. That set off another line of research. Who would a buyer trust to authenticate and complete a purchase likely to go fifty million or more?

I fired off an email to Dad asking that question. As an afterthought, I asked if he knew of any professional thieves he might consider for such a job.

Two nights of hacking took me through Margarita Martinez's bank accounts. Her investment income was enough to support her and ten thousand of her closest friends, but one of her Swiss accounts showed occasional large infusions. There hadn't been any recent large deposits, but a hundred thousand credit payment was dated the day after the museum robbery. The credit was downloaded to a payment card, so there wouldn't be a record of who received it.

I then did searches on Deborah and Malcolm. Deborah came up squeaky clean. Malcolm was another matter.

Over the previous five years, Malcolm Donnelly had repeatedly paid an alcohol rehab program some big money. Further investigation showed the patient was his wife. But that paled in comparison to his gambling losses. The man definitely had a gambling problem—the problem being he didn't win very often.

Donnelly was raking in fifty million a year from Tarden Corp., but his lifestyle and gambling had him going further and further into debt. I thought back to the conversation I overheard between him and Deborah, and realized that Deborah didn't know how deeply in trouble Malcolm was.

For myself, I couldn't even imagine how someone could blow seventy-five million credits a year and have nothing to show for it.

⊕⊕⊕

In spite of leaving Joe Wilson's car parked on the street for two nights, unlocked and with the key in it, no one had stolen it. For some reason, that made me feel uneasy about the state of the universe. Mike and I thoroughly checked it for bombs and trackers, but didn't find anything.

We took the car and Mike dropped me off in the woods a quarter mile down the road from Margarita Martinez's thirty-room bungalow. The weather was lousy, raining and windy. I slogged through the underbrush until I reached her place. Martinez was scheduled to attend a gallery opening that evening. Her full-time staff of six and the six security guards should be my only obstacles.

Before leaving the hotel, I accessed the invoice for her security system on the infonet and familiarized myself with the equipment installed. Instead of a wall, an eight-foot wrought-iron fence stabilized by brick pillars every eight feet surrounded the grounds. Sharp fleur-de-lis spear points topped the wrought iron.

Blurring my form, I jumped up, grabbed the top of a pillar, pulled myself over, and dropped to the ground on the other side. I didn't expect any of the guards to be out in that weather. Keeping to the shadows, I reached the house without seeing or hearing anyone.

A set of French doors led out to the patio. I had no idea how much of the security system was turned on, since there were people active in the house. What I did know was that Margarita was a cat lady, with at least three of the beasts. That meant any motion detectors had to be aimed well off the floor. I disabled the alarm contacts on the door, picked the lock, and crawled inside.

I found myself in a large dark parlor, the sort of place she might use for entertaining two or three dozen guests. Creeping through the room, I cracked the door and looked out into a short hallway. Beyond that, the cross hallway was lit.

For the next three hours, I went from room to room, dodging the occasional servant. Four of the six stayed in their rooms on the top floor the entire time I was there. The butler roamed around, and the cook stayed in the kitchen until she climbed the back stairs to her room. All of the security guards stayed outside.

I established that the paintings weren't in any of the rooms on the top three floors, unless Margarita was stashing them under the servants' beds. Going through the basement took another hour as most of the rooms had locks I had to pick.

After all that effort, the only thing I accomplished was planting two bugs in her office. A microphone would pick up any sounds and transmit them to my server in Toronto. Any activity on the computer from that point forward would also be copied to my server.

I crawled out of the house and over the fence, then called Mike, and walked to our pre-arranged rendezvous point.

"Any luck?" he asked as I dragged my soggy butt into Joe Wilson's car.

"None, but I really didn't expect to find anything."

He chuckled. "No smoking guns lying out in the open?"

"Nope. It wasn't as neat and clean as the mystery script for your favorite vid. Not a stolen painting in sight."

"Rather uncooperative of her."

I agreed.

Mid-morning the next day, I took an invoice down to Deborah's office for the work I'd done so far.

"No. You can't go in there," Jess said, trying to step in front of me.

I brushed her aside, but as I put my hand on the doorknob, I heard sounds from inside that made me pause.

"Is Malcolm in there?"

Deborah's assistant blushed scarlet.

"How does that make you feel?" I asked. "Or do you get off on hearing them together?"

Jess's face turned even redder, and a visible shiver ran through her body even as she shook her head.

"Why don't you go take a break," I suggested. "That way you won't get blamed when I surprise them."

She opened her mouth, closed it, swallowed a couple of times, shot panicked glances at the door, then nodded and fled, closing the outer door to the hall behind her.

I knew there weren't any security cameras in the office, so I blurred my image, blending into the background. Turning the knob, I quietly pushed open the door to Deborah's office. Peering through the narrow opening, I could tell that neither of the inhabitants of the office could see me. Malcolm's back and bare butt faced me, and he blocked Deborah's view. All I could see of her were her legs pointed toward me from the top of her desk.

Slowly and quietly, I slipped into the office and sidled down the wall away from the door. In a small nook created by a corner and a file cabinet, I held completely still. I had to wait another five or so minutes for them to finish.

They sorted their clothing out, and she attempted to put her hair in order using a small mirror from her purse.

"Why is it taking her so long?" Malcolm asked. "I thought the buyers were all lined up."

"She said we need to wait for things to calm down." Deborah replied. "Right now, the Chamber and the insurance company are checking all shipping out of the area."

"Oh, bullshit," he said. "You can't tell me that I'm going to get checked if I drive my private car to Kansas City. Deborah, tell her to quit stalling. I need that money."

"I can give you a loan. How much do you need?"

I perked up my ears. I knew Donnelly was over extended, but of course, the amounts due on his gambling weren't reflected in his bank accounts until he actually made the payments.

"I don't think you can cover this," he said. "At least she can deliver the Modigliani. Tell her to get it done."

With that, he stalked out. Deborah watched him go and shook her head as the door closed. She grabbed her purse and followed him.

I put the invoice on her desk where she couldn't miss it. Opening the door to the outer office, I saw it was empty and unblurred my form. On my way down the hall to my office, I saw Deborah come out of the washroom and go back to her office.

The thought struck me that I'd just missed a perfect opportunity to bug her office. Considering the two conversations I'd overheard, I decided I really should do that.

That evening I checked my recordings of Margarita Martinez's computer and office bugs. The first audio from the office recorded around noon.

A phone rang and I heard a woman's voice, "Hello?"

"Yes. Why are you calling? I told you to just let things sit for another month."

A period of silence, evidently listening to the caller.

"No. Absolutely not. You don't understand. You're not in charge here, and neither is he."

More silence, for a shorter period.

"I'm sorry. I told you how things work. You can't get in a hurry with this sort of thing. Goodbye."

CHAPTER 17

The following morning, the news feed on the screen in my hotel room told of Malcolm Donnelly's wife Winifred filing for divorce. She charged him with adultery, named Deborah and seven other women as co-respondents, and asked for one hundred million credits and the house as her due for a twenty-five-year marriage.

Although the corporations controlled the news, celebrity divorces were open spectator sports. The reporters gave the divorce more time than they had any of the restaurant bombings. They reported her alcohol use, along with rumors of his affairs. Then they speculated on his wealth, and how the divorce might affect Tarden Corp. One reporter discussed their children, including in-depth profiles of all three. It was the sort of thing I normally avoided watching, but that morning I poured myself another cup of coffee and wished I had some popcorn.

Surprisingly, no one mentioned his gambling. Considering that his mistresses' lingerie and kinks were open game, I had to believe he'd somehow managed to keep his gambling secret.

He must have known the divorce was coming. No wonder he was in desperate need of money. The lawyer bills alone would be huge.

The employee parking lot at the museum was closed to visitors when Mike and I arrived, but at least a dozen news media vehicles sat in front of or near the main building. I was naturally camera shy, and it didn't improve my disposition to have photographers shoving their weapons in my face.

"Why the hell do they want my picture?" I asked

Mike as we fought our way into the building.

"They're probably taking pictures of everyone who goes in or out. It relieves their boredom, and who knows, you might be a secret number nine on the philandering list. Then they'll have your picture all ready to go."

I wanted to smack him with something to wipe the snide grin off his face. Instead, I said, "Unfortunately, I could be tied to Deborah if they start listing her sexual conquests."

The grin slid off his face.

We saw Jess in the hall, and I mentioned the rabid badgers of the press.

"Deborah didn't come in this morning," Jess said. "I talked to her and told her not to."

"Sensible," I responded. "Did she okay that invoice I left on her desk yesterday?"

Jess nodded. "Yeah, I got it. I'll send it on to accounting today."

I thanked her and we proceeded to my office. Mike fell asleep in an old overstuffed chair he'd found and brought in, while I started on the improved security for the inventory database.

About two hours later, I took a break to go get some coffee. My route to the cafeteria took me past the main entrance, where I saw a woman in the middle of a profanity-laced tirade against the guards. I stopped and listened, and figured out that the problem was her handbag. They wanted to send it through a scanner, and she didn't want to let them.

The woman looked familiar. Short, stacked, carrying a little extra weight, with silvering blonde hair and blue eyes. She was expensively dressed and I guessed her to be around fifty. Out of curiosity, I moved closer.

Then it struck me. Winifred Donnelly. I had met her once, briefly, a few weeks before, and seen her on the news that morning.

"Ma'am, we have to scan the bag for security reasons. No one is exempt," a guard patiently tried to explain.

Winifred wasn't having it. "Do you know who I am?" she screeched. "I'll have your job. I'll sue your ass and own this whole damned pile of rocks. You just enjoy bullying a woman. Protecting that damned slut who runs this place."

I don't know why, maybe it was the fact that particular guard was unvaryingly cheerful to everyone and greeted me with a smile every morning, but I took pity on him.

"Mrs. Donnelly?" I said, stepping forward. "I'm Elizabeth Nelson, security consultant. What seems to be the problem?"

"He's trying to steal my purse!"

"Oh, now, I don't think he needs your makeup," I said. "I imagine his job pays him enough to buy his own."

"I don't want his grubby hands in my stuff," she grumbled.

"I can understand that, but he doesn't have to touch your purse at all." I had been moving toward her, but when I got within range of her breath, I stopped. It was amazing that she could stand with that much vodka in her.

"Why don't you put your purse on that conveyer belt, and let the machine scan it?" I proposed. "No one will touch it."

"Why? Do you think I have a bomb in there or

155

something?"

"Mrs. Donnelly, I don't think you have a bomb." I wouldn't have put it past her to carry a pistol, but I would have bet my last credit that what she was trying to hide was her bottle. "It's the rules. Even I have to go through scans. You know about the robbery, don't you?"

She swayed on her feet and squinted at me.

"Are you here to see Director Zhukoff?" I asked.

"Give that bitch a piece of my mind," Winifred muttered. "She doesn't have a piece of mind." She broke into a semi-hysterical giggle. "Nothing but a piece of ass."

"Director Zhukoff isn't here," I said. "She called in sick today."

"Ha! Sick of lying and whoring around, most likely." She stood there swaying for another minute, then looked up at the security guard. "Lucky for you I'm in a good mood today." Then she turned and wobbled out the door.

The guard turned and looked at me, his eyes wide.

"Yeah," I said. "Imagine what kind of hell on wheels she'd be if she was PMSing."

He barked out a laugh. "Thank you, Miss Nelson. I appreciate the help."

I shrugged. "No problem." When I turned, I saw Jess watching me from the hallway. I continued on toward the cafeteria, and she fell in beside me.

"You have to deal with her much?" I asked.

"Every time she can't find her husband, or, like today, she gets a load on and decides to come see Deborah."

"Lovely couple. I wonder why she decided to divorce him?"

156

Jess shot me a look, then dropped her voice. "I heard Malcolm tell Deborah that there might be a buyout for Tarden."

"You'd think ol' Winifred would wait for the money," I said.

"Not if she knows an audit would knock down his house of cards."

I stopped and faced Jess. "His gambling."

She nodded.

"How does that affect the corporation?"

She took a deep breath and looked away.

"He's cooking the books," I said. "Embezzlement." In the corporate world, you were better off raping and killing babies on the town square than screwing up a stock's price. The investor class took their money very seriously.

"How in the hell did he get that deep?"

She bit her lip and shook her head. A look of fear blossomed on her face. "Oh, God. I've said too much."

"Yes, you have. Don't say it to anyone else."

That night, I sent my mother an email suggesting that a forensic accountant might find something of value in Tarden's books. If I'd had the time, I would have researched it myself. Trading stocks on inside information could be so lucrative.

$$\oplus\oplus\oplus$$

Deborah didn't show up for work the following day, either. The second morning after the divorce announcement, my phone rang as I was getting dressed.

"Libby?" It was Wil.

"Yeah. How's it going?"

"Lousy. Deborah Zhukoff's dead. Her body was found in an alley this morning."

"Oh, my. Let me guess. My DNA was under her fingernails, she was holding the missing necklace, and my name was written in blood next to her body."

Silence.

Then, "Libby, I know you have every right to be mad at me. I handled things completely wrong. I need your help, and the Chamber is willing to pay for it."

My turn for silence. "That almost sounded like an apology," I finally said.

More silence, then, "Libby, I'm sorry."

"You're sorry for being an ass, sorry that I called your case for being an ass, or sorry for every doubting and suspecting me?"

"All of the above."

"Gee, you know how us blonde bimbos are. I completely forgot already what all of the above entailed."

I heard him take a deep breath. "I'm sorry I was an ass, and I'm sorry I ever suspected you. I'm sorry we treated you the way we did."

"And you want to make it up to me no matter what it takes or how long it takes. Right?"

I could almost hear the gears in his brain grinding, even through the phone.

"Libby, I want to make it up to you." I could hear his teeth grinding.

"And you'll sign that prenup, right?"

"Damn it, Libby," he exploded.

I started laughing. "Okay. What do you need me to do? Remember, though, that you've burned all your chances with me."

"Yeah, I figured that. Where are you? I can send a car."

"Give me the address."

Mike and I took the train and then a bus to an area of town a couple of miles from the museum. We hoofed it to the area where Wil told me to go and found a bunch of police and security cars, an ambulance, and policemen in uniform telling us we shouldn't be there.

After half an hour, someone finally asked Wil what to do about the loud-mouthed blonde who kept asking for him and refusing to go away.

"Don't you know that when you throw a party, you're supposed to leave a list at the door so the bouncers know who to let in?" I asked when Wil finally came to retrieve us.

"I'll make sure my social secretary is informed," he said, leading us toward an alley.

I looked around at the neighborhood. "What was she doing here?" We were in an area of middle-class apartment buildings with a few stores, restaurants, and bars at the street corners.

He shook his head. "Come see."

A garbage truck sat in the alley next to a dumpster. Deborah's nude body lay behind the dumpster. Her front was covered in dried blood, and her face held that look of horrified surprise I had seen too often.

"Dumped behind the dumpster, not in it?" Mike asked.

"Yeah," Wil said.

"That probably means the killer wasn't strong enough to lift her."

Wil cocked his head to look at him.

"Mike used to work for my father at MegaTech," I said and saw Wil nod. I continued, "Deborah wasn't a lightweight. She probably weighed one forty-five, maybe one fifty. Even most men would have trouble lifting her that high. Cause of death?"

"We waited for you. I wanted you to see how we found her." Wil told some of the waiting men to move the dumpster. After they rolled it away, the medical examiner crouched over the body, then eased her onto her back.

"Stabbed, it looks like," he said.

Wil handed us shoe coverings and we put them on, then approached the body.

"See here?" the ME asked, pointing to her abdomen. A deep wound under her breastbone showed evidence of having bled a lot. I knew if the thrust had been upward, it would have hit the heart.

"A lot of stab wounds," Wil said. Indeed, there were multiple wounds to her chest, shoulders, and neck, with a single slice on her left cheek.

"They all look pretty shallow, with the exception of the lower one," the ME said.

Wil looked at me, and I looked at Mike. I didn't doubt that with his experience, he knew a lot more than I did about murder investigations. I usually didn't stick around for that part.

"Looks like a frenzied kill," Mike said. "Or, the frenzy came after the kill, either from frustration or to make it seem like a crime of passion."

"Any idea why anyone would want to kill her?" Wil asked me.

I turned and walked away. He followed me. When we were well away from everyone else, I said, "How

160

much are you paying me?"

"Your standard rate."

"Twenty-four seven, no questions asked?"

"Hell, no. Bill me honestly. I have to account for my budget."

"You're no fun."

"So you've told me."

"How much do you think I can bill the insurance company for?"

He blinked at me. "You think this is connected to the robbery?"

"If I tell you, it might hurt my negotiating position with Mr. Chung."

"Oh, for God's sake. Is money all you think about?"

I lost it and started yelling at him. "Aren't you getting paid for standing here arguing with me? How come everyone thinks I look like some damned charity? I spent days playing games with you people instead of working. Who's going to pay my lawyer bills? I'm fucking innocent, and I have lawyer bills because of you, and you think I'm greedy?" I wanted to hit him. Instead, I unballed my fist, got my temper under control, and said through gritted teeth, "You're the one who called me this morning."

He stared at me, then spun on his heel and walked away, pulling out his phone. He talked to someone for about ten minutes, then came back.

"Chung will pay your standard rates, but only for hours spent on the robbery, not the murder."

"He'll pay for both," I said. "It's a derivative crime, Wil. Deborah and Malcolm Donnelly arranged the theft."

161

He must have had his own suspicions because he didn't look sufficiently shocked. "Do you have proof of that?"

"No, but I have leads. I know who the broker for the art is." He didn't say anything, just stood there waiting. "A woman named Margarita Martinez."

"Great. You're accusing the director of the museum, the chairman of its board of directors, who's also chairman of a large and respected corporation, and one of the foremost art patrons in the city."

"Why didn't they inform the insurance company about the robbery? Why hide it from the media? I'd have immediately posted pictures of those paintings on line. Make things as hot as possible for the thieves. And then there's the method. I know Chung suspects an inside job. Why have David Wilson killed? Deborah tried to tell me that he was dragging his feet on fixing the security issues, but suppose that wasn't true? I'll bet he tried to blackmail them."

I figured I might as well throw that last part in. No harm in deflecting any suspicions about Wilson's death.

"How sure are you?" he asked. "Is this just a hunch?"

I shook my head. "No, I overheard Deborah and Donnelly talking. Twice. Donnelly's got money problems, and they were lovers. He talked her into stealing two paintings, but then he got greedy. The necklace was an afterthought. They planned to plant it on me, but you screwed that up by arresting me before they had the chance."

"So, I did something right?"

"Don't even go there."

"Libby," he said, and the tone in his voice stopped

162

me. "I do owe you an apology, and the Chamber will take care of your lawyer bills."

I gaped at him.

He took a deep breath and continued. "I needed to placate Donnelly and Zhukoff. They were insistent that you'd stolen the paintings. I was hoping that by arresting you, they might drop their guard and make a mistake. I should have told you, but we needed your honest reaction. When I discovered they hadn't told the insurance company—" He gestured toward Deborah's body. "This whole case has blown up now. With Deborah and Wilson dead, I'm running out of suspects."

I wandered around the alley for a bit, trying to figure out if I should forgive Wil or gut him, then told him, "If you ever do something like that to me again, you'll be singing soprano. Understand?" I looked over at Deborah. "Somebody drove her body here. Find her car. Check on Donnelly's whereabouts last night. If he didn't do it, or order it, then he's in an absolute panic."

"Why would he panic now?" Wil asked. "I could see him panicking and killing her, but why panic if he didn't?"

"Because with this robbery, he's let criminals into his life. The kind of people that were only an abstraction before. If someone killed her, then he could be next."

He looked thoughtful. "That makes a lot of sense."

"And if he's nervous, he's likely to make a mistake. Put a tail on him. Deborah was the main contact to Martinez. I'd put a tail on her, too. Things just got a lot more complicated for everyone involved."

⊕⊕⊕

Wil drove us to the museum. I was surprised that Jess wasn't in her office. I didn't even know who to ask if she'd called in. After all, Deborah was her supervisor.

"Have you released news of Deborah's death?" I asked Wil.

"No. We haven't contacted her relatives yet. Her parents live someplace in Iowa, and she has a sister in British Columbia."

He came back that afternoon to pick us up and take us to the ME's office.

"The wound in the belly was the cause of death," the ME told us. "None of the other wounds were life-threatening."

"How many other wounds?" Mike asked.

"Twelve stab wounds and the cut on the cheek. All the stab wounds were fairly superficial except the lower one."

"Trajectory?" I asked.

"Upward." He picked up a scalpel and demonstrated. Then he turned the knife over in his hand. "The chest wounds were made like this." He flipped the scalpel over, raised his hand over his head and stabbed down. "I would guess the victim was lying on the floor when the secondary wounds were inflicted."

"What kind of knife?"

"It appears to have been a kitchen knife. Smooth blade, single edge, about six inches long and an inch wide. The time of death was around nine o'clock last night, as best as we can figure. It was very cold last night, so the body was ambient when she was found."

As we left the morgue, Wil said, "We found her car

164

about a mile from where we found her body. A block from a train station. Her clothes were in another dumpster between the body and the car."

"And the condition of the car?" I asked.

"The trunk is bloody, just like her clothes."

"Did you find any other bloody clothes?" Mike asked. "The killer would have gotten pretty messy."

"No, but I'll tell Chicago Police to keep looking," Wil said.

"Blood inside the passenger compartment? Any evidence from the killer?" Mike continued.

"The forensics people are going through it. We'll see. I'm not sure why the killer stripped her."

"Hoping to delay identification," I said. "Well, that blows that theory."

"What theory?" Mike and Wil asked together.

"That it was a professional hit. Kitchen knife."

"So, you don't think it's connected to the robbery?" Wil asked.

"Oh, it's connected. I'm just saying that a professional hit man wouldn't use a kitchen knife. An art thief might, however."

CHAPTER 18

Wil and one of the Chicago detectives questioned Malcolm Donnelly, who couldn't, or wouldn't, supply an alibi. Winifred Donnelly said she was home all night, but the butler had the night off and the rest of the staff were either gone or in their rooms. None of her staff could say when Mrs. Donnelly came home, or if she did, or if she went out again. I asked if she drove a car, and Wil told me she didn't have a license. As if someone committing murder cared about such things.

When Jess showed up for work the next day, her face was puffy, her eyes red and swollen, and she burst into tears about every five minutes. She had no alibi. She said she'd been at home watching a vid.

Other than me, that exhausted the immediate pool of suspects. Considering Deborah's free-wheeling social life, and her penchant for discretion, the police hit all the bars and restaurants that Jess, Wil and I knew she frequented. Winifred's divorce filing supplied a few more possibilities. Her private investigator had followed Deborah and Malcolm around for months.

Malcolm was less than forthcoming during a second visit from Wil. Privately, I considered Margarita Martinez a suspect, but preferred that no one tip her off that we connected her to the robbery.

For myself, I couldn't see Winifred managing to dispose of the body. Even the ultra rich didn't have people on call for that sort of thing. It might make a good side business, though. I could hire vamps and lycans. Plenty of muscle and an unerring sense of smell. Cleaning up the blood wouldn't be a problem. I could probably get bookings through divorce lawyers.

Deborah's domestic staff said she had gone out around four o'clock in the afternoon and hadn't come back. The calendars on her home and work computers didn't show any appointments. Her phone was missing. The phone company showed her only calls, both in and out, were with the Institute.

The police waited another day, then released the news of Deborah's death.

Chung called me in to his office at the Institute the following day.

"You know that the insurance corporations share a database on art," he said after I sat down in his office. "We track all insured works and those who own or trade in them."

I nodded. It included such works as the Gaugin I found, even though it had been missing for over a hundred years. It still listed works stolen in the twentieth century.

"We also track certain individuals, your father is one, and so are you because of him."

He waited, but when I didn't respond, he continued. "A couple of men on our list, Bernard Carpentier and Edouard Maillard, flew in from France this morning."

"The names don't mean anything to me," I said.

"Carpentier is a very close associate of one of the names on the list you gave me, Georges Hollande. Maillard is the curator of his collection."

Hollande I recognized as head of one of the major crime families in France.

"They came to collect Hollande's painting or paintings," I said.

"That is my assumption," Chung replied.

I wasn't sure what to think. In the conversation of

167

hers that I overheard, Martinez had seemed in no hurry to move the paintings. Did Deborah's death change her mind? Or did it spur Hollande to action?

"We released the list of the stolen art to the media," Chung said, breaking into my reverie.

"When did you do that?"

"The day before Director Zhukoff's death."

That meant either event could have prompted Hollande's action, or the combination of events. I also wondered if that news had anything to do with Deborah's murder.

"Mr. Chung, in your experience, do buyers at this level pick up their purchases, or take delivery?"

He cupped his chin in his hand and got a faraway look in his eyes. "That's an interesting question. If it were me, I'd want the seller to take the risk of moving it to Europe. Too much can go wrong between here and there, and then you're out the money. Even with a legitimate sale, the buyer usually wants the seller to take the risk of shipment. Of course, with a legitimate sale, the shipment is insured. That's not an option in this case."

I nodded, following his line of reasoning. "So, assuming that Monsieur Hollande has experience with such acquisitions, why would he take the chance?"

"Another very good question." The hint of a smile crooked the corner of his mouth. "We can always speculate, can't we?"

I smiled back at him. "He's concerned that things are too messy at this end, so he sent his boys to take charge of things."

"Very reasonable. Another possibility is, he found out the complete scope of the theft, and is interested in one or more of the other paintings," Chung responded.

That stopped me, and I thought about Chung's comments when I first handed him my dad's potential list of buyers.

"Hollande collects both Degas and Monet?" I asked.

"Hollande collects a lot of things. For the right price, he might take all five paintings. He and a man in Russia, who wasn't on your list, are the only ones I could see as buyers for the necklace."

"Mr. Chung, I think we know who organized this robbery. Do you have any suspicions as to who actually executed the plan?"

He shook his head. "No. Right now, I'm assuming they hired locals to do it."

⊕⊕⊕

I went back to the hotel and did some research online. Hollande was implicated in drugs, extortion, human trafficking, weapons, and just about anything else the legitimate corporations wouldn't touch. His legitimate businesses included hotels and casinos. One financial expert estimated Hollande's worth in the thirty to fifty billion credit range.

One thing that caught my attention was a quote from an interview with Hollande. "I enjoy beautiful things—paintings, sculptures, houses, women—I collect them all."

I hated dealing with the mob. The corporations might not care about an individual human life, but they were always profit driven. The crime families didn't need an excuse for anything they did. They might kill someone on a whim or a moment of irritation.

I listened to the recordings through my bug in Margarita Martinez's office, but didn't hear anything interesting. Her email had a message from an anonymous account in France that only said, *Our representatives will contact you in Chicago on Thursday.* That would be the following day.

I called Wil. "Did you put a tail on Martinez?"

"It's on my to-do list. I've been a little busy."

"What are you doing right now?"

"You mean, other than talking to you? I just got out of a meeting with the AIC board of directors. They voted to suspend Malcolm until, as they said, 'questions surrounding the robbery are resolved'. They want me to oversee your remaining work on the network security."

"Meet me someplace."

"Where?"

"Someplace unlikely to get bombed. A place that serves alcohol and real food."

When Mike and I reached the restaurant, he said, "I'm not hungry. I think I'll just hang out at the bar and have a drink." I watched him sit next to a pretty vamp and then turned to look for Wil.

He waved at me from a corner booth, and I wandered over, sat down, and punched my drink order into the automenu.

"The prices are reasonable," I said. "How's the food?"

"The fish is all from natural farms, guaranteed antibiotic free and heavy metal free. The hamburgers are real beef from their own farm. Chicken also."

"Lots of that here in Chicago," I said.

"Not really. Not enough of it, anyway."

I ordered and then told him about my meeting with Chung. "That's why we need a tail put on Martinez. A long-range listening device, too, if you can. If the buyers are coming to town, things are going to get interesting."

"Sure thing. I can tap her phone, too."

I shrugged. "Won't do any good. She uses a special phone for this kind of business, and I suspect it's shielded. I also suspect it has a weird routing that would make it hard to identify."

"Because that's what you'd do?"

"Of course. Don't sell her short. My source tells me she's one of the top brokers in the world. She didn't get there overnight, and the Chamber didn't even know about her."

Wil nodded, but he didn't look happy. "Should I do it right now?"

"The buyers from France will contact her in the morning," I answered. "I'd suggest you have someone out there early. She's going to leave the house around eight."

He stared at me with his mouth hanging open. "How the hell do you know that?"

"Aren't you glad I'm on your side?" I gave him a big smile. "I could have read her mind, but instead, I looked at her calendar. She has an appointment with her hairdresser at ten. The boys from France will be a little jet-lagged, so expect them to get around to contacting her about the same time."

I ate my burger and we chatted.

"I've missed you," Wil said, abruptly, interrupting a conversation about music.

He took me off guard and made me a little

uncomfortable, so I answered, "Why? All the other women in town afraid to go out with you? I keep telling you, take a girl to a bombing, and the word gets around."

"Yeah, that's part of it, I guess." His tone was wistful, and the expression on his face tender. Red flags went off like fireworks in my head.

"Well, I kind of missed you, too. I hate it when men treat me like a girl. I'm much more comfortable being just one of the guys." Oh, Libby. I wondered how long my nose grew on that one.

He acted as if he was going to say something, then with a small shake of his head, didn't. I changed the subject to farms and restaurants and an article I'd read about gardens on roofs of urban buildings.

When we got up to go, Mike came over from the bar.

"I think we have a problem," he said, leaning close and speaking into my ear.

"How so?"

"There was a vamp sitting at the bar when we came in. He paid you a lot of attention, and when you sat down, he left in a hurry. Left a fresh drink sitting there."

I asked Wil, "Are we near the mutie district?"

"On the edge. It really starts a couple of blocks from here."

"Maybe we should go out the back."

Wil raised an eyebrow. "Who have you pissed off that I don't know about?"

"Remember a tavern bombing and a couple of snipers? You weren't the only one paying attention to me that evening."

Mike went back to the bar and spoke to the

bartender, who motioned to a hallway beyond the bar. Mike turned back and motioned to us, and we followed him down the hallway.

We passed through the kitchen, and the staff gave us funny looks, but didn't say anything or try to stop us. Mike stuck his head out the back door and looked around, then continued through.

Our luck ran out when we reached the end of the alley. A very tall, thin man appeared in front of us.

"Keep your hands where we can see them," Gustav Alscher said in his gravelly German accent. "We have you surrounded."

I looked up and saw people on the rooftops. There were sounds of movement in the alley behind me.

"What do you want?" Wil asked.

"Her. Come with me, girl, and we'll let your friends go. Nobody gets hurt."

"Somebody's going to get hurt," Wil said. "I guarantee you'll personally never know the outcome of this."

"Wil, no," I said. "It's okay. I'll go with them." Dropping my voice to almost inaudible, I leaned close to Mike. "I'll call you when I shake free."

Stepping forward, I said, "Okay, let's go."

A man stepped close to me and reached out his hand to take my arm. I spun to face him. "Let's get the parameters of my cooperation straight right now. Anyone who lays a hand on me dies. That's non-negotiable."

"Leave her alone," Alscher said. "She said she'll come. That's enough."

I walked through a gantlet to a waiting van and got inside. Alscher got in the back with me, and we drove away. The driver tried to be cute. He took

173

random turns to try to shake off any tails and confuse me. At one point, he drove in a four-block circle for fifteen minutes.

With a yawn, I told Alscher, "I still know where I am and where the lake is. Tell that fool to just drive before I fall asleep."

Of course, the last thing I would have been able to do was sleep. I was so keyed up that I was almost vibrating.

"Does Carly know that you've snatched me?" I asked out of curiosity.

"There wasn't time to find her," he said.

"So, where are you taking me?"

He didn't answer, just turned and watched out the windows. So, I did the same thing. We eventually left the civilized parts of town and plunged into one of those post-apocalyptic nightmare landscapes such as the one I'd seen with Mike. Very few people out on the streets, and some of them only remotely resembled a human being.

Most people who grew up in a corporate culture, no matter how far down in the hierarchy, never met one of the extreme mutants. At most, they might have come face-to-face with a vamp or one of the more-human-looking lycans. Pictures of trolls and other monsters often didn't do them justice.

We drove past a troll standing on the sidewalk talking to a vamp girl dressed like a street hooker. The man, or at least I assumed it was male, stood much taller than Alscher's seven feet. I would swear he easily weighed four hundred pounds, and it was all bulging muscle. He had skin so dark it was black at night, completely hairless, with teeth that would make the most extreme lycan proud.

Not the kind of guy you wanted to take home to meet the parents, unless you were trying to induce a couple of heart attacks to get an early inheritance. I was pretty confident in my ability to take care of myself. Some nitpickers might even call me arrogant. But the only way I'd take on a troll was with artillery from the next county.

We finally arrived at our destination. A block of row houses, half of them fallen down, and a huge, squat building that I guessed used to be a store of some kind. I wasn't impressed, except by the size of the rat sitting on a pile of rubble, daring me to get out of the van.

Alscher wasn't daunted, throwing open the door and climbing out into the street. The rat held its ground, but didn't attack. I wasn't fooled. Where there was one rat, there were a million, and that had all the signs of an ambush.

"We're here. Come on," Alscher said.

"What about the wildlife?" I asked, fingering my pistol in my purse.

"Huh?" He looked around as though he hadn't noticed there was a rat half the size of a German Shepard ten feet away. "Don't worry," he said, turning back to me. "They don't attack adults."

I wanted to ask how they told the difference. Did they ask to see identification? I crawled out of the van, keeping Alscher between me and the rat king, and followed the driver into the old store. Most of the glass was missing, so the wind whistled through the place. It seemed to go on forever. We proceeded across the floor to a stairwell that led down.

It was dark at the bottom except for two pairs of glowing animal eyes. When my sight adjusted, I realized the eyes belonged to an orange tabby cat and his calico companion, both larger than the rat. One of them yawned, revealing teeth like daggers.

Proceeding through a door, we found light and people. The place looked a bit like a bar in a bomb shelter, though there were some cots and beds. Music played from a radio.

Alscher pulled a couple of beers from a cooler on a long table, popped the tops off the bottles, and handed me one. "I've sent word to Carly. She'll come when she can."

I looked around and wandered over to sit at an empty table. Alscher didn't follow me. None of the people who kidnapped me seemed to pay much attention to me. I guessed they didn't worry about me escaping, with good reason. Where would I go? Outside with the rats? I knew approximately where I was in relation to where I'd been and to the lake, but I had no idea how to get back or tell Mike where I was.

Most of the people, about fifty or sixty, were obviously mutants or had congenital abnormalities. Lycans—also called wolfmen—with lots of hair, people with scales, vamps, and a woman with two heads flirting with two different guys, mixed in with people who looked normal, but probably weren't.

The conversations around me ranged from a discussion of a classic novel, to an argument about revolutionary tactics, to a guy trying to seduce a woman who didn't act very interested.

About half an hour after we arrived, a tall man a bit older than I was pulled a chair next to mine and dropped into it. I noticed there was webbing between his long fingers, and his face seemed elongated, his mouth extending far beyond his short, broad nose. In my mind, I labeled him Horseface. I wasn't interested in ever learning his real name.

"Hi, sweet thing. What's your name?"

"Leave me alone," I said, turning away from him and looking for Alscher. He was standing across the room, talking to three other men.

"That's not a very friendly attitude," Horseface said, putting one arm around my shoulders and sticking his other hand between my legs. "You need to be friendly, otherwise you won't do very well around here."

I smiled at him, batted my eyes, and laid my hand on his arm. He took it as encouragement and, with a smirking leer, squeezed me hard enough to make me gasp. Taking hold of his wrist, I pulled his hand out of my crotch and gently placed his hand on the table. Then I pinned his arm to the table with a stiletto.

He cursed, jumping up and away from me. The table tipped over, dragging his arm down, and he shrieked in pain.

Stepping toward him, I grabbed his shoulders and drove my knee between his legs as hard as I could. His eyes bulged and he dropped moaning to his knees. I knelt beside him and pressed the muzzle of my pistol against his temple.

"You know how you feel when you knock a woman down," I said into his ear, "and then you stand over her, unbuckle your belt, and unzip your pants? You know how that feels, don't you?"

He took a sobbing breath.

"Don't you?" I insisted.

"Yes," he said in a ragged voice.

"You like forcing women, don't you?" I continued in a soft, crooning voice. "It makes you feel strong and powerful, doesn't it? Come on, you can tell me. Doesn't it make you feel fantastic? Don't you hate them? Isn't it great to see them grovel before you? The fear in their eyes is even better than the sex, isn't it?"

He took several deep, panting breaths, then whispered, "Yes."

"Well, I'm going to blow your brains out," I said. He whimpered. "Now you know how those women felt. This is for all of them."

I looked beyond him, adjusted the angle of my pistol a little, and pulled the trigger. Blood and brains sprayed the floor and the wall beyond.

Dead silence descended on the room. No one even breathed.

"I keep my promises," I told Alscher as I walked to the cooler, pulled out another beer, and went over to a table with three couples and an empty chair.

"Anyone using this chair?"

Everyone shook their heads.

"I hate rapists," I said. The eyes of two of the women slid to their companions, then back toward me. The men stared at me in fear and revulsion, leaning back in their seats to get as far away from me as possible.

The third woman simply stared at me. I was fascinated by her exotic beauty. Pale golden skin with fine, tiny scales, straight black hair to her waist, and delicate seashell ears that were half the size of a normal human's. The pupils of her eyes were vertical slits, like a cat. Her anger was almost palpable, but I didn't think it was aimed at me. Hopefully, I'd made one ally.

I took a sip of my beer and looked around. Every eye in the place was on me. While I was trying to project an air of nonchalant kick-ass, I was actually terrified. I didn't know if I had ensured my safety or signed my death certificate. It was getting late, and I'd have to sleep sooner or later.

⊕⊕⊕

CHAPTER 19

Carly showed up around midnight.

"Libby, what a surprise. I didn't know you were here."

"Really? Your buddy Alscher said he told you I was here."

The confused look on her face told me everything I needed to know.

"No, but I don't carry a phone, so he might have tried to get word to me. It's good to see you. Did you think about what I said? Are you going to help us?"

Deep sigh. She looked so hopeful. "Help you do what?"

"We need a leader, someone who can mobilize the masses, give them direction, get them working together."

"I have no idea why you think I would be good at that sort of thing," I said. "I thought you were the leader here." I waved my hand to indicate the room. "Everybody here seems to follow you."

"I'm the prophet," she said enthusiastically. "I see things. I see through things. Delusions, illusions, lies. Like I can see through your disguises. And sometimes I see the future. I've seen you, seen you lead our people to freedom."

She seemed like such a sweet girl. It was disheartening to realize she was delusional. Stark raving mad. Bat-shit crazy.

"Carly, do you ever take anything to help you see your visions?" I asked.

Again, she looked confused. "You mean like drugs? No, never. Sometimes I eat some mushrooms. They help me to relax and lower the veils. But they

180

aren't drugs. Gustav grows them."

Ah. I glanced over to where Alscher sat watching us.

"Carly, I didn't come here by accident," I started.

"I know. It's part of the cosmic plan," she said. I could see where her enthusiasm might be contagious, especially amongst a bunch of losers without much hope.

"No, that's not what I meant. Gustav and a gang of toughs with guns kidnapped me. They threatened to kill the people I was with if I didn't comply."

She shot Alscher a startled glance, but her certainty wasn't shaken for long. "Well, the universe has to work through people. That's why it needs you. God helps those who help themselves, you know."

I tried not to roll my eyes. After a while, Carly and Alscher led me to one of the row houses nearby and showed me to a room on the second floor with a pile of rags in the corner. I assumed that was supposed to be a bed. The chances I would crawl in with the bedbugs and whatever else might be living there were nil.

Luckily, I didn't have to brave outdoors to find the outhouse. They had dug a pit in the basement and placed a board over it to sit on. The stench was lovely, quite in keeping with the rest of the décor. But they also afforded me some privacy, so I called Mike.

If I had a normal phone, he would have been able to track me. But, as I'd told Wil about Margarita Martinez, I used a hardened phone, with every privacy feature known to modern technology.

"Libby?" Mike answered.

"Yeah, it's me."

"Thank God. Where are you?"

181

"Not entirely sure. Area looks like a war zone." I described my general location as best I could. Then Wil got on the phone.

"Describe that abandoned store," he said.

After a while, he told me, "I'm pretty sure I know where you are. Can you get free? Go outside, I mean?"

"Sure. When? Wil, there are rats out there the size of dinosaurs, and God only knows what else. Some of the cockroaches have saddles. And there are trolls."

I thought I heard a snicker.

"It's not funny, damn it. I saw a cat the size of a tiger. This is a scary place."

"Give us an hour, then go outside. We'll pick you up."

"I hope you're bringing a battalion with you. I'm in the fourth row house from the corner, a block from the parking lot around that old store. One hour from right now. Don't be late."

I went back to my room. Pushing the small table there against the wall, I sat on it and leaned back. It wasn't comfortable, but it was the best I could do. Sounds in the rest of the building soon ceased, and I listened to the serenade of a cat and a rat having a disagreement outside.

When the hour was up, I pried loose a couple of the boards covering the window, blurred my shape, and crawled out onto the roof covering the front porch. I hung by my arms while I gathered my courage, then dropped the fifteen feet or so to the ground. I landed awkwardly on the uneven surface, letting myself fall and roll while I covered my face and head with my arms. Graceful it wasn't, and I hurt like hell in several places.

I limped out to the street and looked around. No

one but Carly could see me, but I didn't know if blending into the background affected my scent. I assumed the rats hunted by smell. I'd much rather fight a bunch of thugs than a pack of rats.

My chrono showed that I was on time. I didn't see any movement on the street leading into the neighborhood. Then I happened to look up. About a hundred feet above me, an aircar blocked out part of the stars. I unblurred my form and pulled out my phone.

"I'm right below you," I said when Mike answered.

The sense of relief as I watched the aircar descend was on a par with getting out of the Chicago jail. I was really beginning to hate that town.

A shout came from behind me to my right. I cast a glance that way as the aircar settled on the street twenty feet in front of me. A figure in a dark, hooded cloak ran toward me. I ran to the open door of the aircar.

I jumped in and reached out to pull the door closed when I saw the person running toward us push their hood back. It was the woman with the gold-scaled skin.

"Wait!" I shouted as the aircar began to rise. "Wil, we have another passenger."

One of the things I liked about Wil, when the action got heated, he didn't argue or hesitate, he just got the job done. The aircar dropped back to the pavement.

She reached us and looked up at me, breathing heavily. "Take...take me with...with you," she panted.

I reached out my hand, took hers, and pulled her in over me, then slammed the door. "Go!"

The aircar rose, circled once over the area, then

183

headed north toward a more civilized part of town.

I looked at the hand I held in mine. In addition to the scales covering her skin, webbing connected her long, clawed fingers.

Mike turned from the front seat and gave the woman a thorough inspection, then glanced at me.

"My name's Libby," I told her. "I don't believe we were introduced."

"Miriam," she said. "Miriam al-Azadi. Thank you." She had an accent. Arabic maybe? Softer than what I associated with Arabic.

"Couldn't you have left any time?" I asked. "Were you a prisoner?"

"Alscher's pet. Carly's handmaiden. A plaything. They told me that I couldn't go out in normal society because I'm a monster and they would kill me or lock me away in a zoo. But when you looked at me, and I saw your eyes, I knew they'd lied." The accent was fairly strong, her pronunciation sibilant as she drew out her S's and rolled her R's.

"I don't understand. What did you see in my eyes?"

"It's what I didn't see. No horror, no revulsion, no pity. You weren't even curious. You looked at me in exactly the same way as you looked at the woman beside me."

"Where are you from?"

"I was born north of the Himalayas in Central Asia. My parents sold me when I was very young, and then I was sold again and again. Alscher bought me seventeen years ago in the part of Ukraine called Moldova."

"How old were you when Alscher bought you?" Mike asked in a quiet voice.

184

"Fourteen, I think. He took me to Africa, then to South America. That's where he found Carly. She was just a girl, then."

Slavery was outlawed everywhere, but we all knew it still existed.

"Where are we going?" Wil asked.

"We need to retrieve our things from our hotel," I said. "Then we're open to suggestions. Not the place where you and Tarden Corporation have a million bugs planted, and definitely someplace far from any mutie areas."

Mike gave Wil directions, and he took us to the hotel. We collected our equipment and clothes in less than half an hour, including the time to defuse all the booby traps, cameras, and listening devices I'd installed.

"The Chamber has a safe house," Wil suggested.

"And you don't mind if I short out all of your electronics?" I asked with as sweet a smile as I could muster.

His expression didn't indicate a great deal of support for the idea.

Mike wandered off and made a phone call. When he came back, he gave Wil an address and received a surprised response.

"Are you serious?"

"Oh, yes. We'll be fine there," Mike said.

Wil gave me a look, then looked back to Mike.

"I'm fine with anything Mike sets up," I said.

So, we ended up at Jezebel's House of Pleasure. The grand lady herself met us at the back door, giving Mike a hug and me a big smile. "My, have you grown up."

"Hi, Doreen," I said. "It's been a while." Doreen, or Jezebel, had worked for my mom as a dominatrix when I was in middle school.

She gave us a couple of spare rooms, I paid her a boatload of money, and for the first time in weeks, I went to bed feeling safe. Brothels didn't stint on personal security. It would be easier to break into a bank.

⊕⊕⊕

Mike woke me four hours later.

"Do you have a death wish?" I asked him as I tried to pry one eye open. It was awfully bright. I should have closed the curtains before I went to bed.

"Margarita Martinez left home for her hairdresser's," he said.

"I hope she dies of electrical shock from a hair dryer," I grumbled, rolling over and pulling a pillow over my head.

"Wil called and said he thinks he has a line on the Frenchmen."

I popped up and headed for the washroom. "Why didn't you say so?"

Twenty minutes later, showered and dressed, I joined Miriam and Mike downstairs shortly before Wil showed up. Doreen had tossed Miriam's rags and found some reasonably decent clothes for her to wear. We jumped in Wil's fancy car, and he drove us to his office at Chamber headquarters.

"First thing," Wil said to Miriam when we arrived, "I have several people who would like to meet with Miss al-Azadi to discuss Gustav Alscher and Democracy Now. Is that all right with you?"

She moved closer to me, her eyes asking me for guidance.

"She's not in any trouble, is she?" I asked Wil. My trust in him wasn't at an all-time high.

"Oh, no."

"You just want to talk to her as an expert consultant, is that right?" I pressed.

"Exactly."

"And the rate you'll pay her is how much per hour?"

He gave me as startled a look as she did.

"What are your standard witness fees?" I asked.

"Fifty an hour."

I turned to Miriam. "Is that acceptable?" I doubted she had ever had fifty credits of her own in her entire life. She'd probably never had a bank account or a credit card.

Wide eyed, she nodded.

I winked at Wil. "I think we have a deal. Just tell your people to remember to feed her. Neither of us has had breakfast yet."

Wil chuckled. "Is that a hint?"

"I certainly hope so," I said.

He was pretty good at taking hints, leading us to the building's cafeteria. It was a déjà vu moment for me, with Miriam's reaction similar to the first time I took Glenda to a grocery store. She froze and just stared with her mouth open. That reaction was enough to cement my dislike for Alscher. The corporate system that gave someone like her no choices was already on my general shit list.

I sent Wil a couple of text messages while we ate, and he did a good job at following up on those hints also. When we finished our meal, a woman came to collect Miriam. I handed my new friend a burner phone I carried, and showed her how to punch the speed dial to reach me if she needed to.

With that chore taken care of, I turned to Wil and said, "Lead on, O Great Corporate Executive."

He gave me a sour look, but didn't protest my new title for him. We got on an elevator, and he hit the button for the twelfth floor.

"You didn't tell me you rated a penthouse office," I said. "You sure you don't want to sign that prenup?"

He shot me a frosty look. I would have thought I'd get a little teasing back, but he obviously wasn't in a joking mood.

We got off the elevator and walked to the end of the hall, through a reception area with a receptionist who said, "Good morning, Mr. Wilberforce," and into a corner office with a fantastic view of Lake Michigan. Wilbur's name and title were on the door.

A desk sat off to one side, and a long conference table sat where everyone could enjoy the view. Myron Chung stood from his seat at the table and greeted us. The secretary had followed us in and served coffee for everyone.

"We have a tail on Señorita Martinez," Chung said after the secretary left. "We also have the Frenchmen under surveillance. They are still at their hotel. As soon as they move, we'll be notified."

"Does Margarita know them?" I asked.

"I don't know about Carpentier, but I'm sure she and Maillard are at least somewhat acquainted. He's rather well known in the art world."

"Her bank statements show that she usually has a charge at a place called Gitan Bistro after the one with

188

her hairdresser," I said. "I can slip into a disguise and get a table before she arrives."

Chung's eyebrows rose a bit, and Wil glared at me.

I couldn't figure out why they were staring at me. "What?"

"Bank accounts are private," Wil said.

I shrugged. "If they want to keep people like me out, they need to do more than talk about security. I could fix it for them."

"I think that your height would be an impediment to a disguise," Chung said.

"Gitan is a little too fancy for Jasmine Keller," Wil said.

I waved my hand in the air. "Let me worry about that. Do you have a car Mike and I can borrow?"

"I can drive you."

"Oh, no," I said, shaking my head. "I'm not letting you learn all my secrets. Who knows when you'll decide to arrest me on some trumped up charge? Just loan me a car so I don't have to steal one."

He gaped at me, then looked down and sorrowfully shook his head. "I give up."

"Great! You're going to sign the prenup?"

It sounded like he growled, which I took for a no.

"Okay. Your loss. I'll settle for the car."

Wil took us to the garage in the basement and showed us a beat-up older sedan. "We confiscated it from a drug runner," he said as he handed me the keys.

"Does it come with a tow truck?" I asked, passing the keys to Mike.

"If it breaks down, call me."

Mike chuckled as we drove away. "We won't have

189

to call him. You know he's going to follow us."

"Yeah, but you only have to lose him long enough to dump me off. Let him tail us until we get a couple of blocks from the bistro."

Half an hour later, Mike said, "Get ready."

At the next intersection, he ran the red light, turned the corner, and almost immediately turned into an alley. I jumped out before the car came to a stop, and he drove off. I moved close to the wall and blurred my form.

A couple of minutes later a dark car slowly drove by the alley, and I could see a face in the car window peering toward me. As soon as it passed, I morphed into a richly dressed, chubby, fiftyish woman, six inches shorter than I was, with elegantly coifed brown hair. Stepping out of the alley, I window-shopped my way toward the bistro.

The Chamber operatives who cruised by every few minutes didn't give me a second glance. Neither did Margarita Martinez, who arrived at the bistro shortly after I did. I followed her inside and asked for the table next to hers, where I sat with my back to her.

I had barely opened my menu when two men came through the front door. They matched the pictures of Carpentier and Maillard that Chung had shown me. The host took them to the table next to Margarita's. I was as close to the three of them as they were to each other.

Carpentier was about six feet tall and two hundred pounds. His nose had been broken more than once, and he had a rough air about him in spite of his expensive suit. Maillard was shorter, thinner, and somewhat effeminate, with a long nose and thinning hair.

Two minutes later, two men that I recognized as

Chamber operatives came in and sat across the room from us. The entire circus had gathered in that room. The only things missing were the stolen art works and a dancing bear.

The two men spoke to each other in French, talking about the sights and sounding like tourists. Neither of them spoke to Margarita, though one made a flattering comment about her looks. If you took them seriously, it sounded as though they were excited to tour the AIC that afternoon.

Margarita finished her meal and began gathering her belongings. In fluent French, and without looking at the men, she said, "This is not a convenient time. If your patron is patient, the package will be delivered as promised."

"Our patron is interested in additional packages," one of the men said.

"That is not possible."

"Make it possible," the other man said, his voice deeper and rougher.

"I beg your pardon?" Margarita said, her voice full of both surprise and affront.

"Whatever your bid for the Monet," the first man said, "we'll give you twenty percent more."

"And we don't plan to leave Chicago empty handed," the second man finished. "You have my number. Call me when we can collect our goods."

Margarita didn't answer them and continued on toward the door. Since I had asked for my check when she did, I followed her. She walked toward her car, but a man intercepted her. The reaction he received was quite different from her reserved manner with the men inside.

"What the hell are you doing here?" she hissed.

"Have you lost your mind? Get away from me."

"You're stalling," the man said. "You may be able to sit on that stuff forever, but we need to get paid." He appeared to be around forty, average height and build, with receding brown hair and brown eyes. A completely nondescript, average man that you'd never notice. The perfect look for a thief.

I came within about twenty feet of them before she glanced in my direction. I just kept walking past them toward a fancy car parked beyond hers. Before I passed out of earshot, I heard her say, "Dammit, Jeff. You'll get your money. Things are just a bit complicated right now."

"Yeah," Jeff said, "that Zhukoff broad got killed. Let's see if we can tie this thing up before any more women die."

I turned and took three fast pictures of Margarita and Jeff. He walked away, and she watched him go. Then she got in her car and drove away.

CHAPTER 20

I slipped into the alley behind the bistro and morphed into my Jasmine Keller persona. Exiting the other end of the alley, I hugged a fence and blurred my form, then followed the man Margarita called Jeff.

He walked three blocks to reach a car parked a block away from the bistro, and used a number of other very sneaky techniques to ensure he wasn't being followed. He was very good, but I'm a girl, and I don't play fair.

When he started his car, I unblurred my image, and Mike pulled up beside me as Jeff pulled out of his parking space.

"He's paranoid," I told Mike. "He did everything he could to make sure he wasn't being followed."

Mike nodded. I figured if he was trained by my father, and worked twenty years for him, he knew how to tail someone.

"So, who are we following?" he asked. "That's not one of the Frenchmen, is it?"

"I think he might be the thief," I answered. "He ambushed Margarita demanding money. He also warned her that if he didn't get paid, Deborah Zhukoff might not be the only woman to die."

He gave me a raised eyebrow, and I said, "I don't know. It would be easy to interpret what he said to mean that he killed Deborah, or hired the killer, on Martinez's orders."

Mike looked skeptical.

"You don't think so."

He shook his head. "No, I don't. That was personal. I would believe that Martinez did it herself before I'd look for a professional hitman."

"Unless I wanted to make it look like an amateur murder," I said.

"You're overthinking it." He slowed down and let Jeff squeeze through the light turning red ahead of him. Mike smirked. "He'll get caught by the next light, and he'll be less wary. So, what did you find out inside the restaurant?"

"When Chung first told me about the men from Hollande's organization, he speculated that Hollande might be interested in the entire inventory. From what the Frenchmen told Martinez, that was a pretty good guess. They want the paintings, and they said they would stick around town until they had them. The Chamber men in the bistro will follow them, so I figured we'd follow the mystery man."

Jeff drove out to the far western edge of the city and eventually parked in the driveway of a house in a middle-class neighborhood. He got out of the car, unlocked the front door of the house, and went inside.

"Now what?" Mike asked.

"Back to Doreen's so I can get online and try to figure out who Jeff is."

⊕⊕⊕

Jeffrey Sanderson, forty-two-years-old, born in Chicago, and the registered owner of the car he drove and the house we saw him enter, had no known source of income, according to the databases I searched. I sent the information I found to Wil and Chung.

The Chamber had not returned Miriam to the brothel, so I called her. She told me the Chamber

194

offered her a house and was picking up all her expenses. I called Wil as soon as I finished speaking with her.

"What's the deal with Miriam?" I asked. "Are you arresting her?"

"You wanted us to treat her as a witness, so we are."

"And?"

"She has significant information we can use. But none of it's any good if Alscher gets his hands on her, so we're putting her up in a safe house."

"And you're paying her twenty-four hours a day. Right?"

I heard him sigh. "Of course we are, Libby. I wouldn't dream of shorting her."

"What can I say? I grew up steeped in corporate capitalist ideals. Wil, what's going on with Alscher?"

Another deep sigh. "He's a wanted terrorist, and we've been after him for the past twenty years. Have dinner with me and I'll tell you more."

"Only if the place is certified bomb proof."

He chuckled. "I promise."

Wil took me to the restaurant of a country club. High walls, lots of guards, and metal detectors that went crazy when he and I walked in.

"You depend on a piece-of-junk machine for security?" I asked the guard who collected most of my knives, throwing stars, grenades, and gas canisters. He wanted my bra, but the head of security stepped in. "I don't think that will be necessary for Deputy Director Wilberforce and his guest."

Turning to me, "The metal detectors are only one of our security precautions," the security director said, pompously drawing himself up to his full height in an attempt to look down at me. That failed since he was three or four inches shorter than I was, plus I was wearing heels.

I glanced at Wil, then pulled my pistol out of my purse and set it in front of the metal detector. Then I handed him my card. "I didn't mean all machines are stupid, only that one, which is hopelessly out of date. I would be happy to provide you with a quote for a full assessment of your security measures. I'm sure your clientele would rather be safe than dead."

They all stared at the pistol.

"It's amazing what they can do with some of the modern polymers," I said, picking up the gun and putting it back in my purse. Collecting my other weapons, I put them away as well.

"I didn't realize that was a Marten Stealth," Wil said as we sat down. "I've fired one, but they're very expensive."

"Takes a bit of getting used to because it's so light," I said. I reached down into my boot and showed him the pistol I kept there. "The Mini Stealth is even worse. It weighs practically nothing. But the guns aren't the only things they missed." I showed him a ceramic knife, then put it back in my purse. "Everyone wants to go cheap with security, then they whine when they get burned. If you don't want to pay to protect it, then it probably isn't worth owning." I gestured to the elegant surroundings. "It's not as though they're hurting for cash."

The food was spectacular, almost up to the quality of my mom's chef at her brothel. I mentioned that to Wil, and he laughed.

"I can just see the chef's face when you compliment him on almost being good enough to cook in a whorehouse."

196

I'm not sure what my face looked like, but Wil sobered immediately. "I'm sorry. I said something wrong, didn't I?"

"I don't like that word. It's degrading." It always pissed me off that all the words used to describe prostitution denigrated women. Women didn't invent it.

"I apologize."

Nodding, I said, "You wouldn't know. Tell me about Gustav Alscher."

Wil refilled our wine glasses and leaned back in his chair. "Alscher is one of the most wanted men in the world. He's from an upper middle class family in Munich, Germany. He became radicalized during his university years and rose to the top of an organization called P2P, or Power to the People."

"A lot of kids go wild at university. Most of them settle down," I said.

"And some don't. Alscher was a doctoral candidate when a new voice appeared in P2P, a woman named Olga Schubert. When I say voice, I mean that literally. She was trained as an opera singer, but she also had an incredible speaking voice, and it's suspected she was a strong empathic projector."

"I suspect Alscher is, also," I said.

He gave me a long, thoughtful look as he took a sip of his wine. "And what kind of talent allows you to see that in a person?"

I grinned. "The talent of observation. That, and the feeling he's trying to manipulate me."

Wil laughed.

"No, really. A physical feeling. I mean, he sits and stares at me, and I feel like invisible spiders are trying

197

to crawl under my skin. If that's some kind of talent, then it's one I never knew about. The guy is beyond creepy."

"But you never felt compelled to help him?"

"No, I just want to clock him in the face. But when I watched him around his people in that abandoned mall, he was playing them like a choir. And he's got Carly wrapped around his finger. He has her convinced she's a prophet. He uses psychogenic mushrooms to lower people's inhibitions and resistance."

"Mushrooms?"

"I was told he grows them."

Wil sat back and thought about that for a while, then he said, "Well, back in Germany, he had Olga Schubert. Their organization grew. She spoke at huge rallies, and they began to accumulate some political following. Mutants, anti-corps, even some of the middle class. Then the terror attacks started. Bombings, mostly, but also assassinations."

"Like here."

"Yeah, like here. The German corporations came down on P2P with a sledge hammer. Schubert was killed in a raid on P2P headquarters along with almost two hundred other members. The SWAT teams didn't screw around. They napalmed the building. Over two thousand members were rounded up and either executed or sent to labor camps. Alscher escaped. No one knew where he was until he surfaced here."

"And now he has a new girl to be the face of his movement."

"So it seems."

"What kind of information are you getting from Miriam?"

"My people spent the morning trying to find out if he's planning any more bombings or other operations. They don't think she's holding back information, but she doesn't seem to know very much about their operations. When they ask her about Alscher's movements and contacts over the past seventeen years, she's a font of knowledge. We're waiting for a Russian translator to free up some of her time. Miriam knows several languages, but her Russian is far stronger than her English."

English was the de facto international language of business, but it still ranked behind Chinese and Spanish in the number of native speakers. For all of the international standards established over the past three hundred years, native languages still hung on almost everywhere.

"Is she going to be okay, Wil? You'll take care of her and make sure she lands in a good place?"

He cocked his head and seemed to study my face. "Yeah, I'll make sure of it."

"Thank you."

⊕⊕⊕

Jess called the following morning and said she'd received the routers I'd been waiting on. She also mentioned that Chung wanted to see me. She sounded terrible on the phone, and looked worse when I saw her in person. Her skin was blotchy and her eyes were red from crying. I'd always figured she and Deborah had a thing going, and that Jess took it far more seriously than Deborah did.

Chung wasn't in when I arrived, so I configured and installed the routers, then installed the intrusion trap software I had written. Any hacker coming into the AIC network through either router would find their path blocked by the other router and unable to retreat. The only way out of the trap was to reveal actual location information on the hacker, which set up their eventual neutralization and capture.

I was pretty proud of the program, and even Mom hadn't found a way to compromise it, though she did figure out a way to avoid it after playing with it for six months. Other than my network, and Mom's and Dad's, AIC and a bank in Toronto were the only clients I'd installed it for. Needless to say, I'd switched my main accounts to that bank.

Chung came in around noon, wandering into the old conference room I used as an office. He looked around at the schematics and printouts piled on various tables, and the electronic equipment and cabling strewn about.

"Jeffrey Sanderson," Chung said without preamble. "We seriously looked at him for a heist in Vancouver about five years ago. He was questioned in regard to a burglary seven years ago in Romania." He shrugged. "No follow up in either case. Other than proximity, the investigators didn't see any reason to suspect him."

"Were the goods recovered in either case?" I asked.

"No."

"And that's all you have on him?"

"Afraid so." He looked at me and I thought I saw a twinkle in his eye. "Except for his connection to Karl Nyquist."

I had no idea who that was. "Who is?"

"Sanderson's brother-in-law. Conviction for a

jewelry robbery. He was questioned in regard to the robberies in Vancouver and Romania, but no one saw a link between him and Sanderson. The wedding to Sanderson's sister came later. He lives here in Chicago, too."

He dropped into a chair. "Libby, how many people do you think it took to pull this off?"

It was something I'd thought about a lot. "It could have been one person and a driver, but more realistically, I think two to three inside, plus the driver. Five framed paintings are too much for one person to carry. Hauling them downstairs and outside one by one would take too long."

He nodded, looking thoughtful. "And where would you stash them?"

"A self-storage unit rented by someone who wasn't involved. The chances that Sanderson has them in his garage are nil. Even an amateur would be too afraid to do that, and from what we've learned, Sanderson is no amateur."

"Someone who wasn't involved? I'm not following you."

I grinned. "A friend of a friend has a storage unit. 'Can I store a small package for a month? I'll give him a case of beer.' People at your level always complicate things. Five university students might share a storage unit over the summer."

Chung's countenance cleared. "Ah, I see. Of course."

"You might check on all of their relatives."

CHAPTER 21

Nothing happened for a couple of days on the robbery or murder fronts, so I got a lot of work done at the museum. I called Wil and set up a meeting with him and one of his cybersecurity experts for the following Monday to review and sign off on the work completed so far.

Wil called me back less than half an hour later.

"Chung's French friends showed up at Margarita Martinez's home about five minutes ago. Didn't you say you'd planted a bug there?"

"In her office. I'll check the feed."

"I'll be by to pick you up in half an hour," he said and hung up. His office was downtown, and AIC would be on his way if he planned to go out to Margarita's house.

I logged in to my network and checked the feed from the bug in her office. Right off the bat, I heard people speaking in French.

"Monsieur Hollande is impatient," a man's voice said. "Need I remind you that he paid a good faith fee, and he's beginning to wonder if you are acting in good faith."

Margarita replied in the same language, but her French wasn't that good, and she spoke it with a Spanish accent. "There are complications."

"The complications are entirely on your end," the man said. I thought it was Carpentier. "Do you have the paintings, or not? Our understanding was that you hired the extraction team, not the people at the museum."

"I don't have the painting," she said. "Look, give me until tomorrow night and I can get the Degas for

202

you."

"And the Monet?" a second man's voice said. That confirmed the men's voices for me. The second man was definitely Maillard.

"That is promised elsewhere. As with your patron, a good faith fee was paid for the Monet."

"That is unfortunate," Carpentier said. "Perhaps that deposit could be refunded."

"I can't do that," Margarita said. "Edouard, surely you see why I can't. No one would ever deal with me again. Even Monsieur Hollande would no longer trust me."

Soft mutterings between the two men followed, and even turning up the volume as far as I could, I could only make out a word here and there.

"The Degas. Tomorrow. Where?" Carpentier asked.

"Hi. You ready to go?" Wil's voice sounded, too loud, almost next to me. I about jumped out of my skin.

"Shhh!" I waved my hand at him and pointed to my computer. It was too late. I'd missed it. Wil sat next to me, and we listened to the end of the conspirators' conversation, then I backed the recording up to the point where Wil walked in.

"...dinner at the Shoreside Hotel," Margarita's voice said. "Only Edouard. Eight o'clock."

I reversed the recording a little more, but we had the important part.

"Is there any reason to go out to her place?" Wil asked.

"Now? No." I put my fingers on his lips as I saw the bug was starting to record again. I switched from the recording to the live feed and heard Margarita start to speak again.

"Jeff? We need to meet," she said. We weren't able to hear the other side of the conversation. "Lunch, tomorrow at the Shoreside Hotel. Dress appropriately."

The ensuing silence extended long enough that I assumed she had hung up.

"So, what do you make of that?" Wil asked.

I thought about it for a bit. "I think you should check and see if she reserves a room there."

His eyebrows rose, then he smirked and nodded. "I shall do that."

⊕⊕⊕

I wandered down the hall to the suite of offices the insurance company had commandeered and told Myron Chung about the new developments.

We talked about the various strategies available. I was especially curious if he planned on going after Georges Hollande. I was familiar with Alonzo Donofrio, head of the largest crime family in Toronto. Actually, a little too familiar. Alonzo scared me spitless. So, I was curious if one of the largest insurance companies in the world felt tough enough to take on the mob.

Chung gave me one of his twinkle-eyed half smiles and leaned back in his chair. I seemed to be a source of constant amusement to him.

"I'm going to tell you something, and I'll deny to my grave that I ever said it."

I felt my eyes widen a bit and sat on the edge of my seat waiting.

"North American Insurance does enough business with Monsieur Hollande's various companies that covering a loss of this magnitude isn't worth antagonizing him."

I snorted out a laugh and Chung's smile widened into a toothy grin.

Curious that Wil hadn't joined us, I headed back to my office. Wil was just hanging up the phone when I arrived. He was animated, excited.

"I've got it all set up," he said. "We'll take them all down."

"Huh?"

"The SWAT team will be in place when Sanderson shows up. We'll recover the painting and arrest him and Martinez. Then, when the Frenchman shows up later, we'll pull a sting on him and arrest him, too."

I stared at him. Speechless.

"What?" he asked. I guess he noticed me staring at him with my mouth hanging open.

I pulled it together. "Ya know, sometimes I find myself thinking that you're a rational, intelligent human being. And then you remind me that you're a cop." His face fell. "Why didn't you come with me to talk to Chung?"

"I had things to do. To organize the bust."

Big sigh. "Did Sanderson steal your lunch money?" I asked. "Is Martinez planning on selling something the Chamber is responsible for?"

His brow wrinkled as he tried to figure out what I was getting at.

"Wil, this isn't the Chamber's business. AIC and North American are calling the shots because it's their painting. Their money. Have you forgotten the other five artworks? If you bust everyone, those are gone

205

forever."

He sort of shook his head and then said, "I figured once we have them, they'll tell us where the rest of the paintings are."

"And why would they? Even if you put them in prison for a couple of years, they'll have millions waiting for them when they get out. Cancel the damned SWAT team and come down to Chung's office. Let him explain how he wants to run this thing."

⊕⊕⊕

Jeffrey Sanderson walked through the lobby of the Shoreside Hotel and into the dining room. The maître d' led him to Margarita Martinez's table.

The audio from the bug planted under the table was as clear as if we were sitting there with them.

"So, what's this about?" Sanderson asked.

"Order your lunch first, then we'll talk."

The waitress took their orders, and as she walked away, Margarita said, "The buyer has sent people to take the Degas. I need you to bring it here this afternoon."

"Only the Degas?"

"Come, now. You aren't an amateur. These things take time, but if they're done properly, they are very lucrative."

Margarita placed her purse on the table and dug around in it, pulling out a small mirror, her car keys, and an envelope. She checked her makeup and her hair, then put the mirror and her keys back in her purse.

"There's half a million on the card," she said. "That should buy a little patience. You'll get the other half for that painting after the buyer pays me."

"That will help," Sanderson said. "You understand, it's not me that's pushing."

"I don't care who it is. It's not professional, Jeff. Choose your help a little better."

From my place in the corner, my form blurred into the wall behind me, I saw Sanderson color a little.

"So, bring it where?" he asked.

"Room 332. The key is in the envelope with the credit card. Put it in the closet, close the door, and lock the room. Leave the key card."

He nodded.

They ate their lunch, she paid the check, and they left.

I followed Sanderson. He walked toward his car in the parking lot, and I walked around the corner of the building. Mike had the car door open. I got in, closed the door, and unblurred my form.

"You planted the tracker on his car?" I asked.

"Yes, and the bug inside the car. We were trained by the same guy, remember?"

I felt my face warm. "Sorry. I'm used to working alone. I feel a little antsy about things I haven't done myself."

He chuckled. "No problem. Better to double check than miss something."

Sanderson pulled out of the parking lot and dialed his phone.

"Hi, it's Jeff," we heard from our speaker. "Meet me at Karl's house and bring the package marked five." Silence for over a minute. "Yeah, yeah. I've got money for you. Stop your bitching. Yeah, now. I'll be there in about forty minutes."

Mike and I exchanged looks.

"Damn," I said. We were hoping that Sanderson would lead us to the paintings. Instead, it sounded as though one of his pals would retrieve the Degas from its hiding place.

I called Chung and told him our news.

"Such is life," he said. "We'll put Karl and the third person under surveillance. I've had cases that took ten years to make this kind of progress."

All that comment did was make me feel young and inexperienced.

The tracker on Sanderson's car meant we could hang way back and avoid detection. His car finally stopped moving in the same general area as his own house. We drove down the street and saw his car parked in the driveway of a house in the middle of the block. I checked the address.

"Mike, that's Karl Nyquist's house. Sanderson's brother-in-law."

"I hope you remember all this for the future," Mike said. "Chung has been on target."

"Yeah, I noticed that. Remind me not to steal any art insured by North American."

Mike laughed.

I morphed into Jasmine, and he dropped me off on the next block. I walked into the alley and blurred my form. The neighborhood reminded me a little of where I lived in Toronto. Townhouses on tiny lots with minimal yards. These were a little older and more rundown than mine was. The problem was the lack of room for error. Neighbors everywhere, and very close. For all I knew, twenty people saw me change and then disappear.

Six-foot-high fences separated the houses on both sides from the alley. I made my way to the back of Nyquist's house and pulled myself up so I could see inside the yard. Everything looked quiet. If I didn't know Sanderson had gone inside, I wouldn't have known anyone was home.

I slid over the fence and hugged it as I made my way around the yard to the house. I stuck a microphone on the window and turned it on.

"So, this is all the money we're going to get?" I heard a male voice ask.

"Naw, that's just the money for the first painting. We'll get paid for each one as she gets them sold," Sanderson said.

"Hell, I can live with that," the man said. "Damn, Jeff, that's a million credits for all of them."

"I told you this gig would pay good," Sanderson said.

"So, when Donny gets here, what happens next?"

"We give him his money and get rid of him, then you and I take the painting to a hotel and leave it."

"That's it?"

"That's it. Short and simple."

Twenty minutes later, Mike's voice sounded in my ear. "A van just pulled up in front of the house. Must be Donny."

Through the bug, I heard the doorbell ring inside the house. People greeted each other, then they all trooped out to the van and transferred something into Nyquist's van. What I couldn't hear, Mike described it to me. He was parked a block away, watching through binoculars.

I waited until the three men came back into the

house.

"Here's your money," Sanderson said.

"Damn, a hundred thousand credits. Jeff, I've never seen that much money in my life."

"It's only the beginning," Sanderson said. "Just hang on and be patient. There's more where that came from."

I climbed the fence back into the alley and made my way to the street where Mike picked me up. We drove around the corner as Donny's van pulled away from the curb. We followed him, and I called Wil to tell him the painting would soon be heading toward the hotel.

Donny drove to a bar.

Mike parked the car at the far end of the parking lot and turned to me. "Well?"

I shrugged. "I never really saw him. Tell me about him."

Mike brought out his phone and showed me a picture. "Early to mid-thirties, shorter than either Sanderson or Nyquist, slender." Donny looked as though he might be Hispanic or Italian. Maybe another Mediterranean ethnic group. Dark hair and mustache, olive complexion. One of the pictures included his left hand and he wasn't wearing a wedding ring.

"I'll let him get a couple of drinks in him," I said. "What do you think? Blonde, brunette or redhead?"

He thought about it. While we were waiting, a car drove up. Two women who looked to be Hispanic in their mid-twenties got out and went into the bar. I took careful note of how they were dressed.

Mike shrugged. I shrugged and turned the rearview mirror so I could see myself. I decided on five-foot-five. Straight black hair pulled into a high ponytail. Olive complexion with high cheekbones and a cupid's bow mouth. Brown eyes. Slender with a bubble butt and boobs that were prominent but not too large. A sleeveless white wrap blouse, skintight coral Capri pants, and black four-inch stilettos. I imaged more makeup than I would ever wear. When I finished, I looked at Mike.

"What do you think?"

He was staring at me with his mouth open. "Holy Mother of God," he breathed. I didn't know he was religious. I also realized that he'd never seen me build a persona, only morph to Jasmine and back to myself.

"It's not real," I said. "It's just an illusion. I can't really see it all, so when I get out of the car, let me know if anything looks weird. You know, like I have my ass on crooked or something."

He barked a laugh and then chuckled.

I had to hold the image of the person I wanted to be in my mind, the whole image, from every angle. Then I projected it and pretty much forgot about it. I didn't have to spend much conscious thought to maintain it as long as I stayed awake.

Picking up my purse, I got out of the car, turned a pirouette, and walked back and forth a couple of times. Mike grinned and gave me a thumbs up.

"Wish me luck." I strutted around the corner and headed for the bar's entrance.

Inside, I looked around as my eyes adjusted. As I expected, it was a dive bar, but a clean one. The smell of Mexican food caused my stomach to grumble. Other than the bartender and a waitress, I counted twenty people, and the place could have held five times more. Donny sat at the bar, flirting with the two women I'd seen walk in.

I had an advantage, and I knew it. There wasn't any reason to build a realistic persona. Beautiful was the default. I pulled myself onto a barstool and ordered a margarita, inwardly chuckling at the irony.

"I haven't seen you in here before," the bartender said as he looked me over.

"I'm in town visiting my cousin and her husband. She said this place is okay." I didn't try to fake an accent. I spoke classroom Spanish, but there wasn't a chance I could fool a native speaker.

"Where are you from?"

"Atlanta." Much safer than Dallas. They would expect me to speak Spanish if I was from Dallas.

Sure enough. "Habla usted Español?" *Do you speak Spanish?*

With a self-deprecating shrug and a shy smile, I said, "Poquito." *A little bit.*

I had caught Donny's attention. One of the girls he was flirting with wandered off. The other one looked irritated. I ignored her and focused on him.

Two hours later, I had discovered that the taco basket was delicious, Donny was happy to help me drink my margaritas even though he couldn't hold his liquor worth a damn, and he got very touchy-feely when he was drunk. The last part was exactly what I was hoping for.

"Hey, baby," I said, leaning close to his ear and ignoring his hand on my breast. "Let's get out of here and go someplace more private."

He gave me a sloppy kiss that half-missed my mouth and said, "Sure. That sounds good."

I managed to get him upright and we started toward the door when a tall, well-built man with light brown hair walked in.

"Hey, Karl," Donny said, swaying and leaning against me.

"Jeff wants to see you." Karl shook his head. "Shit, you're drunk."

"Just celebrating a little bit. Tell Jeff tomorrow."

"No, tonight."

"But, this chick's into me."

Karl gave me an unfriendly look. "Another time." He grabbed Donny by the arm and dragged him out of the bar. I waited a minute, then followed them. I watched Karl shove Donny into Karl's van, then he got in and drove off. They left Donny's van sitting next to the bar.

I rushed around the corner to where Mike was parked and jumped in the car. "What happened?" I asked.

"I don't know. No one has contacted me."

"Follow them."

That lasted less than five minutes. Karl took a turn onto a freeway onramp, then immediately took the next off ramp. A truck got between them and us, and they were gone.

CHAPTER 22

I morphed back into myself and called Wil. "Hey, what's going on?"

"A couple of men dropped a crate off at the hotel, took it to the room Margarita reserved, then took off. That was about three hours ago. Margarita and Maillard just sat down to dinner."

"Have you confirmed what's in the crate?"

After a moment of hesitation, he said, "No."

"Why not?"

Silence, then, "You think we should go into the room and check on the painting?"

"Duh. Yeah, I think you should. How do you know we're not being set up? Everything could be happening somewhere else, with Margarita and Edouard as decoys."

I hung up and turned to Mike. "Any ideas?"

"I'm curious as to where those two are going," he answered. I knew he meant Karl and Donny. "I'm also curious as to how Hollande's men plan to take the painting out of the country. It's a little too large to stick in a suitcase, and the airport's being watched."

I thought about it, trying to figure out what I would do in their situation.

"Mike, just because they flew in on a commercial airplane, doesn't mean they plan to fly out that way."

"The train station is being screened, too," he said. "Private plane?"

"How many planes do you think Hollande owns?"

"So why did they fly in commercial?" Before I could even open my mouth, he answered his own question. "Misdirection. They want us watching commercial flights. How many airports in this vicinity?"

Pulling out my phone, I called Wil again. We talked for a couple of minutes, then he said, "Libby, hang on a minute."

I waited. When he came back on, he said, "Chung thinks we should intercept them right after they leave the hotel. He doesn't want to take the chance of losing them."

"I agree," I said. "Make sure they're far enough away that you don't alert Martinez." I hung up and told Mike, "Wil says there are six airports in the greater Chicago area that can land a plane capable of a nonstop flight to France. There are five more within a two- to three-hour drive."

We drove to the hotel and parked where we could see the exit closest to Martinez's room. Mike stayed with the car, while I blurred my form and entered the hotel.

I knew the hotel from my stay there with Dad. Margarita had booked a room at the end of the hall next to a stairway. At the bottom of the stairs were two doors. One led to the hall on the ground floor, and the other opened outside to the parking lot. That doorway was partially concealed from the parking lot by a hedge and a low wall. Someone could drive up in a car or van and block sight of the door entirely. Perfect for loading priceless paintings unnoticed. One might have wondered if Margarita had done that sort of thing before.

I didn't want to meet anyone on the stairs, so I walked down the hall to the elevator and took that to the third floor. With my form still blurred, I squeezed into a space by an ice machine and waited. Half an hour passed before Margarita and Maillard got off the elevator.

They went into the room. Forty-five minutes later, Carpentier came out of the stairwell and knocked. The door to the room opened and admitted him, then quickly closed. It opened about five minutes later, and the two men carried a slim rectangular wooden crate out of the room.

As soon as they disappeared into the stairwell, I followed them.

They're coming down, I texted to Mike.

I stood ten feet away and watched Hollande's men load the crate with the painting into a white rental van. When they finished, they jumped in and drove off. I saw Wil's car follow them out of the parking lot at a discreet distance. Mike drove up, I got in, and he followed Wil.

I sat back and relaxed. There wasn't a lot to see as we traveled through the night, but I got the feeling we were in a new part of town for me. I soon realized that we traveled in a convoy, the van with the painting in front, and at least a dozen Chamber Security cars, including us and Wil, trailing behind.

After about an hour, Mike said, "It looks like they're headed for Midway."

"I thought we were going to take them down before we got to the airport."

"Wilbur wants to get the plane."

I sat up straight. "When did he decide this?"

"While you were inside the hotel."

"Nice of everyone to update me."

The cars in front of us sped up as we entered a gate in a tall fence. The signs pointed left to "Private Aircraft" and everyone took a hard left. Ahead, I could see the Frenchmen's van headed toward a hanger with a plane parked in front of it.

One of the Chamber vans screeched to a stop right in front of the plane. Other cars swung around the end of the hanger. Wil followed the painting, and we followed him.

A man emerged from the plane and stood at the top of the stairs for a moment. Then he raised an automatic weapon and started firing. Everyone in sight dove for cover, and vehicles swerved all over the place.

Mike also swerved, the car skidding and throwing me into the seat belt. He straightened the car out, and drove past Wil's car and the Frenchmen's van, cutting between the rear of the plane and the hanger. I looked out my window as we passed and saw men with guns in the hanger.

"The ground crew's armed," I told Mike.

The car skidded again as he cut to the right, putting the hanger between us and everyone else. We slid to a stop, and he leaped out, a pistol in his hand. I got out my door and crouched low between the car and the hanger.

"Are you wearing a vest?" Mike asked.

"Ballistic corset," I answered. "It covers me from shoulder to crotch."

He laughed. "Good. Watch your head."

"You, too. What are we doing?"

"Recovering the painting. Don't get caught up in peripheral crap and keep your attention on the objective."

I had to laugh at that. It was one of my dad's major precepts.

We faced the rear of the plane, with the hanger on

our left. The thieves' van sat to the left of the plane's tail. I had seen armed men inside the open hanger, people from the plane with machineguns, and most of the Chamber officers were on the other side of the plane from us as well. The area sounded like the New Year fireworks had come early.

"Mike, I'm going to sort of disappear. Can you cover my back and not shoot me?"

He scuttled around the car and said, "I'll certainly try."

I moved to stand in front of him. "This is how I don't look."

His brow scrunched, then I swayed back and forth and his face cleared. "Oh, I see. Or rather I don't. When you move in front of the plane, it disappears. And I can see you move if I'm looking directly at you."

"Exactly."

"So, what are we doing first?"

I phased back into visibility and held out my hand with four mini-grenades, each about half the size of a golf ball. "I thought we'd clean out the hanger so no one's behind us."

"Good thinking."

"I'll go low, you go high," I said. "Don't shoot down."

Creeping along the hanger wall to its end, I blurred my image, primed the four grenades, and threw them inside. A few moments later, they exploded. I waited for quiet, then slunk around the corner. One man staggered upright toward the open front of the building. I fired two shots and he fell.

Two other men fired at Mike as he followed me in. I shot one of them, and Mike shot the other. We disarmed two wounded men, then turned our attention back to the war going on outside.

"I'm going to sneak under the plane and try to get into that van," I said.

"Be damned careful. The walls of that van aren't going to stop any bullets."

I nodded, then realized he couldn't see me. "Okay, going now."

I crawled the hundred feet to the van on my stomach. Standing up, even invisibly, seemed like a bad idea with bullets whizzing all around. At least once, I heard the pop a bullet made as it displaced air directly over me.

What I couldn't understand was why Hollande's men continued fighting. They were badly outnumbered and couldn't escape. Airport and Chicago police were arriving to reinforce Wil's Chamber Security men.

As I crawled under the plane, I saw a man hiding behind one pair of the plane's wheels. He stuck his gun out and fired, then ducked back. He had a direct view of the back of the van I was trying to reach. Taking aim, I fired three shots and watched him slump, his automatic rifle clattering to the ground.

The .380 caliber pistol I used was specially made with a silencer and a built-in flash suppressor. As an assassin and a chameleon trying to be invisible, I didn't want my pistol's muzzle flash to give me away.

After what seemed forever, I reached the van. The driver's side door was open. I'd seen Carpentier bail out and run when the vehicle came to a stop. Raising up and peering inside, I saw Maillard curled up in a ball in the floorboard. Surprisingly, the windows and the windshield were intact. It didn't look as though anyone had wasted time shooting up the van.

I let my form become visible, aimed my pistol at the man on the floor, and said in French, "Monsieur Maillard. I have a gun pointed at your head. Please show me your hands. Move slowly."

He did move slowly, unwinding and sticking his empty hands in the air.

"Very good," I said. "Now, crawl toward me."

When he got close enough, I reached in, grabbed his collar, and pulled him out onto the tarmac.

"Where's the painting?" I asked.

"In the back."

Good. That's where I thought it was. "You're going to help me get it."

"No. We'll get shot."

"Either you help me, or I'll shoot you and then get the painting. I'm not turning my back on you. Do we understand each other?"

The fear on Maillard's face was real. The man was an art curator for a thug, but not a thug himself. I hated watching people beg for their lives. It was so undignified for both sides of the conversation. I pulled a jet injector out of my purse, held it to his neck, and gave him a shot of sleepy medicine. His babbling and crying ceased, and I rolled him under the van, hoping he'd be more protected there, making sure he was clear of the wheels.

I crawled into the van and took a look at the crate holding the painting. No way I was going to lift and carry that thing by myself, even without people shooting at me. I looked back at Mike and waved him toward me. He covered the distance much faster than I could have. Vampire speed.

"What's up?" he asked.

"Do you think we can push this van into the

hanger?"

"Why not just drive it?"

"I didn't want to attract any notice. The electric engine won't make any noise, but I thought that if it just sorta crept into the hanger by itself, no one would pay attention to it. I mean, there are a lot of other things demanding people's attention."

A burst of machinegun fire and a scream punctuated my statement, followed by another fusillade of gunfire.

"Maybe so," Mike said, "but start the engine anyway. If we have to hurry, I want to be able to hurry."

That made sense. I reached in and punched the starter, waited for the engine to come to life, then put the van in neutral. It would have helped if there had been any kind of slope, but airports were pretty flat on purpose.

We started pushing, Mike probably doing more of the work than I was. The idea seemed to be working at first. Until we pushed the van past Maillard's body, I didn't think anyone noticed. Then I heard someone yell, and a bullet shattered the window on the side facing the Chamber forces.

A minute later, it got a lot harder to push. Mike ducked down and looked under the van. "Damn. Someone shot out the tire on that side." A clang sounded through the van. "Shot out the other damned tire."

I pushed the gearshift into forward, and said, "Hang on," and pushed on the throttle. The van picked up speed. It was hard to steer, walking beside it, but I had no desire to sit inside and become a target.

With the engine doing the pushing, Mike took up a position to cover our backs. I heard his gun fire once, and then he ducked after me.

After what seemed like a couple of years, the van inched into the hangar, and I tried to figure out the best place to park it. I managed to steer it in behind some kind of equipment and a large toolbox. Having shut down the motor and set the brake, I leapt into the back of the van and checked the crate.

With a huge sigh of relief, I announced, "Mike, it looks like we got lucky. I don't see any bullet holes in the box holding the picture."

He didn't answer. I stuck my head out of the front window and saw him standing twenty feet away. I didn't know where the guy holding a gun on him came from, but he didn't look friendly. We thought we had secured the hanger earlier. So much for that assumption.

"Come on out, sweetheart," a gruff voice said. "Be a shame if I had to shoot your friend so I can come in after you."

I blurred my form and stepped past the crate to the doors in the back of the van. I threw the double doors open and dropped out of the van, prone on the floor. The guy with the gun half-turned in my direction, and Mike dove in the other direction.

Too much movement, too many people to keep track of. The guy didn't see anything to shoot at in my direction. I shot him when he turned his head back to follow Mike.

"Nice," Mike said as he picked himself up and walked back to where his pistol lay on the floor.

We checked out the shipment, opening the crate so that I could briefly inspect the painting, then sealing it back up again. The war outside continued for another half an hour. We elected to sit it out behind the large toolbox. It would have taken a canon to punch a hole through that thing.

"Come out with your hands in the air," Wilbur's voice finally announced after everything outside went quiet.

I winked at Mike. "You promised you wouldn't arrest me again. I've been good." I yelled, putting a terrible whine in my voice.

The response was too faint for my ears. I looked at Mike and raised an eyebrow.

"He said, 'Oh, for crying out loud'," Mike whispered with a grin.

I raised my voice again. "We're coming out."

I stood, opened the back of the van, and stepped out where Wil could see me.

Wil stood there with an expression on his face that a person might get from eating jail food.

"The painting is in there," I said. "It doesn't appear to be harmed, but of course it will have to be authenticated. I assume Chung will have someone to do that."

Wil shook his head slightly, and the lines between his eyes deepened. "Authenticated? Why?"

"The theft broke its provenance, sort of like a break in the chain of evidence. They'll have to make sure a substitution hasn't occurred." I looked beyond him at dozens of uniformed men milling about. "What is so special about that damned airplane? Do you get to keep it and take it home with you, or something?"

Wil glanced back toward the plane. "We got a tip that Hollande was on the plane."

That stunned me. "Is he?"

He nodded. "Yeah. We got him. And with this

shootout, not only do we have him on art theft, but on murder. He's done."

I sobered immediately. "You lost people."

"Yeah, we did. Me and the cops. We didn't expect that kind of firepower."

CHAPTER 23

I made sure that Georges Hollande didn't see me. He wouldn't have known who I was, at least I didn't think so, but I didn't have Wil's faith that Hollande would never be free again. People with that kind of money and power were hard to keep down. If I ever met him again, I didn't want him associating me with what was surely one of the worst days of his life.

The carnage was terrible. Twenty-five of Hollande's men had died and seven cops, including two of Wil's Chamber Security people. All over a stupid painting.

"I'll bet most of the people who died there didn't even know who Degas was," I muttered to Mike as we drove back to Doreen's place. I was bone tired and couldn't wait for a hot bath and a soft bed.

"Probably not," Mike said.

My phone rang. I stared at the number until I realized it was Myron Chung calling me.

"Mr. Chung. What can I do for you?"

"I think another buyer is here," he said.

"Here? In Chicago?"

"Here, as in the Shoreside Hotel. Frank Gomez checked in about an hour ago. Those same two men delivered another shipping crate to Martinez's room."

"The tall man and the short Hispanic?"

"Yes."

Donny and Karl. "Where's Margarita?"

"She went home after Hollande's men took the painting. I checked with the hotel, and she has the room booked for the rest of the week."

"Mr. Chung, I'm staying about forty minutes from

the hotel. When Margarita leaves home, call me. I'm going to try and get some sleep."

I said to Mike, "I wonder if Wil is going to try and bust Gomez and his plane."

"The chairman of a large corporation? Good question. I'd be surprised if Gomez set off a firefight like the one we just saw. Corporate executives tend to use lawyers to do their fighting."

We slipped into Doreen's through a side door, and I went to my room while Mike headed for the kitchen to get his dinner. I thought about food and decided a bath was more important.

One thing about using a brothel as a hotel. The oils, lotions, and creams in the washroom were exquisite. But as soon as I slipped into the steaming hot water loaded with aromatic oils, my phone rang. Thinking it might be Chung, I grabbed it and answered.

"Libby?" It was Wil. "Where are you?"

"In the bathtub. And afterward, I plan on going to bed. Contrary to popular opinion, I do need to sleep occasionally."

"Oh, sorry. Have you talked to Chung?"

"Yes. He said he'll call me when Margarita Martinez leaves home in the morning. Why, what's up?"

"I'm thinking that we need to find where they have the paintings stashed."

Duh. "Oh? Any ideas how to do that?"

"I was hoping you might."

I bit my tongue. We might try following them, but Karl was smarter than we were the last time.

"I'll think about it. Good night, Wil."

⊕⊕⊕

The following day, I watched Margarita and Frank Gomez eat lunch at the Shoreside's restaurant, then retire upstairs to her room. He was young to be head of a major corporation. She hung on his arm like a lover, and indeed, when she opened the door to the room, he put his arms around her as he followed her in, and she giggled like a schoolgirl.

It took a couple of hours, and if one were gauche enough to listen at the door, the noises coming from inside did not sound like a serious artistic discussion. Eventually, Margarita came out into the hall. She looked a little mussed, and her makeup wasn't as crisp as I remembered.

Turning at the doorway, she said, "Be a dear and make sure the door is locked when you leave."

Before the door closed and she practically skipped down the hall to the elevator, I could see that the bedclothes were quite rumpled. I understood that providing a little extra personal attention when a client paid millions for a painting might make Margarita some men's favorite art broker.

Fifteen minutes later, a couple of men came out of the near stairwell and knocked on the door. Gomez let them in, and in only a couple of minutes, they carried a narrow shipping crate out. Gomez pulled the door closed behind him and followed them down the stairs.

I trailed them, and watched the crate load into the trunk of a limousine. I had to applaud Gomez's class. A painting by a grand master shouldn't have to travel in a working-man's van.

Wil and his team intercepted them only a few blocks away. Another team boarded the plane at the airport and took control of it. All very civilized and quiet. I was glad to see that someone had taken the lessons of the previous night to heart.

Two paintings recovered, two customers detained, but we were no closer to finding the rest of the artworks or arresting those responsible for the theft. Even more maddening, to me at least, we weren't any closer to learning who killed Deborah Zhukoff.

"Mike," I said, "Let's try to find Donny again."

He showed his fangs in a lopsided smile and said, "Sounds like a plan to me."

The license plate on Donny's van had given us the listed address for Donald Chavez. We tried that first. The van wasn't there, but I still walked up to the door and knocked. No answer, so I walked around the house, peered through the windows, and decided he wasn't home. Our next stop was at the bar, and sure enough, we found him at his home away from home. I assumed my disguise from before. I tried to recall what name I'd given him, and couldn't remember.

When I opened the door and walked into the bar, I realized it didn't matter.

"Hey, baby," Donny said, getting up off his barstool and walking away from a woman who was draped all over him. I didn't see him as that much of a lady-killer, so I assumed he was still spreading his newfound wealth around. I gave him a big smile. "Hey, handsome. What's goin on? Did ya miss me?"

He bought me a drink and some tacos, and I steered him away from the bar to a quiet booth in the corner. Over the next hour, I made sure he downed three drinks to my one.

"So, what do you do?" I asked after he was

228

sufficiently lubricated and kneading my breast like bread dough.

"Make furniture and cabinets." I detected a note of pride in his voice.

"Really? Who do you work for?"

"Nobody. Work for myself."

I drew away from him. "Oh. I thought you had a job."

"Naw, it's not like that. I have my own workshop and sell stuff through some of the fancy furniture stores. It's top-quality. Have more orders than I can fill."

"Uh-huh. That's why you're here instead of hard at work."

"Geez. Hey, what's wrong? A guy needs to take a break once in a while. Can't work all the time."

"Yeah, right. Middle of the day, middle of the week. I'll bet you don't work at all. You probably sell drugs or something." I picked up my purse and acted as though I was searching for my coat.

"Hey, baby, don't be like that." He grabbed at my arm.

"I had plenty of losers trying to get in my pants in Atlanta," I said. "I thought you were different. I deserve a guy who can pay the rent and buy me nice things. Someone with a future."

He pulled out a business card and shoved it under my nose, his name plus "Latin-influenced custom furniture and woodcraft" with a phone number. On the back, it showed the logos and numbers of half-a-dozen stores, most of them recognizably corporate.

I left off searching for my coat, which was within arm's reach, and studied the card. "You really own a business?"

229

"Yeah, that's what I been tryin to tell ya." His slurring was reaching a point where I decided he'd had enough to drink.

"So, you could show me your shop?"

"Yeah, sure. You want to see it? Okay, I'll take you over there."

Looking up at him through my lashes, I let a smile grow on my face. "Is anyone there?"

"Naw, nobody. I took the day off and the shop's closed."

I gave him my best wicked smile and purred, "Have you ever done it there? You know, where you work? I screwed my boss on his desk once, and it was hot. Do you have a lot of power tools?" Stroking the inside of his thigh. "Do you have a power tool for me?"

Donny paid and dragged me out to his van in record time. Unfortunately, he acted as though he planned on driving. As drunk as he was, I considered that a disastrously bad idea. Leaning over, I pulled his face around and kissed him.

"Why don't you put it on autopilot? That way I don't get bored." It would also be far easier for Mike to follow the van on robotic control.

Twenty minutes later, we pulled up in front of a business with a parking lot for a few cars and a sign in front. He really did have a respectable business. In spite of myself, I was impressed. Inside was a small display room with a few tables, chairs, and an incredible chaise lounge upholstered in dark red velvet. The work was clean and decorated with what looked to be artistic hand carving.

I walked over and studied the chaise. It was drool worthy. If I couldn't have a man in my life, that piece of furniture was definitely worth my love.

230

"How much?"

"Sixteen thousand."

Love dropped to intense like. Besides, that piece in my townhouse, surrounded by the rest of my furniture, would look like a rose in a field of weeds.

"Show me your shop."

He took me to the back where he had a lot of tools—saws and lathes and other stuff I didn't recognize—and several pieces of half-finished furniture. One corner of the shop caught my eye. Scraps of plywood and pine boards, materials for the paintings' shipping crates. The rough lumber looked out of place among the dark hardwoods he used in his furniture.

"Some nice wood," I said, running my hand over a dining room table that was almost black with red highlights.

"I have it shipped in from all over the world," he said.

Looking around, I asked, "Where do you keep it all? Someone told me once that some woods needed to be kept in controlled conditions so they wouldn't dry out and crack. I don't understand how you'd make furniture with wood like that. Wouldn't it crack in your home?"

"That's why you oil it. But I have a humidity-controlled storage room to keep wood in until I'm ready to use it."

"Really? Can I see?"

He led me to the rear of the shop, where he unlocked and opened a heavy steel door. When he swung it open, I saw stacks of wood in all different shapes, sizes, and colors. Against the back wall were three plywood and pine shipping crates, two about the

231

size of those we'd already confiscated, and a smaller one.

Reaching into my purse, I found the jet injector filled with a fast-acting barbiturate. Then I turned to Donny, put my arms around his neck, and kissed him. He folded me into an embrace and as one of his hands traveled over my ass, I pressed the injector against his neck.

He slumped, and I eased him to the floor.

A quick check of the shipping crates revealed the Monet and the two Renoirs. I pulled out my phone.

"Mike? How far away are you?"

"Half a block."

"Leave the car and come on in. I have the paintings."

We loaded them into Donny's van and drove it to the museum. The look on Myron Chung's face was priceless, but not as satisfying as the one on Wil's face when he showed up.

"If you want to bust the thieves, take the van back to the owner," I told them. "I'm sure Donny will cut a deal."

I wondered if he might be willing to sell that chaise cheap. Legal bills were expensive, and it looked like he might need some money.

⊕⊕⊕

The next morning, Wil took me to breakfast at a bistro with pastries that should have been illegal. They also served real coffee, something hard to come by in the parts of town I'd been frequenting.

"Your buddy Donny is singing all the right notes,"

Wil said as we waited for our food. "His friends, however, aren't saying a word. Nothing to implicate Martinez. Gomez threw her under the bus without a second thought. Says he didn't know the painting he bought was stolen and wants his money back. We also have the surveillance video we took of her and the activities in and around that hotel room."

If they had vid from inside the room, they could probably sell it, but I didn't say that. "That should be enough. At the very least, you can shut down her business. No one will deal with her once word gets out. Assuming she survives Georges Hollande's wrath."

"We're announcing the recovery of the paintings and the arrests this afternoon as soon as we've arrested Margarita. Then we'll have to deal with all their lawyers."

I chuckled. "Better you than me. We still have loose ends, though. The necklace, Donnelly, and the murder. Unless Martinez implicates Donnelly, we don't have anything on him."

The waitress brought our meals, and I dove in.

"Are you starving?" Wil asked.

"Mm-hmm," I said, nodding my head and stuffing another bite of quiche in my mouth. I hadn't eaten since Donny bought me tacos the day before.

Wil laughed. "Well, as to Donnelly, he still has the problem of his gambling debts."

"Nope," I said between bites. "He cleared sixteen million on those two paintings."

Wil put his fork down. "You checked his bank accounts."

"Yep. I assume he got Deborah's share as well."

"Don't you ever think about the fact that hacking

233

into banks is illegal?"

"No, not really. Someone would have to catch me. Besides, I don't steal anything. I only do it for educational purposes."

CHAPTER 24

I talked Wil into hauling Malcolm Donnelly down to Chamber headquarters for questioning. He didn't want to do it. Standard diffidence toward a large corporation's chairman, and all that.

An apartment on the floor below Donnelly's was being remodeled while the owners visited Europe. Immediately after my breakfast with Wil, I went over there, and as soon as Donnelly left the building, I went in.

I showed up as a man wearing a fumigation suit and announced that I needed to spray the place for roaches. The construction workers went home, and I crawled from the balcony of that apartment to the balcony above. Crossing over another balcony took me to Donnelly's. I jammed the alarm contact on the sliding door, and waltzed in.

It wasn't a large apartment. I suspected that before Winifred filed for divorce, he kept it as a place to take his ladies. Figuring I had three hours, I thought I would have enough time to search the nine rooms.

The woman lying in bed watching a vid and eating chocolates wasn't in my plans. From her reaction, she wasn't expecting me, either.

She must have caught movement out of the corner of her eye. I whipped back out of the doorway as she turned toward me. Then she screamed. I could hear my father in my head. "Careless" and "unprofessional" were the two printable words in his imaginary rant. I hadn't taken the time to scout Donnelly's place before breaking in.

I morphed into a likeness of my friend Paul. His

image was stored in my memory and it was quick. That done, I charged back into the bedroom. She opened her mouth to scream again but hesitated. I understood why. Paul was handsome and charming enough that a woman might actually welcome him barging into her bedroom.

Grabbing her wrists in one hand, I looked around for something to tie her hands. The belt of a bathrobe came to hand and I used it, then gave her a shot with the jet injector.

Unable to resist, I whispered in her ear as the drug took effect. "I'm going to make this the sweetest dream of your life."

I didn't find anything in the bedroom. I didn't find anything in the entire house. No necklace. No incriminating papers or files on the computer. I did find a used home pregnancy test cup in the spare washroom. To add to Donnelly's problems, it showed a positive result.

Before I left, I untied the mistress and tucked her in. With any luck, she'd decide I was a dream and not say anything to Donnelly.

Of course, there were tons of places someone could hide a necklace in Chicago. It might be in his office at work, or in his locker at the country club. But people got edgy when their valuables weren't ready to hand or in places they couldn't control. Prior to Winifred filing for divorce, Malcolm was still living with his wife. At least, that's what the news said.

The plans for his estate were available with only an hour's worth of hacking. Nothing too lavish. Forty rooms in the main house, two or three outbuildings, a clubhouse that served the pool and tennis courts, and the stables. He had bought the place twenty years before and never used the stables, at least not for livestock. For all I knew, that was where he kept his haram.

I looked up the Chicago police's interview with Winifred and her servants.

After I spent most of the day on that line of research, Mike said, "You know, breaking into the Donnelly estate and retrieving the necklace is a spectacularly bad idea."

"Oh? How so?"

"What are you going to do with it? How are you going to prove he stole it? B and E is a crime, you know. Donnelly's going to scream that you've been guilty all along and now he has the proof."

His words percolated through my brain as I stared at him. "That's entirely too logical," I finally said.

He shrugged. "Just thought I'd throw that out there before you asked me to help you get in trouble."

"So, what do I do?"

"Ask Wilbur to search the place with the Chicago cops?"

"On what pretext?"

Mike grinned. "The Chamber needs a pretext? Say you're searching for Zhukoff's murder weapon. The wife's alibi has holes you could drive a truck through."

I thought about it. "That wouldn't even be targeting Malcolm at all, would it? He hasn't been to the estate since Winifred filed for divorce. His lawyers wouldn't have any cause to block the search."

"They would be cheering you on," Mike said. "If Wini goes to jail for murder, her divorce claims fall apart. He can divorce her without a fuss or any payments."

I called Wil. He argued with me. It seemed that was all we did. It hadn't always been like that, and I hated it. Then I put Mike on the phone to him. Evidently, they spoke the same language. I wasn't sure if that language was male, or corporate security, or something else, but Mike convinced him.

⊕⊕⊕

The following morning at seven o'clock, Mike and I joined Wil and Myron Chung, along with twelve Chamber Security men and twenty of Chicago PD's finest. A police lieutenant knocked on the front door of the Donnelly mansion and presented the butler with a search warrant. Then he trooped upstairs to present it to Winifred.

As the butler told us, the lady of the house was indisposed. When someone was so dead drunk the cops couldn't wake her up, that was pretty drunk.

We found four safes in the house, one in Winifred's bedroom, one in Malcolm's bedroom, and one in his office. The fourth one was behind a panel behind the dartboard in the billiards room.

"What made you look there?" Wil asked, scratching his head.

I couldn't tell him that I felt the electricity running to it when I put my hand on the wall. "I've seen this sort of hiding place before," I lied.

"Other than asking Donnelly or his wife for the combinations, I'm not sure how we're going to get these open," Wil said, staring straight at me as he said it.

I stared back. "Standard procedure is to contact the companies who manufactured the safes, but you're assuming they're locked."

His eyebrows raised. "They all look locked to me."

"That's because you're not a professional security technician," I said. "I've installed safes for my clients, and I'm willing to bet that the Donnellys left all of these unlocked."

He held out his hand, pointing toward the safe.

Safes with electric keypads were very popular. The companies that marketed them said they were more secure than the old-fashioned tumbler locks. In actuality, they were simply more convenient for the people who bought them. And more convenient for me. I could crack a safe with a dial lock, but it was much easier to just short out an electronic lock.

I touched the keypad, then unlatched the door and opened it. Wil shook his head as he walked over and looked inside.

"Well, well, what have we here?" He reached in and pulled out a plastic bag containing the Lalique necklace. I heard someone gasp, and realized it was me.

"Lieutenant, can we make sure to preserve any fingerprints on this bag and its contents?" Wil asked, holding it up for the cops and everyone else to see.

We continued searching the premises for Deborah's murder weapon. The police confiscated several knives, but I doubted any of them were the fatal knife. Winifred just didn't fit my idea of a killer. Malcolm did, but I hadn't found a knife at his apartment that matched the ME's description, either.

⊕⊕⊕

The fingerprint scan revealed four sets of prints, Malcolm and Winifred Donnelly's, Deborah Zhukoff's, and Margarita Martinez's. The really good news was that my fingerprints weren't on either the bag or the necklace.

"We hit the quadfecta," I crowed. Everyone laughed at me. If trifecta was a perfectly good word, I didn't see why quadfecta couldn't be.

The police arrested Winifred that night, but when they sobered her up, she went completely silent, and her lawyers stepped between her and the police.

Malcolm threw everyone under the bus. The robbery was Deborah and Winifred's idea, and he was an innocent victim. His only crime was being chivalrous for love and helping them cover it up. Margarita was the daughter of Satan who seduced Deborah into the idea. Wil and I were conspirators with Deborah. I kept waiting for him to blame the Pope.

Margarita refused to talk until Wil suggested that she was the prime suspect in Deborah's murder. At that point, she tossed Malcolm into the pot and salted it with information about his gambling debts. The Chamber and its banking partners found a ten-million-credit payment she had made to him, and the nine-million-credit withdrawal and payment he had made to one of Chicago's leading crime bosses.

They began to doubt Margarita's credibility when they couldn't find any trace of the six-million-credit second payment she said she'd given Malcolm.

Wil invited me up to his office. Unfortunately, he didn't have romance on his mind. He sat down behind his desk and asked, "Didn't you tell me that Margarita had put sixteen million credits in Malcolm's Swiss account?"

"I don't think so. Ten million."

He regarded me in silence for a long time, as if hoping I'd get a pang of conscience and magically turn into an honest person or something.

"I could have sworn you told me sixteen."

"Well, how could I have found sixteen when the people who run the banks only found ten?" I half shrugged, turning to the incredible view out his windows.

"I'm wondering how that six million disappeared between the time you told me about it and the time the bank auditors went looking for it."

With a smile, I turned to him and said, "I'm flattered. You must think I'm awfully smart. You've got bigger fish to fry, you know. Margarita says she paid Donnelly six million for the Modigliani. She paid Sanderson one million. Gomez says he paid her fifty million. That's a lot of money floating around unaccounted for. Did you ever find out what Hollande paid for the Degas?"

He took a deep breath and let it out with a sigh. "You're never going to tell me, are you?"

"Admit it. A little bit of mystery makes a woman more attractive, doesn't it? But I'll tell you what I'll do. Make reservations at that bomb-proof country club again, and I'll take you out to dinner. I'll even throw in a night at the opera before I leave town."

I walked over to where he sat, kissed him on the cheek, and headed toward the door. As I opened it, I turned back to him. "It's the least I can do to repay you for setting me up with such a lucrative gig. If you hadn't arrested me, I might have been tempted to express my appreciation in a more personal way."

⊕⊕⊕

That afternoon, I dropped by the museum to give

241

Jessica my final invoice and do the same with Myron Chung.

Jess glanced at the invoice and said, "I'll get Mr. Wiberforce's signature and give it to accounting."

It had been over a week since the murder. Every time I'd seen Jess, she looked like she was just dragging through her day, going through the motions. I didn't think she was sleeping well, and she looked exhausted.

"Are you all right?" I asked.

She nodded, then she shook her head, then she nodded again, then she burst out crying. I took a chance and reached for her. She buried her face in my chest and sobbed.

"You really loved her, didn't you?"

"Yes," she blubbered. "We...we...were...she said..." Whatever Deborah said, I never found out because Jess was crying too hard to tell me.

She finally wound down, and I led her into Deborah's office, made her lie down on the couch, and pulled an Afghan over her.

"You rest, okay?" I waited about five minutes until I was sure she was asleep, then tip-toed out and went down the hall to find Chung.

He looked up as I came in his office. "Ah, Miss Nelson. I've been expecting you."

I smiled and handed him my invoice. He glanced at it, scribbled his name on it, and tossed it on top of one of the piles of papers on his desk. Seeing my raised eyebrow, he grinned and said, "Those are my expense reports. Nothing in that pile is getting lost."

"It's been a pleasure, Mr. Chung."

"It has been," he answered. "Sit down, Miss Nelson. I've been impressed. So have my employers.

They have authorized me to speak to you about ongoing employment."

"That's flattering, but I prefer my independence."

He steepled his fingers in front of him. "I thought that would be your answer. In that case, are you interested in further contractual work?"

"Absolutely."

"Good." He pulled a stack of paper an inch thick out of his drawer. "Read this, sign one copy and send it back to me. The other copy is yours. If you want to amend it, we'll have to send it through the lawyers, but I doubt you'll find anything objectionable. It's a standard contract for independent investigators."

The smile I gave him was completely sincere. "Thank you."

"Hurry," he said. "I can probably keep you fairly busy. The trade in stolen art has become a major participant sport among certain factions of the elite. I guess they get bored."

"No qualms about my family?"

He chuckled. "I'd rather have you and your anonymous source of information on my side."

CHAPTER 25

The news the following morning was all about another bombing. The terrorists hit a teen nightclub and exacted an appalling casualty toll. Between the two bombs set off, the subsequent fire, and the people trampled in the ensuing stampede, the media reported over one hundred killed and another one hundred injured severely enough to be hospitalized.

Watching vid of the aftermath, I saw Wil twice, once with a reporter interviewing him. He looked almost as good on the screen as he did in person.

I went downstairs to get breakfast and found Doreen's employees—the six women and two men who lived at the house—watching the same news channel.

"Most of the victims were under eighteen," a woman on the screen said. "Some as young as fourteen. Area hospitals are calling for blood donations."

Blood shortages were common any time a catastrophe occurred. Vampires paid much better for human blood than hospitals, and usually didn't require testing for mutations or diseases.

Although I was one of the least squeamish people I knew, body parts of dead kids weren't what I wanted to see with my breakfast. I put a plate together and took it back upstairs.

While I was eating, Mike knocked and came in.

"I'm figuring that you probably don't need me any longer," he said. "When are you planning on going back to Toronto?"

"You all packed?" I asked.

"Yeah."

"Well, I still haven't found Zhukoff's killer, and the Chamber is still paying me."

He sat down across from me. "You know it's probably one of the people they've already arrested. Without some kind of evidence, I doubt the killer is going to confess. You may never know."

"Maybe. I keep running all the suspects around in my mind, and none of them feels right. I think I'll start over and approach things a little differently. Divorce the killing from the robbery and see if we've overlooked something."

"Want me to stick around?"

I shook my head and handed him a credit card. "Thanks, Mike. I really appreciate your help. Give my love to my parents."

He keyed the card and looked at it, then back at me with his eyes as wide as I'd ever seen. "Good God, Libby."

"I had a good week, and I figure your contribution was worth half of it. I have a warm spot in my heart for people who help keep me alive."

"But...where...?"

With a smile and a wink I said, "Let's just say that Saint Modigliani blessed us and leave it at that."

My phone rang. Picking it up, I didn't recognize the number, but it was a Chicago area code.

"Nelson Security. How may I help you?"

"Miss Nelson? This is Devon Spiess with the Chamber of Commerce."

"Yes, Mr. Spiess?"

"I need to meet with you immediately. Can you come into Chamber headquarters, or can I pick you up somewhere?"

I remembered Devon from Wil's hospital room and the day he drove Wil home from the hospital. I'd seen him a couple of times since, but he'd been very stand-offish.

"And what is this in regard to?"

"I'm afraid that's confidential."

Okay. Nothing like walking into the spider's web in total ignorance.

"I'll meet you at AIC in an hour," I said.

Mike's smile was tight as I hung up the phone. "I guess I'll delay my trip back to Toronto. Who was that?"

We still had the drug-runner's car Wil had loaned us, so we drove over to the museum and found Devon waiting for us on the front steps. That was okay with me, as it was easier to escape if we were outside.

He nodded to Mike and then said, "I take it you saw the news this morning."

"The bombing? Yeah, I saw it."

"Afterward, sometime early this morning, Wil disappeared from the scene," Devon said. "We got this message a couple of hours ago."

He held out a tablet. I took it and hit play. Gustav Alscher's face appeared.

"This is Democracy Now. We have your Deputy Director, Wilbur Wilberforce. If you want to see him alive, here are our conditions you must meet to secure his release."

Alscher listed a number of improbable things, such as opening schools and universities to all students, regardless of their ability to pay. He also wanted training and job programs for the uneducated from the lower classes. The mutants and poor should be given free health care with clinics and hospitals established in the poorest parts of town. In addition, electricity and clean water should be supplied to all parts of the city, regardless of people's ability to pay for such things.

I doubted that he thought the corporations would actually meet his crazy demands. Asking for billions of credits in charity was too unbelievable to take seriously.

Then he hit what I figured he really wanted—ten million credits and the "release and repatriation of our revolutionary sisters held as political prisoners, Elizabeth Nelson and Miriam al-Azadi."

I looked at Devon. "I assume the definition of repatriation has changed since I was in school. I didn't realize it now meant enslavement to a demented demagogue."

"Everyone with a political agenda defines their own terms," Devon said. "Miss Nelson, you're under no obligation to help us, but I'm hoping you will."

"I'll help, but I'll bill you."

"Fair enough."

"Where's Miriam?"

"The mutie? At a safe house."

"Well, let's go see her. She knows more about Alscher, and where he might be keeping Wil, than anyone else. I assume you want to retrieve him alive."

"If at all possible." Devon allowed himself a small smile. "I know that would be his preference."

"If not, don't you get promoted?" I asked, giving him a sly grin.

"Probably not. I'd just have to break in a new boss."

"Better the asshole you know, huh?" Mike

interjected.

Devon barked a laugh but quickly sobered. He led us to an aircar that took us northwest out of the city. Forty-five minutes later, we set down in front of an old farmhouse surrounded with trees. The nearest structure I saw from the air was several hundred yards away.

Inside, the house seemed clean and comfortable, if a little old fashioned. Miriam came out from a back room, smiled, and hugged me. Then we sat down and discussed our problem.

"They're going to send me back?" Miriam said after I explained Alscher's demands.

"No, they aren't," I told her with an emphatic shake of my head.

"Why not? They think they can work a better deal?"

"We don't plan to work any deal," Devon said. "We're not trading human beings or rewarding a terrorist for killing a bunch of kids. We just want to rescue Deputy Director Wilberforce."

Miriam looked at him with a kind of awe in her face. Considering her history, I think such a concept was new to her.

"I need you to tell me everything you can about where Alscher may be hiding his hostage, and everything about his defenses," I said. "Everything. Don't leave anything out."

Over the next four or five hours, she detailed what she knew, I asked questions, and she told me more. Devon supplied maps, aerial photographs, and other information as needed.

The old shopping mall was the center of Alscher's operation. Within a mile of the place, he controlled several thousand mutants and criminals in his own little kingdom. Carly was a big part of that. He'd feed her mushrooms and have her prophesy at large rallies where mushroom tea was liberally distributed.

The house where they held me was one of the places he stayed, but Miriam told me about two more. One was actually livable, but only a few of his closest confidants knew of it. I could see why. People might start asking questions as to how he got clean water, heat in the winter, and electricity, not to mention food.

It was an age-old tale. The revolutionary who was trying to tear down the system on behalf of the poor, downtrodden masses, really just wanted to be part of the elite he railed against. It made me wonder why he got into the revolution game in the first place.

I said something to that effect to Devon and Miriam, and she shook her head. "No, you don't understand. He doesn't want to join the elite, he wants to rule the elite. Gustav feels he's a superior man, one who is destined to rule. You can see it with some of the mutants he draws to him. He calls normal humans the 'old men.' He preaches that we have evolved beyond what humans were before."

By mid-afternoon, we had as much as Miriam could tell us. We had a good guess as to where Gustav was holding Wil, and the best second and third options. Devon had a force of Chamber Security, Chicago Police, and various corporate security personnel numbering about three thousand men. All were armored and armed to the teeth, and the force included over a hundred attack helicopters.

Corporate response to the earlier bombings had been muted. Deliberately targeting children was a different matter, and people were outraged. Devon didn't say it, but I was aware of the corporations' response to other uprisings, including the one in Europe that Alscher had escaped. I fully expected Alscher's part of Chicago to be a smoking lifeless pile of rubble by the end of the week.

First, we had to get Wil out of there.

"How much time do we have?" I asked Devon.

"Twenty-four hours, maybe twice that long. Alscher gave us forty-eight hours to meet his demands. I don't know if I can hold off the people screaming for his head that long."

I looked at Miriam. "Can I speak with you privately?"

She nodded and led me back to what I assumed was her bedroom. "Are they treating you okay?" I asked.

"Oh, yes. They feed me and take care of me. I can't go anywhere, but I'm used to that. I have as much water as I wish, even to wash, and they've given me all these nice new clothes that even fit. They even let me sleep alone."

I bit my lip at the tone in her voice. Like a kid at an amusement park for the first time.

When I went back to the front room, I said to Devon, "Drop me as close as possible to that house of Alscher's that she told us about. The nice one by the park. I'm betting he wants Wil someplace he thinks we don't know about."

"And drop me near the old mall," Mike said. "They don't know me, and with proper clothing, no one will give another vamp a second glance."

"You don't want to get caught in there if the authorities start bombing the place," I said.

"No, I'll stay for thirty-six hours max, and then

leave." He looked at Devon. "If you decide to go in earlier, I'd appreciate a warning."

"That I can do for both of you. If you find him, where do we set the extraction point?"

Another hour of planning ended with Devon providing me with gas and explosive mini-grenades, a riot gun, and an extra pistol and clips. My purse converted to a backpack, and I stuffed it all away. He wanted to wait until dark to drop us in, but Mike spoke against that.

"I see better at night, and so do the lycans. The mutie community is mostly nocturnal. We want to be in place before everyone wakes up."

The aircar hovered over a five-story building about a mile from an old park. Out of an apocalyptic landscape, the building was the tallest object in sight. I rode a rope attached to a winch down to the roof, and the car rose straight up until it disappeared from sight.

As soon as I entered the doorway leading downward, I blurred my image. From that point on, I planned on staying invisible.

The house Miriam described was near the old park. According to Devon, the park had a terrible reputation—overgrown, crime infested, and a favorite lycan hangout. The entire area around it looked like the ruins of an ancient urban battlefield. The only exceptions were the large houses immediately surrounding the park. When built, they were the homes of an ethnic-African ghetto aristocracy. Devon told me that top members of the city's mutant crime hierarchy held most, if not all of them. I noticed he didn't use the word owned.

All of the Chamber's intelligence, and what we'd learned from Miriam, said that Gustav Alscher had fought through to become the top dog. I wondered if controlling people using empathy was his only mutation. Of course, having a prophet, or clairvoyant, such as Carly, might have helped. Exactly how much and how clearly did she see the future? Did she anticipate me going in after Wil?

It was late afternoon, and very few people were out on the streets. I saw a couple of lycans and a troll, along with a few normal-looking people. That morning, a fierce storm had blown through, but the rain had stopped by the time I hit the roof. Low clouds promised a dark night and the possibility of more rain.

As I approached the houses around the park, I noticed a lot more people, especially lycans. Most were just lounging about, but a lot of them were armed. I stopped across the street from a few guys sitting around a table, playing cards and drinking beer. Two of them had been in the mall the night Alscher kidnapped me and I killed Horseface.

Mike had sounded just like my dad, telling me over and over that I might be walking into a trap. I knew that, and Alscher knew I was a chameleon. In any case, he should be preparing for an assault by the security forces. Anyone with half a brain would expect reprisals for killing kids, but I had doubts about Alscher's sanity.

And always nagging in the back of my mind was the knowledge that Carly could see me. If Alscher was smart, he would have her where he kept Wil. The thing was, Alscher couldn't see me. He couldn't truly understand my abilities. The more I thought about it, the more my head spun in circles. I took the whole line of thought and shoved it away before the distraction immobilized me.

Slipping past the card players, I noticed they all had weapons. Not just small revolvers, but assault rifles and heavy-caliber automatic pistols. The kind of firepower to meet an incursion by Devon's forces, and very nasty if turned on Wil and me. Being invisible and being invulnerable were two entirely different things.

I passed the houses and entered the park, where I had to proceed very slowly because I couldn't see fifty feet ahead of me. The obstacles included overgrown bushes and trees, waist-high grass, dry now in winter, and tangles of rose bushes so thick as to cause some major detours. I just hoped I didn't step on a sleeping lycan. Or a snake. I didn't know if Chicago had snakes, but the idea of a snake as big as the rats...

I forced myself not to think about such things. It was bad enough that I kept seeing what looked like the entrances to dens, either lycans or rats or something else.

Eventually, I worked my way in behind the large house Miriam identified as Gustav's. Most of the houses in the area showed some activity, but that one had some outstanding attributes. Gustav must have hired my father's decorator. I thought the piles of sandbags around the heavy machineguns were an especially nice touch.

That level of paranoia made me wonder about electronic security. I spent the next two hours carefully scouting the perimeter of the house and yard, looking for laser projectors and electric wires. Tripwires, pressure plates, or even something as crude as landmines or other booby-traps, could seriously derail my mission.

Other than a single tripwire circling the property, I couldn't find anything. My luck held as I slowly inched my way across the back yard past all the guards, then through a back door when no one was looking that direction. I found a set of stairs off the kitchen leading down. The basement was Miriam's best guess for where they'd be keeping Wil.

Creeping down a set of dark stairs, I came to the bottom and found a small space with two locked doors. The smell of decomposing human was overwhelming, and I switched out my normal filter mask for a gas mask. It took about five minutes to get through three locks and open the door to my left. Two of the men inside were dead, and had been for some time. The third man was a vampire and he was barely alive. It appeared the three of them had been locked up together and forgotten. Vampires were tough, and the evidence showed he was the likely cause of his companions' deaths. Neither of them were Wil.

The other basement room was thankfully empty of corpses. It had the unique ambiance of a torture chamber, with plenty of dried blood and a number of tools and devices that I wished I'd never seen. My sympathies for the poor, downtrodden revolutionaries faded fast.

Back up the stairs. It took another half-hour of inching my way through the house, dodging the attentions of the people wandering in, out, and around, to discover that I was in the wrong place.

I stood in a hallway and heard Gustav say into a phone, "I don't care. I want a guard on him twenty-four hours a day. Yes, one outside the room and two inside. Tom, they're going to try and break him out. I don't care what happens outside, those guards stay put."

It took me another hour to get out of the house, across the yard, then back across the park. I contacted Mike to tell him about overhearing Gustav talk about Wil.

"I'm pretty sure they're keeping him at a house near the mall," Mike told me. "The place is crawling with armed men."

It was well past dark and a lot of the night dwellers were out on the street. Wanting to make better time, I assumed the illusion of a vampire woman and openly headed for the old mall at a jog.

CHAPTER 26

If I hadn't seen Mike's disguise when he donned it, I probably would have walked right past him. Using only the cosmetics I had in my purse, he managed to turn himself into a man looking a hundred years older. He had gray hair, appeared shorter, and walked with a limp. A couple of rips and a lot of dirt rubbed into his clothes, and he blended into the local scene as naturally as the roaches.

"Hey, sailor. Looking for a good time?"

He jerked around and laughed after seeing me. "Now, that is your most attractive persona to date," he said.

I sat down beside him on a crumbling pile of bricks that had once been a porch. "Where's this house you told me about?"

"Down the street there. See the guys on the front porch?"

They were hard to see in the twilight, but I could see their outlines. It was the house where I had been kept prisoner.

"See the boarded-up window on the second floor?" I asked. "That was the room where they held me."

"So, assuming he's in there, how are we going to get him out?"

"You're as bad as Dad is, always asking hard questions. This would be a good time to reveal that you have a teleportation mutation."

He chuckled. "I've been around the back, and there's another contingent of guards there. Compared to the night we picked you up, there are a lot more people with guns wandering around."

"Gustav is expecting us. I think we're going to have to just kill everyone and then run and hope they don't catch up to us."

Mike stared at me. "Gosh, Libby. That's brilliant. It's too bad you were born so late. Napoleon would have treasured your genius."

"It's a gift," I said, feeling my face flush. "You have any better ideas?"

After staring at the house for a couple of minutes, he gave a deep sigh. "Unfortunately, no. Do you think you can get inside before all the shooting starts? It would help if you can secure the hostage before they kill him."

"I heard Gustav give orders for one guard outside the room and two inside. We're assuming that's the house. The other house I visited was guarded even heavier than this one, but that's where Alscher was."

Blurring my image, I used the side railing of the porch to climb to the house's roof. It was slow going, but I was mostly out of the direct view of the men on the porch or any passersby. Crawling along the porch roof, being extra careful of loose shingles, I made my way to the window I climbed out of a few weeks before.

They'd nailed the boards back up, but not with any skill or precision. I slid a heavy-bladed knife under one and pried the corner loose as quietly as I could. A beam of light from inside showed through, but the gap wasn't wide enough that I could see anything. I continued to loosen that board and the one next to it so they'd be easy to rip off. The third board— the one I hadn't messed with before—was stuck on a lot better.

I could get through the narrower opening, but I doubted Wil could. He outweighed me seventy or eighty pounds, and the man's chest and shoulders were massive. After trying without success to get the board loose quietly, I decided that if he wanted to go out the window, he could kick it out himself.

Momentarily unblurring my form, I turned and waved to Mike, then blended back into the background. Pulling the riot gun from my bag, I waited for my signal to charge in and probably get shot. I swore to myself that if the damned man inside didn't say thank you, he would wish I left him there.

I knew there were at least two armed men, and maybe more, waiting for me. The riot gun—a sawed-off semi-automatic ten-gauge shotgun with a twenty-shell magazine loaded with double-aught buckshot—was meant to even the odds.

It felt as though I waited there forever, then a series of explosions sounded from the back of the house. Ripping away the loose boards, I dove through the window. Two men across the room from me leapt to their feet. I fired at the one directly in front of me, and the shotgun blew him backward, splintering the door behind him as he crashed into the hall. Swiveling the muzzle, I shot the other man as he raised his gun.

An explosion behind and below me signaled that Mike was still on the job. A lycan with a pistol looked through the doorway, and I blew his head off.

Wil lay on his stomach on the bed, his wrists and ankles bound with zip ties. I pulled out my heavy knife again and cut through them while trying to keep an eye on the door. Dropping a pistol with a couple of spare clips on the bed, I moved to the window and peered out.

The porch roof had collapsed, and there were a couple of big holes in the porch as well. There wasn't any place to land if we jumped out the window.

Between the shotgun and all the explosions, I couldn't hear very well, but it seemed as though a lot of people outside were doing a lot of shooting. The plan was for Mike to toss a bunch of grenades at the guards in the back and then in the front of the house, then some gas grenades inside, and hightail it for the extraction point.

Wil was rubbing his wrists and ankles, trying to restore circulation. He tried to stand, swayed, and sat back down again. I handed him a gas mask and he put it on.

"This has to be the dumbest thing I've ever seen anyone do," he said. "But in case I don't get the chance later, thank you. I didn't know you cared that much."

"The Chamber's paying me."

"Ah, I should have known." I couldn't see his mouth, but the skin around his eyes crinkled like it did when he smiled.

"Can you walk yet?"

"Yeah, I think so."

"Can you use that pistol left handed?"

"Sure. Why?"

"Roll up your sleeve and give me your right arm," I said, moving next to him. He did as I said, and I pressed my bare left arm against him. "Help me bind us together."

I had a couple of leather straps with velcro. One went around our forearms, the other around our biceps. I raised our hands over our heads, and worked our elbows up and down.

"No matter what, as long as I'm uninjured and awake, do not lose touch with me. Skin on skin. Understand? Follow orders, and hopefully, we'll get out of here intact."

He saluted with the pistol in his left hand. "Yes, ma'am, Commander Libby."

"That's Princess Libby to you."

With a chuckle, he said, "Yes, Your Highness."

I was nervous as hell, unsure what his reaction would be as I blurred us. My best friend Nellie and I discovered the trick when we were very young. We were the queens of hide-and-seek. I had never tried it with anyone else. As long as Wil and I maintained skin contact, my illusion included him.

I heard a sharp intake of breath, then, "I can't see you anymore." He paused, then, "I can't see me. Are we invisible?"

Waving our arms back and forth between his face and the window, I asked, "Can you see the motion?"

"Yes."

"We're not invisible, we just blend into the background." I stood and pulled him up with me. Moving in front of the window, I blocked it from his sight. "If someone is looking at us, don't move. Don't stand in front of a light or an open passageway."

"Got it."

"Don't get in a hurry. We can't do that anyway, tied together like this, but keep in mind that we're practically invisible unless we move. So, we move very slowly. You cover the left flank, and I cover the right. We have to go about a mile to reach the extraction point. Everybody outside has guns and wants to kill us. If we don't get out of here quickly enough, your people will kill us when they attack. Any questions?"

"None at all. Sounds like a stroll in the park."

An involuntary shudder ran through me. "Thankfully, we don't have to go through the park."

"How many times have you done things like this?" he asked, a note of incredulity in his voice.

"You mean, snuck into an armed camp to rescue a hostage from a bunch of homicidal maniacs?"

"Yeah."

"That would be never. Do you truly think I'm stupid enough to try something like this twice? If I get through this without dying, or at least peeing my pants, I'll be shocked. Next time, you're on your own."

The gas from Mike's grenades was much thicker on the first floor and we didn't encounter anyone until we opened the back door. I fired the riot gun three times to clear the area, and swiftly pulled Wil after me around to the side of the house where I stopped, our backs pressed to the wall.

The gunfire had quieted, but my shots set off a new round of firing. Most of the mutants weren't trained in any way at all, so giving them guns and no command structure wasn't the brightest idea Alscher ever had. I didn't know what they were firing at, and neither did they, but bullets whizzed around for the next five minutes. I wondered how many casualties they were inflicting on themselves.

When the shooting died away, we started moving away from the house and the mall. The entire area was like a hornet's nest, or maybe like Toronto's entertainment district on New Year's Eve, only with guns. The inhabitants of the area who weren't armed seemed to be out for the entertainment, and a lot of drinking and partying was going on. Instead of worrying about the authorities, it seemed everyone was celebrating the bombing the previous evening.

If I hadn't had Wil to worry about, I might have morphed into another form and tried to sneak away. Unfortunately, he was very recognizable, and I

261

couldn't take the chance.

We were sidling down an alleyway when my phone buzzed. I pulled it out and saw it was Devon calling.

"Talk."

"I can't hold off any longer," he said. "My boss, Wil's boss, has ordered the air assault to start at dawn."

"Got it." I hung up and called Mike. When he answered, I asked, "Where are you?"

"About a hundred yards from the extraction point."

"The assault is going to start at dawn."

"Okay. You all right? Need any help?"

"No, I think we're fine. Thanks, Mike."

"What's up?" Wil muttered as we set off again.

"Your boss is going to nuke this place in about three hours."

"Oh, okay. I thought maybe it was something we had to worry about."

We had to cross a broad boulevard at some point. I wished I had more knowledge of the area, and Wil admitted he hadn't spent much time down there himself. It hadn't seemed like much of a problem looking at a map. Unfortunately, the map didn't show that we had to traverse a mutie entertainment district. Think of a bunch of dive bars, strip clubs, and hookers along a stretch of road half a mile long. Then downgrade your definition of dive bar about ninety percent. A lot of places had stills operating right out of the back door.

The problem for us was a lot of light. Most of the bars had portable generators or gaslights, and at least a couple of places looked as though they'd hijacked an electric line somewhere. Combine that with a couple of thousand people wandering around, some of them armed, and we had a predicament.

Mike had to have crossed through there, but he hadn't warned me. Of course, he probably strolled right through without a second thought.

We watched the street for about ten minutes as I furiously tried to think of a way to get through. I'd already shown Wil that I was a chameleon, a mutant, so that horse was out of the barn. Fewer than a dozen people knew about my morphing ability. If he ever told anyone in security or law enforcement, my career would be toast. I'd have to go straight and work for a living like everyone else.

I couldn't see a way around it, though.

"Take off your mask. We're going to have to bluff our way through." No one on the street wore a filter mask. They were too expensive for anyone in this part of the city. Even if you could afford one, you were asking to be mugged if you wore it.

I started stashing guns in my backpack and finally pulled off the straps binding us to each other.

"If this works, I hope you remember that you owe me your life," I said as I unblurred my form and turned to face him. "I'm going to tell you a secret, and you can't ever tell anyone else. Do you understand me?"

"Sure, Libby. Hey, we're on the same side." He reached out and tenderly stroked my cheek. "I haven't told anyone about the six million, or any of your other shady deals." And then he leaned forward, pulled off my mask, and kissed me. When he drew back, he stared into my eyes as though he could will me to trust him.

I took a deep breath and nodded. "I'll trust you.

263

What we're going to do is pass you off as my boy toy. Stick close to me and only look at me. Don't go looking around and showing your face to people. Okay?"

I looked around to make sure no one was watching us, then morphed into a troll. In less than a second, in his eyes and anyone who happened to be watching me, I grew two feet and put on two hundred pounds. My hair turned black and grew down to my butt, and my skin darkened to a milk chocolate color. My only clothing was a G-string and sandals.

Wil's eyes about popped out of his head. I put my arm around his shoulders, pulled his face into what he would see as a basketball-sized boob, and said, "Come along, now. Momma Lib got big plans for you tonight, Sweetcheeks."

I dragged him out onto the street with me, heading for an alley where it appeared we could get away from all the lights and people. As we walked across the street, people cleared a path for us. No one wanted to cross a troll.

We hit the sidewalk on the other side of the street and were less than fifty feet from the alley when Carly and Gustav walked out of a bar right in front of us. We almost ran over them. They turned to us, and Gustav took a hurried step backward, but Carly just stopped.

"Hi, Libby."

"Crap. Grab her," I said.

Gustav looked back and forth between me and Carly. "Libby?" he asked.

"Yeah, that's Libby," Carly said.

Wil lunged at Carly, but Gustav said in a weird sort of voice, "You will leave her alone. Grab Libby."

Wil turned and grabbed my left arm in a grip like

a steel vise. I looked in his eyes, and they were blank, his face expressionless.

"Bring her," Gustav said.

Wil turned to follow him, pulling me along.

I pulled a knife and threw it at Gustav. He dodged, but the knife lodged in his thigh and he sprawled to the ground. Wil shuddered, the light came back into his eyes, and he let go of me.

"Grab her," I said again, pointing at Carly.

Wil grabbed her by the arm.

"Bring her," I yelled as I broke into a run. I didn't bother to turn and see if he followed me. I could hear his footsteps pounding behind me.

A bullet ricocheted off the building above my head as I ducked into the alley. It would have hit me if I really was as tall as a troll. Turning, I saw Wil round the corner with Carly thrown over his shoulder. I stopped and pulled the riot gun out of my pack.

"Keep going," I shouted as he reached me. "I'll catch up."

I backed down the alley after him. A couple of men with guns dashed into the alley, and I pulled the trigger repeatedly until they both went down. The alley we were in crossed the alley behind all the bars, and kept going past the next street. I had to shoot two more men before I reached that street.

Looking around, I saw Wil heading away from me with Carly screaming bloody murder and pounding on his back with her fists. I dropped the troll persona, blurred my form to make it harder to shoot me, and broke into a run to follow him.

The woman he was carrying slowed him down, so I caught up with him after a couple of blocks.

"Hey, stop for a minute," I said as I drew even

265

with him.

We slowed to a stop and I dug the jet injector out of my bag. Carly continued ranting and calling for help until I pushed the injector against her neck and gave her a shot.

"She should be a little easier to carry now."

"Thanks. Why do we want her?"

"Because she's the prophet Alscher is using to rile up the muties. Ship her off to Siberia or someplace, and things will probably calm down. Hell, get her away from Alscher, fix some of the weird ideas he's fed her, and she might be useful. She may be a real clairvoyant."

"Which way?" was all he asked.

The sky was lightening in the east when we met up with Mike at the extraction point. True to his word, Devon was there with an aircar to pick us up.

As we rose into the air, I saw a bunch of red lights flying toward us from the direction of the lake. They dropped in altitude, and then a minute or so later, red streaks preceded the bright fiery flash of explosions erupting from the ground.

Battle and carnage in the mutant district continued for three days after our escape. The fighting spread, and more security forces airlifted in, but things finally calmed down. Democracy Now was broken, and anyone who might have advocated for mutant rights was cowering in a basement, hoping the next bomb missed them.

I had been an observer, sitting in the strategy discussions and hanging around the war room. I didn't really have any business being there, but no one threw me out. I think because Devon and Wil let me be there, everyone else seemed to think I had some sort of undefined position.

At least a dozen times, I thought about leaving, but I couldn't just walk away and pretend it wasn't happening. Instead, I went off by myself and screamed and cried sometimes, and I cursed Alscher on a regular basis. He knew what had happened in Germany, and it was being repeated in Chicago. I had warned Carly. The corporate soldiers didn't discriminate. Mothers with children and other innocents were caught in the assault along with the terrorists.

The Chamber posted a dead-or-alive reward for Alscher, but they didn't find his body and he wasn't among the prisoners.

CHAPTER 27

A couple of days after the corporations declared victory and told their troops to stand down, I asked Wil out to dinner at that fancy country club and bought a new dress.

"They have lobster," I said, looking at the menu. "I had a lobster once. Looked like a big bug, but it tasted good. Kind of messy to eat, though. Oh, they only have the tails. I wonder why."

He laughed. "The tails are easier to eat, and the shell will be split already."

"Really? Maybe I'll order that. With all the money I made rescuing you, I can afford it."

"Yeah, you really got rich off of me. The accounting department called me this morning. They said you told them to send the checks for all of the work you did for the Chamber to a charity to help the mutants in southwest Chicago. I did some checking. That charity was only set up yesterday, with a single three million credit deposit. It has a rather suspicious name."

"How could I resist contributing to something called the Modigliani Charitable Trust?" I asked. "Wil, Alscher went about things the wrong way, but what he wanted for people, such as education and decent living conditions, wasn't wrong."

"You're going to ruin your reputation as a stone-cold bitch."

"Shhh. It will only ruin my reputation if you're a blabbermouth."

Wil held up his glass and I clinked mine against it. Taking a sip of my drink, I decided to confront the elephant in the room head on.

"So, now you know I'm a chameleon. A mutant. Not the sort of woman you'd take home to mother."

He cocked his head in that way he had and asked, "Is that what you think? That I wouldn't be interested in a woman with a mutation?"

"Well, interested, probably. You're a man. What man wouldn't be interested in Miriam? She's gorgeous. But I can't imagine her at a charity reception." I looked down at my drink and played with the little umbrella. "But you're also a corporate climber, and when you reach VP, you'll want a wife who can give you normal children and entertain in a sedate, conventional way."

"With a conventional prenup that preserves all my wealth."

I laughed. "Of course. That's why I wouldn't want you to read the prenup. I'd put clauses in there that you couldn't divorce me if I have kids with flippers instead of feet."

Wil shook his head. "Do you want to get married?" He looked very serious.

That sobered me. I thought about it while the waitress came and took our orders.

"Not really," I said after she left. "Not right now, anyway. Maybe someday. To the right man. I wouldn't do it just to get married, no matter how rich he was." I winked at him. "My mother proved that a single girl can have a baby if she wants, and I know how to make my own money."

He didn't look relieved. Instead, he leaned closer, staring straight into my eyes, and said, "I'm not interested in getting married right now, either. But when I do marry somebody, she won't be the perfect corporate trophy wife. She'll be someone so unique and wonderful that I can't live without her. Someone who loves me as much as I love her."

My mouth was really dry, so I tried to take a sip of my drink. My hand shook so badly that I set it back down.

"I...I think that's what most girls really want," I said.

The waitress showed up with our wine, and I excused myself to the ladies' room. By the time I got back to our table, I had my emotions under better control.

Wil took me back to my hotel, and things almost fell apart at my door. I gave him a quick kiss, and he took it to another level. Or maybe I did. Or we did.

Finally, I managed to pull away from him and pant, "We can't do this."

"Why?"

"Because I have a train to catch tomorrow, and I still need to pack."

"That's a lousy excuse."

"It's the only one I can come up with." He leaned in to kiss me again, but I pushed him away. "No. Not like this. Not when I'm leaving." I touched his lips with my fingertips. "If I slept with you tonight, and it was the only time, if I never saw you again, it would break my heart. Do you understand?"

It seemed as though he looked at me a long time, then he said, "Yes, I understand."

"If you're really interested, come visit me. Come when you can spend some time. Let's get to know each other. Right now, I know how you react under fire, but I don't know how you relax in the evenings, or what you do with your time off. I'm not always a kick-ass bitch. I'd like you to know that side of me, too."

"That makes sense." He leaned forward and

kissed me on the forehead. "Good night, Libby."

⊕⊕⊕

Wil and Miriam came the next morning and drove Mike and me over to the museum. I'd submitted all my final reports and invoices to AIC, the Chamber, and North American Insurance. All my equipment and tools were boxed up for the train trip home.

We were taking Miriam to Toronto with us. To my surprise, she planned to become a courtesan. I told her I'd introduce her to my mom.

"Men have been selling me all my life," she told me. "Men have gotten rich selling me. I have no skills. I can't read or write. I really don't mind sex, and I'm told that I'm good at it. Now it's time for me to get rich."

While Wil and Mike carried all the stuff out to the car, I wandered down the hall.

"Hi, Jess. How are you doing?"

"Hi, Libby. I'm okay, I guess." To my eyes, she didn't look okay.

"Are you going to be staying on here?"

"I'm not sure. They've asked me to stay until they can find a new director. I don't know whether I'll stay here, or maybe go out to San Francisco or Vancouver. I've always liked it out there."

"Why did you do it, Jess?"

The blood drained out of her face, and she stared at me. She swayed on her feet, and for a moment I was afraid she might faint, but she reached out and put her hand on the desk to steady herself.

"It couldn't have been because of Malcolm. You've

271

always known about him, and known Deborah was bi. And I can't imagine you didn't at least suspect about the robbery. So, what was the tipping point? What sent you over the edge?"

Tears escaped and ran down her cheeks. She turned away, walked to a chair, and sat down facing me.

"I begged her not to do it, not to go along with it. But she said that she owed Malcolm. She said that she'd bail him out, and then she'd resign and we'd go to Vancouver. We had the money to start a gallery, and with her reputation and connections, it would have been a success."

I watched her wringing her hands, totally defeated.

"Then Malcolm, that bastard, went behind her back and had Margarita steal five paintings. Deborah was furious the day after the robbery. He told her it would be all right because he'd concocted that ridiculous plan to plant the necklace on you."

She looked up at me. "I told her that was wrong. The museum, the insurance company, they're big institutions. No one was really getting hurt. But you're a person, an innocent person, and you didn't deserve to pay for Malcolm's screw-ups."

Jess bit her lip and looked down at her lap. "Deborah said she would tell Malcolm that she was quitting. He could do whatever he wanted, but she wanted out. She told me we'd go to Vancouver."

The woman's composure completely broke, sobbing and gasping. "I found plane tickets for Deborah and Malcolm in her desk. They were going to run away to China. She was leaving me. I called her, and she came to my condo. I confronted her, and she laughed at me. She told me she was in love with

Malcolm, not me."

"And you stabbed her."

"Yes." She sat doubled over, her arms across her stomach, and sobbed.

I turned around and walked out. It wasn't as though I owed Deborah anything. The bitch had set me up.

"You're ready to go?" Wil asked when I met him in the hall.

"Yep. This may be your city, but personally, I like Toronto. I never get blown up there when I go out to eat and the rats are smaller."

On our way to the train station, Wil said with a smirk, "You know, I contracted you to find Deborah Zhukoff's killer. You never fulfilled the contract."

"Sure I did."

He turned to me. "You know who killed Deborah?"

"Yeah. Read the contract. You didn't say I had to tell you who it was."

"Geez, Libby!"

"Hey, don't go getting all official on me. Just take my word for it. Justice is served. The guilty party is paying."

How painful would it be to go through life knowing you had killed the one person you truly loved? I couldn't imagine, but I figured Jessica was paying enough.

⊕⊕⊕

Nellie was singing *Cry Me a River* as I nursed my second drink and tried to decide what, or if, I wanted

273

to eat.

Paul, The Pinnacle's manager and bartender came over and asked, "Is Nellie okay?"

"Yeah, why?"

"She's singing too many sad songs tonight. Happy people are better for business, but before I said something to her, I wanted to check."

"She's okay. She came over while I unpacked this afternoon and I was telling her about Chicago. I guess both of us are in a mood."

He nodded. "Lousy business, that. Were you mixed up in it at all?"

I bit my lip and looked up at him. "Yeah, I was a little too close."

Paul and I had known each other since elementary school. He put his arm around my shoulders and gave me a hug. "Any time you need someone to listen," he said and gave me a quick kiss on the top of my head. "Tell her to pep it up a little, okay?"

The corporate controlled news clamped down on events they didn't want people to know about. They hadn't done that with "The Chicago Insurrection." They broadcast the massacre far and wide, and the message was loud and clear. The corps didn't care what individuals or even groups did most of the time. Challenging the corps was another matter.

Sometime later, Nellie was singing an upbeat dance number, and I was eating poutine when James's voice said, "I didn't know you were back in town."

I felt a happy bump in my chest and a smile spread across my face as I turned to him, stood, and threw my arms around his neck.

"I just got back last night. It's so good to see you." I took his hand and drew him to an empty chair. "Come sit with me."

"I'm crushed that you didn't call me right away," he teased.

With a chuckle, I said, "I assumed you'd know by mental telepathy. C'mon, don't tell me you're the only man in the world who can't read women's minds."

He roared with laughter. I signaled the waitress and ordered him a drink.

"If I buy you a drink, will you forgive me?" I asked with a flirtatious grin.

"I will if you'll agree to go out with me this weekend."

I leaned forward and kissed him on the end of his nose. "That sounds like an excellent idea. Let's go someplace without any bombs."

If you enjoyed **Chameleon Uncovered**, I hope you will take a few moments to leave a brief review on the site where you purchased your copy. It helps to share your experience with other readers. Potential readers depend on comments from people like you to help guide their purchasing decisions. Thank you for your time!

~~~

Get updates on new book releases, promotions, contests and giveaways! Sign up for my newsletter at brkingsolver.com.

Coming late spring 2017
Book 3 of the Chameleon Assassin Series

Other books by BR Kingsolver

The Chameleon Assassin Series
Chameleon Assassin

The Telepathic Clans Saga
The Succubus Gift
Succubus Unleashed
Broken Dolls
Succubus Rising
Succubus Ascendant

BRKingsolver.com
Facebook
Twitter

Printed in Great Britain
by Amazon

12969633R00159